# Secrets of the

## Arlene Pearson

Dedication

*For Arlene Elizabeth Smith*

# Contents

# Chapter 1

*Penshaw Monument was never completed. Had it been given a roof, there surely would never have been a parapet at all...*

*Easter 1946*

Amelia followed Ed and his mates up the steep slope of the green hill which had a majestic Greek temple set atop of it, with patches of blazing azure sky and white clouds shifting behind the gaps in the solid stone pillars. Calves aching from climbing up the seventy wide steps, she wrinkled her nose as the earthy aroma of cows and wild garlic wafted over from the surrounding greenery.

Ed trailed a little behind the others, his shoulders slumped. She had to put things right. She hadn't meant any of it. Her heart was racing, and her breath was coming in short gasps but she didn't want to stop to rest. She had to speak to him. She shivered, despite the sweat lacing on her brow, stealing a quick glance back down the hill. Daddy must never find out she'd been here today.

*All around her, crowds of families were gathering on the grassy slope leading up to the monument for the traditional Easter egg rolling race. Their homemade eggs had either been wrapped in onion skins and boiled so they looked like mottled gold or hand painted in bright colours. Scrambling up the various levels of earth steps, little girls hummed and skipped in their Easter bonnets and little boys with scrubbed faces, and newly polished shoes gleaming, shrieked and raced each other to the top.*

She forged on, hoping to catch his attention but her heart sank as the boys were swallowed up by the doorway in the eighteenth blackened sandstone column, jostling to be the first to climb the secret spiral staircase to the parapet and their favourite pastime of doing circuits around the top of the monument. They loved to scuttle over the pediments, ignoring the gaping abyss in the middle over the solid stone slab base below. There were no handrails or barriers.

Ed was always the leader because he was as sure footed as a mountain goat.

Soon she was halfway up that circular staircase herself, perspiring uncontrollably despite the coolness inside the pillar as she felt her way round and round, up and up in the darkness, scraping her knuckles on the ancient gritstone. At a couple of places, she passed slits hewn out of the stone providing chinks of welcome daylight. Finally, she looked up and clambered through the heavy grille onto the top of the monument, blinking at the dizzying blueness overhead.

It took a moment for the world to right itself and wiping her wet hands on her dress, her hungry eyes raked the scene and sought Ed. Ah, there he was. Her heart leapt in her chest just at the sight of the back of his head, hair so dark it was almost black. He was about to climb over the protective wall of the first walkway, shadowed by another boy. One of his mates was lounging on the roof with his feet dangling over the edge of the peak and another was standing upright on it.

Annoyingly, people kept getting in her way, pointing out the pit heap and the spire of Durham Cathedral to each other and telling her to slow down. She elbowed her way through them and called out to him, feeling her heart thump so fast in her chest it hurt, but he was moving farther away up the peak, eager to reach the other side.

'Ed!' she called, her voice sounding shaky and unlike her own, the blood rushing in her ears. She saw his back stiffen and he turned around. He slowly moved towards her, so she was looking up at him. She could see the beads of sweat on his face and the way his blue-black fringe parted and flopped onto his broad forehead was enough to make her heart turn over.

'Amelia. What the hell are you doing up here? It's not safe.' he said. Heat filled his gaze, making her skin tingle as eyes like burning coals bored into hers. She longed to feel his arms around her waist.

A skylark treaded a patch of air overhead, it's melodic chirping mingling with the calls of the children and the tinkle of their laughter.

His mates tittered in the background and broke the spell. 'Eee, look who it is.' One struck a pose. 'It's the Lady of the Manor.'

'I...I had to see you,' tears pricked behind her eyelids as she forced out the words. 'I came to say I'm sorry.' Her throat felt dry. Ed stood with his hands by his sides, his palms grubby and his shirt hanging out. He almost whispered, glancing behind him at his mates. 'But I thought you wanted nowt more to do with me? You made it quite plain yesterday I wasn't good enough for yer.'

'Bet you can't beat me,' someone said. 'I'm the winner so far. Final race lads?'

The two lounging on the peak groaned. 'We're out. Go on Ed or he's the winner.'

Amelia moved closer. 'Those things I said…I'm so sorry. Don't go, I need to talk to you,' She reached up to clutch at his arm and clung on with both hands. 'I love you Ed and I know you love me. Please say you forgive me.'

'Look lass, not now. We'll talk later, I promise.' He shook her off.

'Later might be too late. Wait. Please, wait a minute.' Without thinking, she hitched up her skirt, knelt on the rough stone and hauled herself up from the safety of the walkway so she was standing next to him on the parapet, wiping the blood from her grazed knuckles on her skirt.

Whew, it felt high up here and a bit wobbly and the sky seemed nearer, a bright, bright blue with everything sharp edged and sparkling. She hadn't realised but this peak must only be a few feet across. Ed moved closer and put his hands on her shoulders and she felt her legs turn to jelly. 'Go back down the hill for now.' He turned his head. 'I can't let him win.'

She twisted towards him. She could smell the heat of his body; his nearness made her feel dizzy. 'You've got to listen to me.' He leaned down so his head was closer to hers, speaking quietly and she felt his warm breath on her ear. 'Amelia. Go back down the hill. We'll talk later on. I promise.'

'But…' Hot tears scalded her cheeks and she dashed them away.

He turned and made to follow Dougie who was waving him on.

'No. Wait!' Amelia screamed at his back. She lurched a couple of steps after him, flinging her arms around his stiff back. He removed her gently and made to go.

'Oooh!' Amelia screamed and stamped her foot so hard a pain erupted in her ankle. She grabbed at his shoulders, pulling him back. 'If you'd only listen to me. It's really important.'

8

It all happened so quickly. He prised her off, turned and then he lost his footing on the stonework, stumbled, rolled over … unable to grab a handhold of anything, his knuckles white, eyes wide.

*On the bank below, the children at the forefront shoved and jostled to form a raggedy posse, being restrained by parents and jumping up and down, arms poised, precious eggs clutched and ready to be rolled down the hill. Some looked rather bewildered, others were practising bowling moves as if at a cricket match and nearly knocking others over, freshly scrubbed faces strained and contorted with the effort. All was silent for one moment and then came the cry:*

*'Get Ready.'*

*'Get Steady.'*

*'Go!'*

*Shrieks abounded as the fragile eggs left hot little hands simultaneously, arms flailing, then they were airborne and sailing over the summit in a fluid, graceful procession through the silken air. It was a thing of beauty, like a golden shower of fireworks dispersing in all directions in glorious chaotic profusion with the hordes clapping and cheering in their wake.*

The nearest boy reached out his hands to him, thinking Ed was larking about as he neared the brink of the peak, but the very next minute he rolled over the edge of the monument and fell seventy feet onto the slabs of rocks below. His cries splintered the air then there was silence.

*Some of the eggs cracked and cannoned off earth steps and exploded into myriads of shattering tiny fragments before they had a chance to reach the bottom of the hill. Howls of laughter erupted as others were caught in-flight by the jaws of leaping, playful dogs, tails waving. Loud barking and yelping noises mingled with the bellowing of the watching crowd.*

The world seemed to halt on its axis, then she heard clapping and cheering as if from a long way off. Her heavy limbs refused to move and it was as if she was in a dream. She was aware of suffocating terror, a voice screaming that didn't sound like hers at all and pain all over her body as arms grabbed her and pulled her back down to safety. Then everything went black.

When she came to, she cried out loud because she knew it was all her fault. Oh, good lord, she'd pushed Ed off the monument to his death. Or as good as. She'd killed her beloved Ed, the lad she loved.

For the rest of her life, the sounds, smells of that day would follow her from the monument and stay with her for ever, sneaking into her dreams and reminding her of what she'd done…

*Meanwhile, the procession of happy, laughing families linked and hugged each other and wound its way back down the winding, sandy path of the hill, eager to see whose egg had survived and rolled the furthest…*

# Chapter 2

*Autumn Drive by the Staiths was once an old disused, industrial site which was regenerated by inclusion in the Gateshead Garden Festival in 1990…*

*Spring 2015*

Verity normally loved Saturday mornings since Jeremy and his shaggy little dog Pedro had moved in with her and Tom, her white Persian cat. They'd been engaged since last year and were saving up to buy a house together. Although she'd always been very happy living on her own in her modern, chalet style house that was ideally located on the banks of the River Tyne, she told herself that she was ready to move on and looking forward to starting over with him in a place that was theirs together.

The sunlight streaming through the kitchen window glinted on her engagement ring, making it sparkle and she couldn't help but smile to herself. Yes, they were now engaged but not in a big rush to get married. Well, at least she wasn't. She was in fact quite content with the way things were at the moment.

Even the animals managed to tolerate each other. Verity had been worried at first that her disdainful Tom would be jealous of his cheeky little Pedro, an adorable little grey and white Bichon Frisse but he simply ignored him. Tom, who'd appeared in her garden one day, looking scrawny and underfed, had never left. Now he was a beautiful, white-haired, graceful creature who thought – and rightly so - that he was in charge.

She was pretty certain she'd found the one in Jeremy. Just looking at him made her heart lift. He sported the messy surfer look, being very tall and broad, with a mane of bright, sun bleached hair which refused to be tamed and mischievous, cornflower blue eyes which sparkled when he was up to something, which was often.

They had history together too, being a disastrous romantic encounter when they were both very young. Then they'd met again by momentous chance many years later when Jeremy came to work for Verity as a temporary Personal Assistant to her Conference Manager, and she had fallen in love all over again.

On Saturdays as they liked to chill out after a busy week at work. After rising late and enjoying morning coffee in the sun-warmed conservatory overlooking her garden, they would stroll along the riverbank past the monolithic structure looming out of the sandbanks, along to the communal hub cafe. Jeremy always said their flat white coffee and bacon sandwiches, eaten whilst sitting overlooking the waterside, were to die for.

This morning was different though. He drained his coffee and jumped up. 'Are you ready? I've got something to show you. Something that just can't wait. It's a short drive away.'

'Aren't we going along for breakfast?' she said, surprised, watching as he let Pedro out into the garden, promising him a proper walk soon.

She hardly had time to run a comb through her straight dark shoulder-length hair which was still damp from the shower and apply some lip gloss and grab her handbag, he was in such a hurry.

'It's okay, there's a teashop where we're going,' he said as they pulled out of Autumn Drive, leaving the house and the blue and white *For Sale* sign behind them.

'Where are we going?' she asked as the contemporary Angel of the North flashed past, wings outstretched. 'Not another house viewing?'

Jeremy chuckled. 'Maybe. You'll soon see.'

'You know I'm not keen on surprises,' she reminded him.

'I think you'll like this one,' he said quietly, half to himself.

Verity recognised the small village they were approaching and her heart sank. 'So why are we going to George's house?' Please, not here. Not this place...

Jeremy had been living with George, his stepdad in a tiny terraced house in a village a few miles away, that was until he'd practically moved in with Verity. George had sadly just passed away a few months previous.

Her fiancé shook his head, curls bobbing as he turned right at the roundabout below a green hill with a Greek Doric temple perched on the top of it, standing sentinel against a backdrop of bright blue sky with only the merest puff of candyfloss cloud. Soon they were parking by the roadside below it. The very sight of the age-old pillars of blackened sandstone made Verity shudder.

'I know how you feel about this place. But I've just got to show you something. I know you'll understand when you see it. Please?'

Before she had a chance to change her mind, he was out of the car, holding her hand and pulling her along a country lane, away from the general footpath which led along to the tearooms, with the hill and monument on their left-hand side, hidden by the trees at this point. She didn't feel quite so bad if she couldn't see the old temple. Jeremy suddenly stopped and stood still.

In a clearing, cosying into a sunlit space under the scoop of the hill, stood a cottage. Or rather a house, Verity thought, intrigued despite herself, a house built of golden stone with three chimneys rising up from the slated roof, and two levels of neat, white edged windows, winking in the sunshine. There was a front door in the centre with the numbers, 1744 etched into the stonework panel above it. It was totally beautiful, however she couldn't stop shaking inside. If only it were somewhere else.

She couldn't comprehend what on earth they were doing in this place? She hadn't been for so many years and she didn't want to be here now.

But how could she tell him that when he was obviously so excited and eager to please her? She wanted to run away and her mouth felt dry.

Jeremy ushered her up to the front gate and opened the gate which was set in a wall built from large uneven stones, like part of a wall built by the Romans. The gate groaned and then they were standing in a tiny yard with a winding pathway.

'What are you doing?' Verity looked around her, her legs feeling weak.

Jeremy grinned at her. 'Oh, please V, just come and look at the secret garden.'

He pulled her along the enticing track out of the yard which opened up onto a large lawned space, flanked by immaculate hedges and apple trees on two sides. The stunning side end view of the end of the Greek temple, trees reaching up to it, made her catch her breath, the emerald hill on which it stood falling away below into tangled greenery.

The strong glare from the sun hurt her eyes, and caused her to involuntarily raise one hand to her forehead to combat the brightness.

13

The ancient bricks appeared to turn to gold under the sudden burst of brilliant sunshine.

She couldn't bear it any longer. 'Jeremy….' She could hardly speak, her tongue seemed to be sticking to the roof of her mouth, but she knew she had to say something.

'Verity, what's wrong? I'm so sorry. If I'd known coming here would upset you so much, I would never have brought you. I just hoped…'He indicated a stone bench, but she pulled away.

'No. I've got to get away from here,' she whispered, feeling like a big black cloud had descended upon her. 'I feel faint.' She was filled with a sense of foreboding, like something terrible was about to happen. But then she knew it had already happened.

She pulled her hand away and retreated through the back yard to the country lane and hurried back to the car. She leant against the door, taking huge gulps of air.

Jeremy ran after her, slightly out of breath and put both arms around her tightly. 'I could really use a coffee,' she said.

Verity still felt rather shaky as they reached the nearby tearooms at the foot of the hill. They entered a long, cosy room with lots of chatter and laughter going on. It was an airy, converted barn with lots of golden, exposed beams. She was vaguely aware of white walls and light wood and long windows with prime views of course, of the monument.

Stomach churning, she waved away the delicious array of deep pies, quiches, deep sandwich cakes, scones but Jeremy's eyes were on stalks.

'You don't mind if I have something, do you?' he said.

'You get what you want, I'll just have a strong Americano,' she shook her head at his suggestion of something to eat and made for the back of the room. She chose a table in a
quiet space where she deliberately sat with her back to the window.

She hadn't wanted to come in here but thought she'd be all right if she could sit without seeing a view of *it*. Instead she looked at the colourful paintings and posters covering the walls and stacked up in the corners for sale. She sank into her seat and took deep breaths, oblivious of the friendly hubbub of noise surrounding her. It was obviously a comfy haven for meeting up for a gossip.

14

Jeremy lowered himself into the seat opposite her and set the Number 17 on the edge of the table where the waitresses could see it. 'What a lush place, I've ordered you a piece of Victoria Sandwich cake, honestly V, I do think you need to eat something.'

Verity shook her head again. Jeremy took her hands across the table. 'Do you really hate this place so much? Can we at least talk about the cottage?'

'Oh, have your food first,' she said wearily as a friendly waitress appeared with a huge slice of quiche and salad for Jeremy and the most enormous slice of sponge cake for Verity which she immediately thought would have fed three people.

'How can I eat when you're in this state? Oh, go on then.' He fell to eating whilst she sipped at her coffee and toyed with her cake, thinking it might choke her, watching Jeremy tuck in. Not much got in the way of Jeremy and his scran although he never put on weight. Must be all that nervous energy he expended. When at last he'd finished, and putting down his knife and fork with a, 'That was scrumptious,' Verity tried to compose herself and took a large gulp of cooling coffee.

'I'm so sorry for being insensitive.' He reached under the table and clasped her hand.
'I'm such an idiot.'

'No, no, it's just me,' she shrugged.

'What did happen that day?' he asked. 'Could you tell me about it? You've never told me the full details. I would like to hear the whole story.'

She pushed her plate away to the edge of the table but held onto her coffee mug. 'I suppose it's silly to still feel like this about something which happened so long ago.' She took a deep breath. 'Okay. Way back in 1946, a terrible disaster took place,' she gestured with her thumb behind her towards the monument. 'Up there.'

'Go on,' Jeremy said softly.

'It was Easter Monday and a few young lads, aged about fifteen or sixteen years old, climbed up there to the open rooftop. They often used to go up there. They'd hurry up the secret staircase in the eighteenth pillar, emerging onto the parapet and it was their favourite thing to run right the way around it.' She wrapped her fingers around her mug.

15

'There was no roof you see, because the structure was never finished. The parapet was open to the elements. One story goes that the funds ran out before it was completed in honour of the Lord of the Manor.' She leant forward. 'Anyway, the lads would hurry along one walkway, scramble up onto the triangular peak to get across to the other side, then run along the other walkway, scramble over the peak and repeat. Again, and again. They used to see how quickly they could do it. The peak was only about ten feet across with no handholds, it was completely open and utterly treacherous.'

She paused for breath and pushed her coffee mug away. Jeremy's eyes never left hers.

'On this particular day, one boy was about to follow his mate round for one last winner takes all circuit whilst the other lads were sat with their feet dangling over the edge of the peak, egging them on. Then, the boy who was following his friend, somehow stumbled and rolled over on the narrow peak.'

She paused again. 'His mates thought it was all part of the show and continued giggling and shouting to spur him on. Only he didn't get up but rolled a bit further and fell off. He fell right over the edge of the monument.'

Jeremy's deep blue eyes widened in horror.

'Yes, Verity went on, playing with the menu, turning over the picture of the monument on the front so it lay face down on the table. 'He fell seventy feet onto the solid stone slab below to the horror of all the spectators.'

'Wow, no way,' Jeremy breathed. 'How horrific.'

'Yes, and it's haunted me ever since. It was the only accident in the whole history of time on the monument.' Verity fiddled with the menu again. 'The spiral staircase was closed after that to the public for over sixty years.'

'That's a terrible story,' Jeremy said slowly, 'but it was a long time ago.'

'Some things you can't quite put aside though.' Verity said. 'Especially when it was my grandfather who was the boy who fell from it.'

16

# Chapter 3

*February 1946*

Amelia walked briskly alongside the line of slender poplars, catching the movement of the late afternoon sunlight as it chased frosty shadows across the hill and turned the landscape to gold. She sighed as she walked under the green shade with the monument behind her, warming her frozen fingers in her fur lined gloves.

She'd felt restless. It was the half term holiday from her private school for girls, and she'd forced herself to go outside for a walk around the estate, however she'd soon strayed beyond the grounds to catch a better glimpse of Penshaw Monument. She was always drawn to it, probably because people seemed to have such fun up there, sledging down the hill in winter and picnicking in summer, and the air was always alive with laugher and excited voices. It was such a happy place to be.

Her father was always telling her she had no right to ever be bored. How dare she? She had her schoolwork and her books and she could ride the horses in the stables anytime she liked. She could go anywhere in the grounds. There was a maze and orchards and lots of sculptures. What girl wouldn't be happy with all that she had? It was true she'd never wanted for anything and she would often feel guilty and try harder to please her father.

It wasn't that she was bored, she was just lonely at times and craved companionship of her own age. She did find it difficult as none of her school friends lived nearby and her father never liked them around anyhow. She had learnt how to be happy being left to her own devices and after what had happened to her mother, she didn't dare complain too much.

Knowing it was time to head home before her father missed her, she did an about turn and walked quickly back home to Monument Manor. Entering the house, she hurried up the sweeping staircase which led to her bedroom, discarding her gloves, hat and coat along the way. Then she heard the unusual sound of faint voices and laughter. She stopped, listened for a second and feeling curious, made her way back downstairs. Sounded like it was coming from the kitchen where Bertha, the cheery Assistant Housekeeper, was always game for a bit of a chat and a gossip.

Amelia followed the long, cool solid stone flagged passageway, which was the old Butlers Passage, along to the scullery where it was always warm and cosy despite the cool blue walls. Amelia always thought blue was a strange colour for a kitchen but apparently it went back to their ancestors who said it was to repel flies. The first thing to catch her eye as she entered were the burnished copper pans gleaming gold on the shelves and the second was through the kitchen window, the sight of a few youths sitting on the low kitchen wall with their backs to the vegetable garden. They were giggling and fidgeting, swinging their legs idly as they chattered. What were they doing there?

At the solid oak table, a boy was poised on a kitchen stool, stuffing his face with a doorstopper sandwich of homemade bread and cheese, whilst Bertha was busily wrapping up wedges of game pie and rocky scones in white paper bags.

'There,' she was saying. 'That'll keep you lads going for a little while on your adventures.'

'Hello,' Amelia ventured, her boots tapping on the stone floor.

Bertha looked up but the boy ignored her, concentrating on his food.

'Hello, there Miss Amelia. Have you met my son Ed?' Bertha said proudly, smoothing down her pinny.

Amelia shook her head, not trusting her voice. From the way that Bertha was talking
she had thought that her words were meant for a much younger boy, however this one looked
about her age and she couldn't stop staring at him. She'd never seen anyone quite like this
boy. Even though his head was bent over as he concentrated on the demolition of his huge sandwich and brushing flailing crumbs from his grubby trousers and scuffed shoes, she could see he was worth looking at. He had wild hair so dark it looked almost blue-black, untamed into any sort of submission and a look of fire and devilment clung to him.

He nodded then, briefly in Amelia's direction and she caught sight of angular cheekbones under flopping hair. He jumped lightly off the

18

kitchen stool, the same one she sometimes sat on to watch Bertha smooth luxuriant jam and cream on her sandwich cakes and was soon engrossed in stuffing his pockets with the home-made goodies. His white school shirt was half hanging out of his trousers and his tie was all awry.

For a second, he stood illuminated in a diagonal slice of sunlight cast through the sash window and Amelia caught her breath. He was taller and more streamlined than she'd first thought, and for once she was lost for words. Something stirred within her heart and she knew in an instant that she was on the brink of something wonderful. Change. That was it. Her life was about to change for ever. She was never going to be the same again. Her heart was beating so fast she thought it was going to burst right out of her rib cage.

She couldn't speak as for one instant his brown eyes rested upon her and she was sure, softened, and for one single moment, she saw an answering flicker of something like unexpected appraisal, or was it a kind of knowing or understanding? Then it was gone. Had she imagined it? She felt faint.

'Ta mam, see you later,' he dashed off the words over his shoulder as he hurried through the open kitchen door to join his mates outside, his pockets bulging. Then he turned and came back in. Amelia waited with bated breath, thinking he was going to say goodbye directly to her but her heart plummeted as he ignored her and addressed his mother.

'Mam, can you take my school bag home please?' Then he was off again.

Amelia tried not to rush over to the window to watch, but her eyes snapped in that direction. There was definitely something in the way he moved. A sort of graceful energy which made his mates look gawky. He didn't look back.

Amelia heard the pointer on the kitchen clock shift forward and she looked at the time. He left at exactly twenty five past five. Oh, if only time could stand still, just so as she could think about what had just happened and maybe hold onto him for just a bit longer. Then, forgetting herself, she ran to the corner which they called the Pastry Room to get a better view, resting her arms on the marble slab underneath the window.

19

'Where are they going?' she found her voice after what seemed an age.

'Where do they always go?' Bertha laughed, shaking her head.

Amelia didn't know. She just continued staring at him as he jostled his mates off the wall and away into the trees, with Ed way out in front. Then she couldn't see them any longer as the woods claimed them, obscuring them from sight.

'Up to the monument of course.' Bertha gestured to the hill behind the woods.

'Oh,' Amelia whispered. 'I see.'

'Piece of cake Miss Amelia?'

Amelia sat on the stool Ed had just vacated. It felt quite warm. 'Yes, please. I can't think why I haven't seen him before?'

'To be honest, your father doesn't approve of the lads hanging around the place. And our Ed never sits still for long anyhow. In and out. Always on the go.'

'Does he often, er call in then?' Amelia traced a pattern with her finger in a patch of icing sugar on the bench.

'Just on baking days.' Amelia filed this thought away for future reference. Baking days were Tuesdays and Fridays. When Daddy wasn't around. 'He's a good runner, you know.' Bertha wiped it away and placed a large slice of cake in front of Amelia with a flourish.

'It certainly looks like he runs everywhere.'

'I mean he's a good athlete. A sprinter. He wins all the races at his school's sports day.' Bertha's smile was wide.

Amelia had never met a boy who ran races. In fact, she had never met a boy that looked like Ed. But he had practically ignored her. Barely noticed she was there. And that was something she was unused to. She usually had an effect on boys. She was the one who did the ignoring. Apart from today. Still, there had been that one moment when he had noticed her. She hugged herself inwardly at the fleeting, precious memory they'd shared. She couldn't wait to see him again.

Her brain began to flood with ideas. She envied their freedom so much. She knew she could scramble through woods and climb trees and hills with the best of them. She could be a bit of a tomboy when she had the chance. Mainly when her dad was away. She could show

Ed how daring she was.  Not just a boring girl. She had a feeling she'd never be bored again.

Next time she vowed she'd go with them.  Or rather with *him*.

And that was how it began.

# Chapter 4

*2015*

That evening, back at Autumn Drive, Jeremy was stretched out full length on the sofa, his pale blue baggy jumper harmonising against the light grey cushions, his feet bare. Balanced on his knees was a pile of papers, being one of his student's manuscripts he was trying to mark but it was obvious to Verity his mind wasn't on it. He wanted to carry on the conversation they'd had earlier in the tea rooms.

'How old is Grandad Ed now?' He shifted the manuscript onto the floor. 'Can't believe he wasn't killed outright.'

Verity looked up from the book she was reading. 'Oh, let me see, his birthday's coming up. He'll be eighty-six.'

'So, he survived the fall and managed to live to a ripe old age.' Jeremy swung his long legs onto the floor, his bare feet narrowly missing Pedro who was curled up fast asleep, never far from his master.

Verity nodded. 'Oh yes. It was apparently one of those falls which defied explanation. He did suffer great injuries to his back and broke both of his legs, but he recovered and lived a normal life. He's a tough old so and so.'

Jeremy let out a low whistle. 'Incredible!'

'Actually, it's a few weeks since I've seen him. He's just moved into an Independent Living flat and it's probably time I paid him a visit.'

'What did you think of Monument View?'

'I loved it, apart from the location.'

'Ah, I know you were never keen on visiting George's house in Penshaw.

Verity had liked Jeremy's stepdad George very much, a lovely man, who had unfortunately just passed away after a very short illness and Jeremy was using the proceeds of his house to go towards a property for the both of them.

Jeremy looked sad for a moment and his eyes clouded over. 'I miss Dad so much.'

'I know you do.'

'He was a good man.' He looked down at his forearms resting on his knees. 'It was the Estate Agent dealing with the sale who mentioned that Monument View was for sale. I walked along to have a look and just fell in love with it there and then. It's perfect for us.'

He glanced over at Verity but she didn't comment, just raised an eyebrow.

'I couldn't help it V, but I had a wonderful idea,' Jeremy said, jumping to his feet. 'A couple of ideas, actually. There's a huge sun-room at the back leading out onto the garden. I thought I could probably use it for my Creative Writing workshops. What a location.' Verity could see the light in his eyes. 'Learning and creating stories with that view straight in front of you. How inspiring would that be for my students?'

Verity turned a page. 'For them, maybe.'

'And,' he pressed on, 'I even thought about taking them on tours of the monument as part of the course.'

'Marvellous.'

'Oh, Verity I'm so sorry, going off on a tangent. I didn't mean to upset you. I'm an idiot.'

'The place gives me chills when I think about what happened up there. It's always haunted me since I was a kid.'

'Of course, it was a terrible thing to happen.' Jeremy squashed down onto the sofa next to her and rested an arm along the back. Tom groaned on the other side of her and moved along slightly.

'It had a profound effect on me. I used to have nightmares about the place.'

'I can imagine,' Jeremy looked sheepish. 'I'm so sorry, you know what I'm like, I do things and I don't think about the consequences. But I do mean well. Come on, Verity, you've got to admit that it's a good idea.'

'Have I?'

'Oh yes, think about it. For one thing, it's only twenty minutes' drive for you to work and well, it's just perfect for me to work in. All that space for my students.'

'Anyhow, you know I can't stand surprises. You promised me that there would be no more after the last one.'

Jeremy pulled a face and bent down to pat Pedro.

'Ah, yes, that was a big one.' Verity shook her head. 'An exotic, stunningly beautiful ex-wife and a shaggy dog. I remember it well. Them both turning up and throwing my whole world into utter chaos.'

'To be fair, you did know about her, just you didn't know that she was going to turn up.'

'Oh, be quiet.'

'And the dog situation turned out okay. You love Pedro.' Pedro gave a little grunt at the sound of his name.

'Luckily for you he got on with my cat.'

'So, you see, something good did come out of the surprise.'

'You've got an answer for everything.'

'So, will you think about going back to have a look around? I just know you'll fall in love with it as much as I have. Our own place at last. No more excruciatingly house viewings.'

Verity sighed. 'I just wish it wasn't so near the monument.'

'Just imagine V.' He turned in closer and grabbed hold of both her hands in his warm ones so that the book fell to one side. 'We can get married sooner. No excuses about not having a house.'

His eyes burned into hers as he moved closer to kiss her. Why did he always make her feel as if the bones had been taken out of her legs and turned them to jelly?

'Okay, okay, I'll think about it.' She wondered if she was being silly. If Grandad Ed could get on with his life after enduring what he had, surely she could get used to living near the place? She really wanted to make Jeremy happy and it was obvious how much he loved this cottage. Was it too much to ask?

'Yes. Hurray!' Jeremy hugged her again, then jumped up, disturbing Tom again. 'You know you won't regret it.'

'Hey, I've got to sell my house first. And I haven't agreed to anything yet.'

'I know, I know.' He pulled her to her feet so that her body was held closely against the length of his and they embraced again. Then he said,

'Only, you won't take too long to think about it will you? It's just that they want a quick sale and I don't want anyone else snapping it up.'

# Chapter 5

It was Sunday evening when the house phone rang. Verity knew it was her father as he was the only person who ever rang on that number. He'd moved to Yorkshire around twenty years ago and they hadn't had a lot of contact over the years, apart from birthdays and Christmases, if then.

She just wanted to forget about her unsettled childhood and any contact with her dad always brought it back to the fore and made her feel uneasy, despite the fact that she was now a successful Conference Manager, organising high profile events throughout the UK. She now owned a house of her own, instead of being passed from relative to relative's houses when he couldn't be bothered to look after her. The past couldn't drag her down now.

She answered warily as a phone call from him seldom occurred unless he wanted something. Which he did. He wanted Verity to attend her grandfather's 86th birthday party in a week's time.

'Birthday party? Yes, of course, I'll go.' She felt relieved. That wasn't a problem although she had an immediate vision in her head of tiny china cups and pink and yellow fondant fancies melting all over mismatched vintage tea plates. 'I was thinking of paying him a visit soon anyhow. Haven't seen him for ages. I suppose I'll see you there then?'

'Well, actually I can't make it. I'm glad you're free though as he hasn't got many relatives left.'

She hardly listened as he launched into a convoluted story about family things that were going on which were making it impossible for him to get away. The usual rubbish. Her dad never changed. His tirade ended with, 'He prefers you anyway.'

'Load of rubbish.' But she secretly felt pleased as she had a lot of time for Grandad Ed.

He was now living in a flat at Sand Steps, which she hadn't visited yet. It was ideally located on the clifftops of a tiny coastal village in Northumberland. Described as independent living, the residents had access to as much, or as little, care as they needed.

Her dad had kept falling out with both Grandad Ed and her Grandmother Lil throughout her childhood, as he was wont to do with most people and there were long stretches when they didn't visit for months on end until they fell in again. She had happy memories of a cosy terraced house with a miniscule rose garden out the front with pale pink roses forming an archway over the doorway. She used to love picking up the fallen petals and Grandma Lil would show her how to make perfume.

Grandad Ed had a reputation of being strict, very unlike her own father. She could remember Grandma Lil saying he liked to think he was the boss of the house and he worked in the Lamp Cabin at the local pit. He couldn't be a miner because of an accident he'd had when he was younger.

A phone call from her dad always left her feeling unsettled, so she did what she often did at these times and dug out some old photographs of her mother which were in a very old box at the back of her wardrobe. She felt that all her childhood was contained inside.

She settled herself in her conservatory with Tom purring away beside her and picked out her very favourite, a precious photograph of her mother, aged around fifteen, all gangly arms and legs, posing with a guitar in front of an open coal fire.

Her mother, named Adele, had died when she was just a baby and her father Micky had moved on pretty quickly to a succession of various aunties. She had never gone short of food or a roof over her head, but she always felt that she was never shown any real affection and felt the loss of having a mother acutely.

She'd lived with various relatives including Micky's sister Auntie Doris, or whoever was willing to take her, until she was fifteen and met up with her mother's brother Uncle Bobby, who in turn introduced her to Grandma Anna, her mam's mother with whom Micky had had a major estrangement in Verity's childhood. Oh, yes, another one. Micky, whom Grandma Anna described as feckless, was relieved Verity was off his hands at last when she moved in with Grandma Anna and she herself felt that her life had only just begun at this point.

Unfortunately, her lovely Grandma had passed away just over a year ago, having been in a home specialising in dementia for the last few years. Verity still felt her loss keenly and knew she always would.

She would always be glad for the happy time she'd spent living with her.

There was an old photograph at the bottom of the box. She pulled it out. Oh no, not the flipping monument again. She shuddered a little, then looked again and had to admit to herself the grainy black and white picture was quite magnificent. Mesmerised, she couldn't recall ever having seen it before. Maybe it had been shoved in there and forgotten about.

The picture focused on the open walkways at the top of the monument. The huge, blackened stone slabs ran lengthways, edge to edge, around the gaping, exposed space in the centre where the roof should have been.

There was a triangular arch at the end and she was surprised to see that a couple of young men were actually standing up on the peak which could only have been a few feet across. Goodness it was so high up, it made her feel dizzy just looking at them.

The protective wall must only have been around three foot tall and she shivered again and wondered whereabouts her grandad had fallen from. There was no panoramic view to be seen, only a blurred and cloudy white background.

At the end of the walkway, and with their backs resting against the protective wall nearest the slope of the masonry, a young couple posed for a camera shot, arms around each other's waists. Their faces were very grainy and Verity used a magnifying glass which was also in the box, to have a closer look.

Verity believed the boy to be her Grandad Ed, aged around sixteen, sporting a shock of thick black hair and a wide smile, gazing at a fragile looking, slender young lady, whom Verity was sure wasn't her grandmother. Lily had straight hair and a robust physique, whilst this wisp of a girl had beautifully arranged, tumbling blonde curls. She was the only female in the picture and it looked as if the youths standing on the pediment were also posing, one was sitting with his legs dangling above the yawning roof space.

They made a very attractive couple, despite the age of the picture and it was easy to see they had eyes only for each other. Her curiosity piqued, she wondered idly what had happened to tear this vibrant young couple apart? She looked at the date on the picture but could only make out 1946. She then found a torn newspaper cutting about the accident which was torn in the middle. All that was left were the following words:

*It was suggested that iron railings with spears should be added at the edges to prevent people getting round and if this was not possible, that the place be locked up and the public not admitted. The spears were never added, so it was locked up and barred to the public from that day onwards.*

She winced and placed the cutting back in its place at the bottom of the box.

# Chapter 6

Sand Steps was a white building perched on a steep rocky outcrop on the very edge of the sea, surrounded by a solid brick wall and dropping away to treacherous sandstone-coloured rocks below. To the right the beach and sand dunes were drenched in the afternoon sunlight, the grey blue sea turning azure at the horizon.

On entering the light and airy Reception area, she noticed that there was a hairdressing salon and a beautician's shop with a gorgeous white and green floral window display. There was also a notice in the window which made her look twice - *Toenails cut in residents' rooms on request.*

She was directed out to the sunken courtyard garden which directly overlooked the vast expanse of sea. All was silent for a moment. Then she heard it, a soft swishing sound, the gentle roar of the surf as it moved over the rocks and lapped upon the shore. She could smell the tang of salt in the air.

Grandad Ed was sitting with his back to her on a bench looking out to sea, sucking on his pipe, legs stretched out in front of him, with a little Yorkshire terrier cuddling into his left side.

He turned at her approach and she saw that he was wearing a brightly patterned Hawaii shirt under a smart, yet worn dark jacket and a checked cap. His face was weather beaten, with a deep cleft in his chin. He eyed her from deep brown eyes under thick, black rimmed glasses.

'Hello Grandad.' Just the sight of the little dapper chap that he was made her smile.

'You came then. About time too.'

'How are you keeping?'

'Grand. Sit down bonny lass. Budge up Tiny, you're taking up half the bench. Give the lass a bit of room.'

She sat down and he gestured with his pipe out to sea. 'The tide's away out.'

'Isn't this such a beautiful spot?'

'Oh aye, I love to sit out here. Do you know, on stormy days, the sea nearly comes over the top of that wall?'

He removed his pipe and at forward to take a closer look at her. Verity wondered if it was even lit or was it just something for him to do. 'Sorry it's been so long.'

'Don't you worry about that. By, you're looking well, lass.'

'Thanks. So are you. I brought you these.' Verity handed over a supersized pack of Fisherman's Friends lozenges which she knew he would really appreciate. 'Happy Birthday.'

'Ta,' his eyes lit up as he took them and shoved them in his inside jacket pocket. 'I'll hide them. Don't want them lot getting at them,' he stabbed a gnarled finger in the direction of the building, chuckling at the thought. 'They're all gannets in here, you see.'

'How's Tiny?' Verity reached over to stroke the little dog. 'Are you even allowed to have dogs in here?'

'Oh yes. Dogs are allowed. He's no bother. He's getting on a bit now though, like me.'
Tiny sleepily rolled over so he was lying on his back between them and put his paws in the air.

'You're honoured,' Grandad Ed looked pleased. 'He remembers you. He wants you to tickle his tummy.'

Verity obliged, feeling warm, silky soft, warm fur with only a couple of knots.

Grandad Ed laughed. 'Ha, you're the only one who gets away with that.'

He moved his pipe to the other side of his mouth. 'Anyhow, I'm pleased you've come early because I wanted to talk to you in private, like.'

'Really? What about?' Verity continued stroking a sleepy Tiny who half closed his eyes in contentment.

Grandad Ed looked around. 'Good, there's no-one else coming yet.' He moved closer and she caught a whiff of sweet tobacco. 'That smells nice.'

He sucked on his pipe, chuckling, 'That beautician you know, she loves the smell of this baccy.'

They laughed together at that, then he continued. 'Nay lass, I want to talk to you about the monument.'

Verity shivered slightly. 'The monument? Why? Doesn't it bother you, talking about it, considering what happened to you?'

30

He laughed softly to himself. 'No, I had some right good times up there. Them was the days. I used to climb over the peaks you know, with nothing to hold onto. Me and me mates had some great fun up there. I was never scared of heights.' He paused, then continued, 'In fact I was never scared of anything.'

Verity looked at him in amazement. It surprised her that he never talked like a man who'd suffered a terrible accident, spent weeks in hospital, and then months in a wheelchair before making some semblance of a final recovery. He seemed to be half talking to himself as he continued.

'People couldn't believe it when I told them I used to run right around it. I was the fastest you know. They couldn't understand why I wanted to do it. Devilment I suppose.'

He grinned showing remarkably good teeth for his age, although they were slightly tobacco stained.

He paused. 'Did I ever tell you what happened up there?'

'Bits of it. Not really because it used to upset me. Tell me again. What did happen, Grandad – on that day?'

'Well, if you're sure you want to hear it?'

She nodded.

'They thought I was dead as first. I was lucky I wasn't. The doctors said because I was young, nearer to childhood than adulthood, my bones were more flexible and I was luckier than if I'd been older. I got away with two broken legs, a broken arm, loads of broken ribs and a bruised back.'

Verity shook her head a little, bemused. This visit was proving to be very different to what she'd imagined. 'Didn't it put you off going back up there?'

'Nah, it didn't put me off at all. I was devastated to see that they'd closed it off though.' He paused to suck on his pipe again. 'Put me out of action for quite a while though. It meant that I couldn't go down the pit and so I ended up with a job in the Lamp Cabin instead.'

'What exactly was that?' Verity asked, interested. Why hadn't she ever taken the time to really listen to him before?

'The Lamp Cabin was where the miners would come in, hand me a brass numbered tally and I would give them a lamp, attached by a cable to a heavy battery. The oil lamp was fitted to their belt and off they went. Now, if that man's tally was hanging up, I would know he was down the pit.'

'Was it very hard work?'

'Not as hard as the lads working down there. I knew everybody. It was still a dirty
job mind you. I used to come home and Lil would have the tin bath ready in front of the fire.'

'Anyway, let me get to the point,' he fished around in his jacket pocket and pulled out an old photograph. 'Look at this.'

Verity hesitated before looking. It was very similar to the photograph she'd found in her box a week earlier.

The young couple posing on the walkway of the monument, holding hands and gazing into each other's eyes. That young girl again.

'Who was she?' Verity sat forward.

'Her name was Amelia Temperly. Lady Amelia Temperly.'

'Ooh, Lady? Was she your first love?'

'Suppose she was. She was the daughter of the Lord of Monument Manor. My mam was the housekeeper there. She was a grand cook. Amelia used to follow me about at first and then well, we were sort of courting they called it in those days. I fell for her in a big way. She was a right bonny lass and a proper tomboy, although she didn't look it.'

'What happened to her?'

'Well, this is what I wanted to talk to you about. I never saw her again after my accident. She just sort of disappeared. I tried but was told I had to forget all about her.' He stopped to suck on his pipe again.

'Then I met Lil. The light of my life. Bright red hair she had. She hated it but I used to call her Red, even when we got older and her hair faded to blonde. Eee, we used to argue like cat and dog but how I missed her when she went.' He chuckled to himself and there was a silence.

Verity stared at the photograph.

'Oh, aye. The thing is you see, on that day, Amelia and I had had a big row beforehand. She liked all of her own way and she was jealous of my mates. She gave me a right telling off for something, said her dad said I wasn't good enough for her.'

'Why are you telling me all this now?' Verity shook her head.

'I want you to find her for me.'

'What? Are you kidding me?' Verity's head was ringing and she just couldn't comprehend quite what he was asking her to do.

'Nah. I'm deadly serious lass. She must have been wondering all these years and I felt right bad about it. I did try to find her after it happened but it was as if she'd totally disappeared.'

'Why me?'

'Well, I couldn't ask your dad because he's useless and only thinks about himself. And the rest of his brood are like him. Apart from you. You were always kind and sensible. As a kid you were forever asking Lil if you could help her, like picking the fallen rose petals to make perfume.'

Verity immediately felt a pang of nostalgia for the past.

'And I liked your mam. She was kind too; you take after her. You're your mother's daughter, for sure. She was far too good for the likes of him.'

Verity shifted position at the mention of her mam, feeling her chest tighten. 'So why now?'

'Well, I couldn't when Red was alive, could I? She'd have skinned me alive. What a temper she had on her. I'd never have dared mention Amelia to her when she was alive.' He paused and stroked Tiny as he jumped in his sleep.

'Not that I wanted to. 'Now, I kind of want to put right a wrong. Besides lass, you know they say that before you die your life flashes in front of you?'

'Don't talk like that. You're not dead yet. You could live a lot longer.'

Grandad Ed chuckled. 'Who knows? I somehow feel that time is slipping away…like the tide. Me and Tiny, I think we're not much longer for this world.' The little dog's ears pricked up at the sound of his name and Grandad Ed stroked his head. 'Anyway, I keep having visions of the past. So vivid, like it was yesterday. As plain as day, like.'

33

Verity heard voices and turning her head, saw a couple of relations she barely recognised stepping out of Reception, laden with cards and brightly wrapped presents. One of them was carrying a large blue, bobbing balloon and they were all laughing and shouting. Verity heard cries of 'There he is!' and 'Come on, let's go and fetch him.'

Grandad Ed looked out to sea and sighed. 'Oh lordy. Here they come. There's no peace for the wicked. The only reason I agreed to have this party was so that I could get you to come. I don't like any fuss you know.'

Verity looked around at the hordes making their way towards them, all shrieking and talking over each other. Then someone stumbled and they all stopped to wait, laughing loudly. Probably drunk all ready if they were anything like her dad. Grandad Ed tightened his grip slightly on her arm, his gnarled hand weather beaten.

'Will you do it then, bonny lass? For me?'

'How can I? It's crazy…I don't know if it's even possible.'

'Course it is. Look at Long Lost Family and all that. A smart young lass like you, you'll know how to use the Tinternet surely? I know you work with computers.'

'Well, yes, but…have you considered that she might be…'

'Dead? Aye, I have. Well, she will be eighty-five if she's a day. Nearly as old as me. But at least I'd have tried. Go on lass, for me. Please. Before it's too late. Here.' He fished out of his seemingly bottomless inside jacket pocket a folded over, battered bundle of papers which he pressed onto into her hands.

'Here, there's some info in there that should help you. Names and that. Quick, put that lot in your handbag before them lot see. Don't tell that bloody lot, will you? Keep it as our secret.'

Verity nodded, wincing at the swear word.

'Promise me lass, you'll think about it?'

Wearily Verity nodded again. 'All I can say is, I'll think about it.'

'Champion,' he grinned again and put his pipe back in. 'And if you need to speak to me about anything, you can telephone me. Reception will ring my room.' He stood up and his knees buckled under him. 'Do you promise, bonny lass?'

Verity grabbed his arm to steady him. 'Yes, I promise. I'll ring you.'

'Only don't be too long about it mind,' he sucked on his pipe. 'Oh, lordy. Here. they're nearly upon us. Let me escort you to my birthday party.'

'Can I just ask one thing? Why is it so important that you find Amelia? After all
these years?'

'There's something in particular she needs to know. Something very important. Oh, and you can give her this.' He handed her the black and white photograph of the young couple against a backdrop of Penshaw Monument.

Grandad Ed straightened up. 'So many memories. As I said, I've been thinking about the past a lot. And I might not have a lot of future left. I just want to set the record straight, like.'

'Rubbish,' Verity intervened, 'you look as strong as an ox. I just need to know what it is you want me to say to her?'

Grandad Ed picked up the little dog who snuggled against his jacket, moved his pipe to the other side of his mouth and stared straight into Verity's eyes.

In the intervening silence, she heard the shrieking alarm cry of the terns as they plunge dived far out to sea, mingled with the chattering of advancing guests. Then he spoke again and she had to listen hard to hear his words as the babbling grew nearer still.

'I want you to tell her that I'm alive.' His brown eyes burned into hers. 'Oh and that she didn't kill me.'

# Chapter 7

At home after work, Verity's thoughts of Jeremy overwhelmed her. The house seemed so quiet when he was out. The truth was, when she was with Jeremy she felt at peace, she felt whole and even though he angered her at times, she always missed his presence when he wasn't there.

She looked out upon the garden, the earlier rain showers had disappeared and the sun slanted upon the apple tree at the back of it with the garden seat underneath, the spot where Jeremy had first made his feelings known as the apple stalks fell almost soundlessly in the evening breeze and a blackbird sang so sweetly from the top boughs.

Her heart and mind welled up with warmth as she remembered that time, a blistering feeling which made her feel warm from top to toe. She'd never felt like this about anyone else. The hours stretched out before her. Why didn't she had to go and find him and tell him that she was willing to have a look around Monument Cottage? She knew exactly where he'd be on this lush Spring evening.

He'd be at the cricket club. Fellridge Cricket Club had been one of the venues where he'd performed his play *Not Quite Cricket* recently and Jeremy and his team had gone down a storm. He'd fallen in love with the place there and then, a rural country building with a cricket pitch and tennis courts and a raft of warm hearted, loyal locals.

Jeremy had played wicket keeper for a cricket team in Hampshire for a time when he was at school and was hankering after joining the cricket team next year. It was the icing on the cake for him that the house which he'd set his heart on was within walking distance.

She walked the short distance and soon she stood before the impressive old building which directly faced the emerald green cricket field. It was a former school, a one storey high, listed building with six white painted attic windows burrowed below a steeply pitched, red roof. Her eyes were drawn upwards to the one single spirelet in the centre of the roof, which stretched up into the blue beyond. The smell of freshly cut grass wafted over the pitch.

Surprisingly, it hadn't been raining here much and the afternoon match had taken place. The cricketers must be all getting changed in the adjacent pavilion and there was only Jeremy in the bar. He was stood, pint glass in hand, holding court with two of the barmaids seemingly hanging onto his every word, Pedro sat at his feet. Verity smiled inwardly, she wasn't surprised or dismayed at all by this. People always gravitated towards Jeremy.

In the beginning maybe it used to irk her. When he first came to work for her, she had been annoyed at the little groups who clustered around him at the water cooler and at the steady stream of females who walked past their office at regular intervals with no reason other than to have a gape at the tall, golden haired beach boy lookalike who was doing Verity's filing. Their company hadn't seen anyone quite like him. She was well used to it now and knew that was just the kind of person he was. A peoples' person. Easy to talk to and interested in everyone. But it was her he loved.

'Verity!' he spied her across the room, everyone else melted into the background and she knew at once by the look in his eyes that he was delighted to see her.

He kissed her on the cheek in greeting. 'Hello. Come and sit down,' he ushered her over to a quiet table in an alcove behind the glass case of gleaming cups and trophies.

'What do you think of the new décor?' he indicated the pale lemon walls which somehow didn't clash with the velvety blue seating and red carpet. 'Do you like the new lights, don't they reflect well off all the mirrors? Sorry, I'm gabbling. I'll get you a drink.'

'Prosecco please.'

She smiled to herself as he bustled back to the bar. He returned with a little bottle of prosecco and a wine glass. 'Dare I hope we're celebrating?'

He opened the bottle and poured the shimmering liquid so quickly that the fizz threatened to spill over the top. 'V? Does this mean we can buy Monument Cottage?'

'It means I'm ready to have a proper look around it.'

His smile lit up his face. 'That's amazing.

'I know how much it means to you.'

'Not as much as you do. I know you'll love it though. You won't regret it, V, I promise.'

'I hope not,' she thought to herself, smiling as they clinked glasses.

38

# Chapter 8

'I can't wait to show you the pubs,' Jeremy said the following day as they zigzagged through back streets, to finally emerge in the centre of the village. 'I just love this village.'

'Pubs? I thought we were going for a look around the cottage?' Verity said. Not that she minded. After another long day inside at the office, it was so good to be out walking in the fresh evening air.

'We are, they're on route. Here's my favourite,' he enthused as they reached a cream walled building with black edged windows. A horseshoe of green grass sprawled in front of the pub, housing picnic tables and overflowing flower tubs. A tall sign on a pole swayed like the sail of a ship in the gentle breeze.

There was also a second pub, tucked neatly behind the first one. Verity noticed a slanting segment of the monument, looming over the rooftops from its elevated green hill.

'Fancy that, two pubs right next door to each other,' she remarked. 'No wonder you love this village.'

'It has its merits. For a real ale man like me. In fact, with the cricket club nearby, how could things possibly be any better?' Laughing, he tucked her arm more tightly under his and hurried her on, past pretty cottages and a riding school, until, on a sharp bend going down the hill, they crossed the road over to a wide ascending path with fields sloping down to the bottom of the valley. She noticed one of the fields was triangular in shape like a shiny green boiled sweet wrapper, perfectly pristine and seemingly without any livestock grazing there. So, this was the approach to the other side of the monument.

Instead of climbing the steps, they took a downward, woodland path which led them to the bottom of the hill and the path Verity recognised.

Jeremy was practically skipping along, holding her hand. 'Here we are again,' he beamed.

Verity looked upon the house in the clearing, cosying into the curve of the hillside and took a deep breath. Close up, it looked more distinctive than she remembered. The stonework was a pale golden beige against which tiny decorative patterns meandered, the edged

39

borders and crisscrossing triangles mingling in their warm reddish and brown tones, all ultimately reaching up to join the green slated roof.

'Wow,' she said in amazement. 'I never noticed before, but the stonework reminds me of the cricket club .'

'That's because it was built to match the church and the cricket club , both listed buildings.'

Verity thought it was very characterful. Jeremy unlocked the porch door and jumped over the step, landing in a tiny porch. She followed him slowly along a little passageway which led them along to a square, surprisingly modern kitchen complete with sash windows.

'The windows are new, just made to look old,' Jeremy said.

There was an expectant stillness in the room, as if the empty house was sizing them up.

They hurried from room to room, Verity becoming eager to see what was next. Jeremy led the way, flinging open doors and creating wafts of air. It was certainly a cottage full of surprises. One feature was the secret space under the stairs, where the curving part of the stairway protruded downwards in the centre. Verity peered inside. It was as if she was looking at the house turned inside out. She could see the shadow of Jeremy's legs as he bounded upstairs.

Part of the house was really old, much older than the rest, being the room to the right of the front door. The walls were thick and there was a fireplace in there, leading up to the third chimneypot on the right of the roof. Verity followed Jeremy up onto the landing, the sunlight casting a crazy myriad reflection of prism like shapes upon the staircase walls. She could feel the heat on her back radiating from the sun warmed window halfway up the stairs as she climbed.

Closed doorways beckoned. 'Goodness, how many bedrooms are there?' Verity asked, marvelling at how much space there seemed to be.

'Four,' Jeremy said, 'but wait until you see the end one.'

'Just slow down a bit, I don't want a whistle stop tour,' Verity chided him.

The first room she looked in was a good size, airy with a walk-in wardrobe. She had to admit her heart was lifting. She loved this room. It had a good feel to it.

'This is lovely, this has got to be our room,' she enthused. And it was on the front so it didn't have a monument view, but overlooked the lake and landscape of the country park. It had an elegant old fireplace as well and a tiny en-suite. 'That's for me,' she thought.

'Whatever you say,' Jeremy's voice was hopeful.

The last room was dual aspect, huge and drenched in sunlight. 'Well, do you want to change your mind?' Jeremy asked when he saw her face.

'Not a chance,' Verity was looking at the view. 'Not for me.'

'I was hoping you'd say that. I can use this room as a study. The light is fantastic.'

'Feel free.'

'You know, you'd hardly even know that the monument was there, unless you wanted to see it of course,' he went on tentatively as they caught a glimpse from the passage window.

'Yes, I'd be fine as long as I don't walk along the landing.'

Jeremy smiled, his eyes crinkling.

At the side of the house was a tiny, paved area set out with garden furniture, surrounded by trellises and borders housing a glorious profusion of flowers. Verity caught a waft of sweet summer perfume, probably the sweet peas, with their fleeting scent. Purple and white edged passion flowers climbed up a trellis whilst hanging baskets adorned the fence and overflowed with trailing lobelia, delicate white daisies and bright pink and purple pansies. It was a fabulous assault on the senses.

'Wow, what a beautiful space,' she breathed as she wandered along the crazy paving. 'I had no idea that this was here.'

'Awesome, isn't it?' Jeremy beamed. 'I thought you might like to sit here and have your morning coffee,' he indicated the seating space in the trellis area.

Fine, she thought, I can sit out here with my back to the monument.

A proper country garden lay beyond with a lush lawned space with another seating area at the far end complete with impressive monument view, which she knew Jeremy had in mind for his students.

'There is a regular gardener,' Jeremy said, seeing her face. 'He only lives a few minutes' walk away and keeps it all in order.'

41

Verity breathed a sigh of relief. She was used to deadheading roses and cutting grass and that was about it. 'Thank goodness for that. I don't mind a little bit of gardening but this is something else.'

'I've already spoken to him he's happy to continue coming along.'

'Sounds like you've got everything covered,' she said. She didn't want to let him off the hook that easily, although she had to admit to herself the house had worked its magic. She felt at home already. It was totally idyllic. She still wasn't sure about the close proximity of the old Greek temple but she'd have to get used to it. After all, if Grandad Ed could get over falling off and actually still think fondly of his dare devil antics up there, maybe she could move on too? Thoughts crowded into her brain.

'And just look at what we've inherited,' Jeremy showed her a tiny plastic greenhouse complete with laden tomato and chilli plants. 'Think of all the hot sauce I can make. And next year I want to start with proper allotment beds so I can grow loads of veg.'

Verity shook her head. 'Another idea.'

There was a light rush of wings as a tiny sparrow flew past and landed on top of the apple tree further down the garden, breaking forth into a lovely interlude of piercing yet sweet, birdsong.

'Well, what do you think?' Jeremy asked.

Verity hesitated. She thought that she loved it, she felt at home but she didn't want to voice those thoughts just yet. There was a silence in which she thought Jeremy looked as though he was holding his breath. Maybe the house was too.

'I'm not sure,' she said slowly. 'Just wondering how Tom is going to fit into the picture. And Pedro.'

Jeremy laughed. 'They'll both adapt, don't worry.'

'Maybe I could get used to it.'

Jeremy's face lit up. 'I know we'll all be very happy here.'

'One thing first of all we need to get absolutely straight,' she put both her hands on his chest, feeling the warmth under his faded blue t-shirt and looked into those cornflower blue eyes.

'Anything. What is it?'

'No more surprises. Please?'

'I promise. Are we good then?'

Verity nodded slowly. 'I think so.' She still couldn't help but think, how much did she really know this man she was engaged to? But she did love him, that was for sure.

'So, will you move in here with me?' Jeremy flung out an arm back towards the house.

'I might have to,' Verity said. 'The estate agent rang this morning. My house is sold, it's too late to back out now so I've got nowhere else to go.'

'Brilliant. For whatever reason you decide to move in I don't care, just as long as you move in,' Jeremy said, moving closer and she felt the softness of his hair as it brushed her cheek.

'And now you've made a decision, would this be a good time to talk about the wedding?'

Verity felt herself stiffen slightly. 'One thing at a time, please. Let me get used to *now* first.'

Jeremy sighed and then kissed her. She felt his arms gather tightly around her waist and they folded into each other whilst the wood pigeons cooed in the background and the little bird on the apple tree sang fit to burst and Monument Cottage glowed in the evening sunshine in joyful welcome.

# Chapter 9

What was it about the thought of seeing Ed that flustered Amelia so?
She prowled about her room like a caged lion as the clock moved so
closely she was sure it was going backwards. Then at last it was time
and she ran down the sweeping staircase and out of the house to meet
him where the diagonal line of poplar trees met the open parkland, safe
in the knowledge that her father was out to dinner until late this
evening. She was supposed to be in the library room doing a school
project.

Although she was a little scared of her father and he was rather strict
with her, she loved him dearly, after all it had been just the two of
them since her mother had died when she was only four years old. He
was tall and enigmatic, good looking too. He had been a military man
and was now a landowner and a local politician. He was the one
person she wanted to please and to do that she had to suppress her
giddiness as he called it and her daydreaming and put her back into her
schoolwork. He wanted her to train to be a teacher.

Trouble was, she was only really good at art and had no idea what she
wanted to do with her life. She loved to spend her time drawing and
filling sketch books with drawings. At her girls only private school
she was taught how to dance which she hated, she would much rather
be roaming over the estate, settling wherever she saw fit to draw
whatever caught her imagination. She particularly loved the bluebells
in the woods and the daffodils. The monument was also one of her
favourite subjects and she had lots of drawings of it, captured from
many different angles.

Still, her father was the last person she wanted to think about now.
Thrusting her hands into her coat pockets and pulling down the hood
over her blonde curls, Amelia strode across a little bridge over the
river and felt her heart race as she grew nearer to their
meeting place. The air felt damp and the smell of wild garlic mingled
with the first, light

raindrops. Dusk was imminent and birds were calling to each other. How she loved this time of day.

He was there already and she was cheered to see he was without his friends. Her heart felt light as they fell easily into step. Together, over the last few weeks they had explored some of the hundreds of acres of the sprawling Monument Manor estate with its ancient woodlands, river walks and open grassland. Sometimes they had an entourage with his mates tagging along (although they probably thought she was the one doing the tagging), although more often than not as in the last few days, they were on their own.

Amelia had taken the opportunity to show him the labyrinth and the statues along the tree lined avenue, the stables, the old swimming pool which had fallen into disrepair but they always seemed to end up back at the site of the monument.

She stole a sidelong glance as they walked, feeling suddenly shy. He seemed younger than her in many ways, although he was about to leave school and go down the pit like his father, who had once been a rag and bone man and his brothers. He wanted to stay on at school, unlike her he loved maths and algebra and solving problems; however, his father had told him he had to earn some money and help to look after the family. His mother only worked at Monument Manor part time.

'Look at all the rooks grazing on that field,' Ed pointed out. Amelia was constantly surprised at his knowledge of wildlife.

'Could be jackdaws as well. After a day foraging in the fields, just before dusk we'll see them all flying in a flock back to their rookery.'

'So where is their rookery?' Amelia was interested.

'See that clump of tall trees at the side of the monument?'

Amelia nodded.

'That's where they'll be nesting; all settling down for a good sleep among the branches.'

'So how come you know so much about birds?'

'Just used to listen to my da when he took me for walks as a kid.'

It was just another thing that she loved about him, his enquiring mind and ability to retain information.

Soft, sifting rain was now falling as they climbed the hill and reached the summit.

'I want to show you something.' Ed's eyes danced. He grabbed her hand and led her through the doorway of the eighteenth pillar, and they felt their way up the stone spiral staircase in the darkness. He pushed open the round metal grille overhead, wriggled through it and reached down to help her up onto the loft space.

At the top, instead of walking out onto the parapet, Ed turned to the left. There was the outline of a door in the thick stone which she hadn't noticed before. He put his back against it, it swung open and they climbed up a couple of stone steps.

Ed flicked the torch around and Amelia saw they had entered a long, oblong space under the pediments, which must have stretched along the whole right-hand side of the structure, a secret chamber with walls hewn out of the same heavy sandstone as the pillars. There was just enough room to stand up in, although there appeared to be more height towards the middle which must have been where the two peaks met.

There was a stone ledge all the way around and a couple of vertical slits hewn out of the rock, just like the ones on the way up the spiral staircase and not which didn't let in a lot of light. There was a strong musty smell.

'What is this place?' Amelia breathed, gazing around her.

'It's a secret room.'

Amelia let out a long breath. 'How exciting! Do you think that it's duplicated on the other side of the monument?'

'No, there's no door on that side. This is the only one.'

The torch flickered and Amelia tripped on the uneven floor and would have fallen had Ed not caught her with his arm around her waist. Holding her tight with one arm, he balanced the torch behind him on the ledge so they weren't in total darkness.

Time really did seem to stand still, Ed's eyes burned into hers, such a look of longing which she knew was mirrored in her own. Eyes give away the real truth, Amelia knew that he might try to hide his feelings and pretend he was only interested in sport and his mates, but she was sure that now there was no looking back for either of them. She could feel the heat of his body and simply melted into the warmth of him. Oh, the sweet clean smell of fresh, youthful sweat mingling with a clean soapy scent and on his breath, the faint aroma of the black bullet mints that he so loved.

'This is incredible,' she breathed, her heart beating fast. 'A secret staircase – and a secret room!'

'Yes, I thought we could meet here and no-one would ever know about it,' Ed said, his breathing becoming faster. 'No-one ever looks this way.'

'What about your friends?' Amelia gasped.

'Nah, they're more interested in being on the outside. They've never even noticed this room. No-one comes here.'

'Except us,' Amelia whispered and wrapping their arms even more tightly around each other, they sat down in one movement, onto the stone ledge, her back against the rough stone, their lips finally touching. Her young heart was so full with love, she felt it must surely burst.

Much, much later, they ventured down the staircase and back to the main platform of the monument. Amelia sat down on the cold stone between two pillars and swung her legs like a child, dreamily looking out at the rolling greenery of the landscape in front of her, obscured only by the pit heap. Dusk was falling gently now.

'Look,' Ed pointed to the skies. 'Didn't I tell yer? There they go.'

'Oh, it's the rooks.' Amelia watched as the shapes outlined against the darkening sky tumbled and turned from across the fields on their short journey to reach the tall trees to the right of the monument.

'Hadn't we better be getting home?' Ed said.

'Please, just a few more minutes,' Amelia almost sang the words and held out her hand. She was so happy she felt as if her heart would burst. 'Come and sit next to me.' He sat and they watched the traffic droning by at the bottom of the hill, headlights flashing.

'I nearly forgot, I brought you something,' Ed said, fishing in his inside jacket pocket. Amelia thought it was amazing what his pockets held. Torch, the black bullet mints, penknife. Sometimes provisions, as she'd witnessed, usually from the manor house kitchen. And what was this? He brought out something wrapped in tissue paper.

It was sticky and Amelia, eagerly unwrapping the paper was charmed to see that it was a tiny, coloured fish, fashioned from the boiled sweets type of confectionery, glowing green with gleaming silver scales and gills. It smelt divine and reminded her of childhood treats at a sweetshop with her mother.

47

'It's so beautiful,' Amelia breathed. 'I'll treasure it.'

'You're meant to eat it,' Ed laughed.

'Oh, I don't know if I could, it looks so pretty. Where did you get it?'

'My granny works at a sweet factory,' he said proudly.

'No wonder you've got a sweet tooth,' Amelia carefully rewrapped the treasure and placed it carefully in her purse.

'They're allowed to keep the offcuts.'

'Well, I certainly can't see anything wrong with this one. Thank you.'

'It's all right.'

'Oh, I feel bad, I haven't brought you anything.'

'Yes, you have, you've brought yourself.' They gripped hands urgently as they embraced again. Ed pulled away and produced a penknife from one of his pockets. He stood up and began to carve their initials on the innermost side of the eighteenth pillar. E.T. loves A.T. Enclosed in a heart shape. Amelia laughed in delight. He loves me too, she thought delightedly.

'There,' he said, satisfied. 'And it's away from most people's prying eyes.'

'I couldn't give a monkey's who sees it,' Amelia announced, flinging her arms wide as if to embrace the moment.

'We're very different folks, yer know, aren't we?' Ed said unexpectedly, sitting down next to her again, but not touching.

'What do you mean?' Amelia laid her head on his shoulder but he shifted slightly away from her, replacing the penknife in his bulging inside pocket with his other treasures.

'I mean our backgrounds.' Ed gazed straight ahead. 'I live in a two up two down terraced house in Fence Houses and you live in Monument Manor.'

'So what? What does it matter?'

'It means that I'm going to work down the pit and you will get married and become a grand lady.'

'Ed, that's utter rubbish.'

'My dad says you're a spoilt little rich girl.'

'He's mostly correct. What does your mother say?'

'She doesn't mind you.'

48

'I like your mother very much. I wish she was the only housekeeper instead of having two.'

'Yeah, she's okay. You know, you can't get stirred in our house.'

'I wish I'd had some brothers and sisters.'

'You wouldn't if you had mine.'

'You don't mean that.'

'I do. Nah, I don't really. Just gets a bit overcrowded at times.'

'Your house sounds so much more fun than mine. You're very lucky.'

He chuckled. 'You really are a poor little rich girl aren't yer?'

'Am I?' she leaned closer for another kiss. 'I will smuggle you into my house one day soon. You'd love my room. It's called the Lavender Room and the walls are said to be six inches thick. Oh, and there's meant to be a ghost but I've never ever been scared in there.'

'What happened to your mam?' Ed asked. 'My mam said she died young.'

Amelia swallowed. 'Yes, she died when I was four.'

She shivered slightly and Ed jumped up.

'Look, sorry we've been out long enough. Come on, you're freezing. I'll walk you home.'

She sighed, gazing at the etching on the pillar. 'Do we really have to go?'

'Fraid so.'

'Ed Turnbull, this has truly been the best day of my life. I could just stay and talk with you for ever.'

'Same time tomorrow then?' She nodded as he pulled her up to her feet and they began the trek back down the green hill, the gentle rain caressing their upturned faces, arms around each other, leaving the monument standing sentinel on the top of the hill behind them.

# Chapter 10

It was the first thing Verity saw from the landing window every morning, except when the mist rolled in off the coast and then it wasn't visible at all. It was also the last thing she saw each night before she closed the stairway curtains. It was all lit up then, as at the base of each eighteen stone column was an enclosed new floodlight, which bathed the whole temple in a golden glow.

The new high-tech lighting could be programmed to shifting colours for special local and national events. On Remembrance Sunday it was immersed in a glowing red. She was kind of growing used to it being there. Good job, because she couldn't escape it.

She'd only been living here for only a short time but it already felt like home. She'd moved in with most of her furniture and her cat and settled straightaway. She especially loved the master bedroom with its walk-in wardrobe under the eaves, which was spacious enough to house all of her clothes and shoes with ease. She welcomed the way the birds woke her first thing in the morning, their eager twittering floating down the chimney of the bedroom fireplace.

It was Friday afternoon and she'd finished work at lunchtime and the whole weekend stretched ahead like the lush lawn in the back garden.

Jeremy was cooking his specialist, spicy version of Chicken Chilli Pasta with fresh chillies he'd started growing himself on her conservatory windowsills at Autumn Drive and then transferred to flowering fruition in the greenhouse at Monument View. Delicious smells were wafting from the kitchen. Verity wandered far down the garden, glass of wine in hand, with Tom swishing against her ankles and revelled in the warmth on her face. The sun was hot and she rested her glass on the table Jeremy used for his creative writing classes and stretched languidly, half closing her eyes against the bright sunlight.

The bookends view of the monument complete with pediments and four pillars, seen from the third side of the garden, made her catch her breath. She moved along to the end of the lawned area to gaze upwards, the strong glare from the sun hurting her eyes, and causing her to involuntarily raise one hand to her forehead to combat the brightness. She felt compelled to raise her head to gaze upwards, above the wooded area and scrubby trees on the hill, then the monument filled her view.

The sandstone appeared to turn to gold under the sudden burst of brilliant sunshine, with an azure blue sky behind it forming a formidable backdrop.

Then, for one split second, a movement, right up there on the parapet caught her attention. There was someone up there. Someone moving fast. She followed the tiny backlit silhouette as it moved over the peaked pediment, which was totally open to the elements. Then it turned and ran back the other way…

She gasped, her hand going to her mouth. Her neck was hurting and she found her heart was beating very fast, surely it was dangerous up there? She wanted to call out in warning but of course, she was too far away. She was filled with a sense of foreboding and knew without a doubt, that something terrible was about to happen up there…But, then it had already happened, hadn't it?

Then the sun dipped behind a cloud and the world went darker. Verity blinked hard and when she looked again there was no sign of anyone or anything up there. The figure had gone and the angled view of the monument and its end pillars stood sentinel, the roof empty. Jeremy joined her and as his arm slipped around her shoulders, the world seemed to steady itself again.

'It's an amazing view, isn't it?' he said.

'Phenomenal,' she mouthed, no sound coming out.

'What is it? You look spooked. Are you okay?' Jeremy looked concerned.

'It's just I…I thought I saw something…someone up there. 'Hurrying. Over the top.'

Jeremy studied her face. 'Really? That's strange, I didn't think the roof was open weekdays. The National Trust only do public tours at certain times, usually on Bank holidays and weekends.'

'Must have been a trick of the light then,' she whispered, turning her back on the monument. He didn't understand, he was probably thinking not this again…

Jeremy took her hand. 'Probably, it's very bright.'

'Maybe it was a ghost?' she whispered, half to herself, sitting down heavily with her back to the scene. She felt chilled although the sun was warm on the back of her neck. She took a large gulp of her wine, as Tom jumped into her lap. Or was it just her imagination?

# Chapter 11

*It was rumoured that Penshaw Monument was to be sold to Aristobulus Onassis, and shipped to Greece, stone by stone to replace the Temple of Theseus and large quantities of coal dust were to be imported from the North East to preserve the stones by regularly spraying them with it so that the structure would last at least 500 years...*

Verity thought about the girl who had maybe also once walked here, long ago in another summer, who also caught the movement of the sunlight chasing across the swell of the hill across the landscape, turning it to gold, then darkening almost instantly as the sun dipped behind the clouds. Maybe she had walked slowly under the long line of poplar trees which shaded and separated the parkland from the road? She took deep breaths and inhaled slowly as she walked under the cool green shade with the monument behind her.

She had decided to confront her demons and join one of the National Trust tours to the parapet. She was going to be one of the tiny, backlit figures she had glimpsed (maybe?) from Monument Cottage's garden. So why was she walking in the opposite direction? The truth was, with time to spare she'd decided to walk around the park first. And gather together her courage. It was one thing learning to live with viewing the monument from her window but actually setting foot upon it was another matter...

She couldn't put it off any longer so she abruptly turned around, breathed a deep breath and began to walk the other way until she joined a lot of other people scrambling up the winding, steep steps of Penshaw Hill, tagging onto the queue at the top. She had a ticket and a time slot so didn't have to wait long.

She could see people hurrying over the stone summit to the eighteenth pillar with the door in it, where some national trust officials were supplying them with hard hats and instructions. Then she'd see them disappear through the doorway and eventually emerge on the top and wave down to the crowds below.

She drew her blue fleece jacket closer around her body against the biting wind, watching the clouds shift across the bright sky behind the dark pillars. For health and safety reasons they were only taking five people up at one time which meant approximately fifteen people per hour at ten minutes each.

More people kept arriving with their dogs to have a look at what was happening. Children played gleefully on the summit, jumping up and down from heavy stone to grass.

Listening to people's excited voices as she waited and catching snatches of conversation, she gathered that this visit meant an awful lot to them as their relatives back throughout the generations had already been up onto the top of the monument. Like her own. There was definitely a buzz in the air.

Then she was first in the queue. Her anticipation grew and she took deep breaths as she walked across the heavy stone squares to the eighteenth pillar. There was a steel framed door in the pillar which was open and within, she could see a collection of white hard hats piled up and the gaping, dark entrance to the spiral staircase. To the right, through the gaps in the pillars she could see way below the cars moving round the roundabout, a green circle in the middle surrounded by a round, white ribbon of road. And was that the sea in the distance, way off on the horizon?

Their group were supplied with white hard hats with attached head torches and she was the first to ascend the stone, spiral stairway. At once she felt very alone. And it was cold. There was no handrail, and it would have been very dark without the head torch.

Clutching at the roughened walls, she came across welcome slits of light every so often, [1]hewn out of the stone. The very small, uneven steps seemed to go on and on, round and round she climbed, her heart beating furiously. Her head torch kept going out and she would have been plunged into full darkness if it wasn't for the intermittent gaps. She kept going and counted seventy four steps.

At last, she saw daylight and as she emerged through a half moon shaped grid onto the top of the monument into bright fresh air, she heard a voice say, 'Watch your head.' Too late as she banged her hard

---

[1] *Taken from Sunderland Site Page 018*

hat. 'They all do that,' the voice continued and someone helped her up into dizzying brightness and startling blue sky and she felt a rush of air.

She was aware of someone watching her and heard the voice again, a young man brandishing a camera. 'Ouch. Did that hurt?'

'No, I'm fine,' she lied, feeling momentarily flustered.

It was absolutely awesome, yet dizzying once out on the walkway. For a second, she wished Jeremy was with her, holding her hand. Thoughts whirled around her head, snippets of research she'd looked at beforehand, this was Sunderland's highest landmark at sixty six feet high and there were walls of three feet on either side of the parapet.

She turned away to text Jeremy as he had made her promise to do so as the very first thing, she did up there, so he could attempt to take a video from the cottage garden below. It was futile to tell him it wasn't worth it; she'd only show up as a matchstick speck. 'I can zoom in on you V.'

He'd wanted to accompany her but she'd insisted it was something she wanted to do alone. The text was delivered. *'I'm on the parapet now.'*

When she looked up the journalist was standing grinning at her. 'Texting your boyfriend? Mind if I take a photo for the local paper? Oh, you can take your hard hat off first.'

Verity obliged, glad for the brief respite before she had to move on along the walkway.

'Just stand with your back to the wall. That's great.' She felt the rough stone at her back, and the wind clutched at her hair but she didn't really care what she looked like.

'That's a good shot.'

'Thanks.' She doubted that, what with her hair all over the place, and moved along, as the next person started to emerge from the crescent shaped grille. She guessed he was taking photos of everyone, there was no reason to believe hers would be the one that made the newspaper.

It took a while to sink in that she was standing on the very same stones her grandad had climbed over all those years ago and there was a vast gaping hole in the middle where the roof should have been and

55

where the accident happened… No, don't think about that now. That was then and this is now. This is a totally different situation, Verity talked sharply to herself. She breathed deeply and began to walk along very slowly, her eyes drawn in all directions.

The ancient stone slabs beneath her feet were blackened and roughened, yet preserved with coal dust, although the pits were long gone. In front of her was the greenery and silver of the lake at Herrington Park and the circle of bright flowers that was the roundabout below, if she twirled around, she could see the Nissan factory and slowly rotating wind turbines in the opposite direction. The sky seemed brighter than ever with only a few wispy clouds.

Walking along to the end of the parapet, she saw the open pediment, the triangular facing on the left side which only looked around ten feet across, and imagined how exhilaratingly dangerous it must have been for her grandad as he scurried across the middle, open to the elements, the wind rushing around him, with no support at all on either side, laughing and joking with his mates.

The wind whipped at her hair as she took photos and someone pointed out the tiny square that was Durham Cathedral. A strange feeling of elation took hold of her as if anything was possible. However, she had expected to feel it certainly wasn't like this. She was looking down on all the world. Suddenly she understood what Grandad Ed had meant. This was actually a magical place. It really was. She just wanted to absorb the moment.

After ten minutes which raced by, it was time to go back down the spiral staircase, waving her hand at the friendly journalist as she re-entered the darkness beyond the grille, where she gave back the white hard hat and torch and received a certificate to say she'd been up to the very top of Penshaw Monument.

She'd done it. And she felt elated. So elated she didn't feel like going straight back down the hill. She walked slowly across stone summit, across the diagonal line stretching from one corner to the other, taking photos at each point and then jumped down onto the grass.

She walked around the structure again very slowly, two tiers of stones forming a step up to the platform, past the floodlights which from above looked like white squares, placed at regular intervals, with

56

the glass broken in some of them round the back where the hillside fell away to woodland. She just wanted to take it all in.

She started idly reading the graffiti etched in some places. Then she saw something which made her stop still and her stomach somersault. Second stone up on the inner side of the fifth pillar, south side of the monument. It read: Ed loves Amelia. 1946. No way. This couldn't be happening. What were the chances? She transcribed the outline of the words with her eager fingers, scraping her knuckles but not feeling a thing. The years fell away and with shaking hands, she fished out her phone and took a photo. And another because the first one was bound to be blurred because of the shaky hands.

In the background she heard happy voices calling as children ran across the square stone platform, their squeals echoing as they searched the four corners for the most accessible place to jump down to ground level. She heard dogs yapping and almost choking with excitement as they strained against the restraint of their leaders to run free and birds chirping joyfully overhead.

Her ears however, were deaf to the voices of that other time when the lovers whispered soft words and laughed with each other, their sounds barely audible and carried away on the evening breeze, clinging to each other in the half light, Amelia's curls falling over Ed's face, scribing their love on the cool solid stone.

Verity stood there for ages just gazing at the inscription, in fact in the end she sat down and kept on looking. It couldn't be another Ed and Amelia, it had to be *her* Ed and Amelia. She just knew it. She stayed there for quite some time. Surely this had to be a sign?

She couldn't quite fathom that the old man with his scented baccy and rheumy eyes had once been the dashing young Ed who'd etched their names on the blackened tablet of stone beneath her fingers. And what about Amelia. Was she even alive?

Later that evening, Verity was looking at the photograph of the graffiti on her mobile phone, when Jeremy burst in on her thoughts. 'Hey V, I see you made the papers.'

# Chapter 12

Verity had promised to ring Grandad Ed and let him know her decision, but it was easier said than done to get in touch with him by phone. So, the following Friday afternoon she finished work early and drove straight to Sand Steps.

After the heat of the office, the clean salty air and the sweep of the cliffs plunging down to the sparkling blue sea in front of her was heartening.

Grandad Ed was in his usual place, outside in the courtyard overlooking the sea with Tiny at his side, a checked cap perched precariously on his head.

'Well, bonny lass, this is a surprise,' he struggled to stand up, pipe balanced at one side of his mouth.

'Don't get up Grandad.' She bent down to stroke the little dog who was trying to run around her in circles but couldn't quite manage it and began pawing at her ankles instead.

'I'll sit next to you. They're going to bring us some tea out.'

He was beaming all over his face, his deeply lined cheeks ruddy from the sea air. 'Why didn't you just ring me? Not that it isn't grand to see you.'

'Ring you? You're never around. No matter, I've come up with a solution,' Verity produced a box from her handbag and opened it, holding up a mobile phone. 'This is for you.'

'Eee, what is it?'

'It's a mobile phone Grandad.'

'Eh? You've got to be joking bonny lass. What would I want a mobile phone for?'

'So I can ring you and you can ring me.'

'Get away, at my age, how am I supposed to work one of them?'

'Erm, what's that in your jacket pocket?' Verity pointed out a half-hidden television remote. 'From what I've been told by Hanna, you're very good with gadgets. In fact, more than good.'

'You've been talking to my mate Hanna, then?'

'Yes, I saw her on my way in.'

'She cuts my nails for me. Aye, I'm the only one who can work the remote in the lounge. This one's from the little telly in my room, I carry it about in case someone takes a fancy to it.' He looked around surreptitiously. 'You've no idea what they're like in here. Stuff goes missing all the time.'

'I'll soon teach you how to use it. All you have to know is how to answer it and how to ring me. 'Here, I'll show you.'

Grandad Ed chuckled. 'By, you're very bossy aren't you? You're worse than them in there.'

'You should hear what they say about me at work.' She moved closer along the bench.

'See, all you have to do is swipe your finger like this to answer. I'll ring you from my mobile now and you can have a practice at answering.' She thrust the phone into Grandad Ed's hands and rang the number.

He swiped and jabbed at the button to answer with a gnarled finger. 'Hello, hello? Tiny's ears pricked up but he didn't move.

'Hello!' Verity replied.

'Hello, hello?' he said loudly, beginning to laugh, clearly at the absurdity of talking on a mobile device when the person was sitting right next to you.

'There you are, you see, it's easy. I've set it all up. You've got the hang of swiping straightaway.'

'Quick hide it, that nosey one's coming.' Verity looked around, she hadn't even heard the lady approach with the tea and tiny iced biscuits, but Grandad Ed had heard her footsteps.

'Well, there's nothing wrong with your hearing is there?' Verity said, pouring the tea from a vintage flowered teapot.

'Eh?' said Grandad Ed.

'You'll be able to hear the ring tone I've set up for you with no bother. I'll be able to let you know what stage I'm at in looking for Amelia.'

'Does this mean you're going to help me?'

Verity sighed. 'Yes, I do believe it does.'

'Champion. A1. I'm right pleased.' Grandad Ed shifted his pipe and grinned widely.

'I've set you up a WhatsApp Group as well so I can send you some photos.'

'Really?' Grandad Ed chuckled. 'I don't know. A What Group? Don't be getting too technical, mind.'

'A WhatsApp Group. Yes, you can take some photos too if you want. Of Tiny maybe?'

'Well, aye, I might like to do that.'

'I thought so. Look, I've put a couple of photos on for you to start off.' Verity showed him WhatsApp pictures of Pedro and Tom.

'Have you've got a dog of your own?' he looked with interest.

'No, Pedro belongs to Jeremy, my, my partner. Tom is mine. But we all live together.'

Grandad Ed laid his pipe across his legs along with a packet of Clan tobacco. They sat companionably whilst he refilled his pipe and Verity drank her tea from the delicate china tea cup and ate a yellow and white swirled iced biscuit. Tiny moved from Grandad Ed's side for a second to sniff and hoover up the crumbs, before regaining his position.

Verity laughed. 'You two are inseparable, I can tell.'

'Aye, he even sleeps in my bed.'

'No way.' Verity wouldn't let Pedro up on hers and Jeremy's bed, she insisted he had to sleep in his basket at the foot of the bed. 'Is that allowed?'

'Oh aye, he thinks he's a person you see. He dives right under the covers and comes up when he gets too hot.'

Verity tried not to look horrified as he went on to say, 'He burrows right down to the bottom of the bed and sleeps with his head on my backside.'

She couldn't help laughing at this image this brought forth in her head and soon the pair of them were chortling away, Grandad Ed puffing away on his pipe and Verity pouring them both more tea and giggling. She felt sad to think of all the time she had missed out on with this side of the family because of her dad's temper.

'I haven't had such a good laugh in ages,' she said, wiping her eyes.

'Does you good lass, to have a bit laugh now and again.'

Verity tried to compose herself. 'Look, I've put a picture of myself and Tom on the phone as a screensaver so you'll know it's me ringing you.'

'Eee, that's very clever lass. Not that anyone else will be ringing me.'

'Well, they might if you want them to.'

'No, I don't want you to go and give my number to anyone else mind.'

'What about Micky?'

'Definitely not Micky. Nowt to do with him. Don't want him knowing my business. You're nothing like him you know. I think you take after your mother.'

Verity felt the usual stabbing pang at her heart at mention of her mother but all she said was, 'Fair enough. Just you and me then?'

'Aye. And if I get stuck with the phone, I'll ask Hanna. I can trust her. She helps me out with the computer sometimes if I want to look at the football scores.'

'That might be helpful. So, we're good then?'

'Aye. But how do I pay for the phone? Them things won't be cheap.'

'Oh, you don't have to worry about that. I've set up a contract in my name.'

'A contract? You mean, you're paying for it?' Grandad Ed sat up straighter. 'I can't let you do that. I've got some money.'

'No need. It's all sorted. I don't want any money, honestly. I mean it. I'll get cross, mind.''

'All right, bossy boots.'

Grandad Ed pulled out a faded white handkerchief with a curly blue 'E' embroidered in the corner and wiped the corner of his eyes. 'I can't tell you how happy I am that you're helping me out, lass.'

Verity thought, oh please don't let him cry.

'Can I ask what made you decide to help me?'

She sighed and showed him a photo on her phone of the graffiti on the monument. 'I think it was this photograph.'

Grandad Ed gave a sharp intake of breath. 'I remember that day so well. Well, that part of it. Does this mean you've been up there?'

She nodded. 'Yes, on a National Trust tour. They opened the spiral staircase to the public in 2011. I forced myself to do it.' Not that she had a lot of hope of actually finding Amelia but it was just the fact that she could do this one small thing to help him.

He took his glasses off and wiped his eyes properly. 'I can't quite find the words but it means an awful lot, bonny lass, to know that you're doing this for me.'

'It's a pleasure,' Verity told him, feeling choked up inside. And it was.

# Chapter 13

Amelia had smuggled Ed in via the back stairs. Grabbing his warm, dry hand, she pulled him along behind her, shushing him whilst giggling. Ed winced and stopped still as he tread on a creaking floorboard which reverberated in the stillness of the afternoon.

'It's just saying hello,' she whispered over her shoulder.

'What if he's down there?'

Amelia thought how on earth could someone who was so fearless, possibly be scared of a mere mortal like her father? 'No, I told you, he's away. And the housekeeper thinks I'm not back from school yet. We've got ages.'

Ed began to move his feet again.

'Come on, it's just here.' She stopped abruptly in front of the last door on the landing.

She opened the door and pulled him in, shutting the door behind them, giggling, a little out of breath. Sunshine poured in crazy crisscrosses onto the polished floorboards, warming the whole room.

'Oh, I do love my room,' Amelia flung out her arms. 'Isn't it absolutely divine?'

Ed was busy removing his grubby sandshoes, then he slowly turned around in a circle, taking in what was around him.

She watched him. What was he thinking as he looked around at the richly papered lavender sprigged walls, the delicate lilac and ice-white floating drapes on the four-poster bed, the gilt-edged mirror and frilly skirted dressing table with the ornate green glass hairbrush set sparkling as the sun caught it?

Ed breathed out, then gave a low whistle. 'By, this is posh, Melly. 'She smiled at the shortened version of her name which only he used. 'It's so different to mine, I've got to share with my two scruffy brothers.'

'Everyone calls it the Lavender Room and says it's haunted.'

Ed crossed over to the wall behind the bed and tapped it. The walls are very thick,' 'No-one outside would hear a ghost rattling on his chains.'

'It's supposed to be a White Lady.'

'It usually is.'

'Ghosts don't scare me. My mother always used to say that it's the living you should be frightened of.'

'You don't know how lucky you are, Melly. You've even got your own bathroom; we've still got an outside netty.'

Amelia shrugged, she'd never really thought that she was lucky, she supposed she just took it all for granted.

He crossed to the latticed window. 'Can I open it? It's a bit stuffy in here.'

'Here, let me.' Amelia flung back the sash window and opened it wide, letting in a waft of fresh spring air which stirred the filmy lavender curtains. 'That's better.' The heady scent of sweet summer flowers assailed her senses and she inhaled deeply.

'Oh, don't those flowers smell simply delightful?'

'Sweet peas, I'm guessing,' Ed said and looking down where sure enough, there was a trellis with the fragrant blooms climbing right up to the windowsill. The stark side view of the monument, etched against the bright azure sky, caught his attention.

Amelia leaned out next to him. 'Oh, wouldn't it be heavenly to be able to smell them all year round?'

'I can show you how to cut the blooms so that they'll last longer.'

He produced a small object from his shirt pocket and placed it with a flourish on his roughened palm. Amelia stared. 'What's that?' It flashed silver in the sunlight.

'It's a penknife.' Ed straightened his shoulders. 'My grandad gave this to me as soon as I was old enough. It's my most prized possession.'

'Watch!' He leaned out over the windowsill and began snipping away whilst she held onto his other arm tightly so he couldn't fall, watching intently. 'Look, these ones with the pods are the ones you need to cut off. See?'

'Be careful. How do you know so many things, Ed?'

'I take notice of what folks tell me, that's all. My mam showed me how to do this. She loves sweet peas.'

'So do I.'

'Well, do this regularly then. But it might be best to do it from the ground. Have you got a vase?'

64

Amelia found a little porcelain jug and filled it with water from the tap in her adjoining bathroom.

'Here you are.' Arranging the blooms in the jug, she immediately buried her face in the posy of luscious purple and pink sweetness. 'Heaven.'

'Watch out for twitchibells.'

Abandoning the posy as the centrepiece of her dressing table, she kicked off her shoes and twirled around to fall backwards onto the bed. 'Come on Ed. Lie next to me.'

Ed joined her on the lavender coverlet, lying a little apart from her, his arms stiff down by his sides. Amelia moved closer and laid her head on his chest. She could feel his heart beating and smell the fresh air of the outdoors on his clothes.

He closed his eyes and wriggled his feet in their holey socks. 'By, this is comfy. I can't believe I'm actually doing this. Me, Ed Turnbull, the kid from Pithead Terrace lying on a four-poster bed in Monument Manor.'

'Oh, Ed, isn't this wonderful? Just lying here next to each other. With the magical smell of sweet peas and the warm breeze wafting in. I will remember today for ever. The first time I smuggled you into my room.' Amelia liked to recollect on their firsts.

She sat up and bent over him, letting her soft hair fall onto his face.

'We haven't got much time. I wanted to talk to you, Ed.'

'Melly, you're always talking to me. In fact, you hardly ever shut up.'

'Don't be cheeky. No, I mean, about the future. Our future.'

'How do you mean?'

'When we finish school and when we're married.'

'Married?' Ed sat up, his back very straight.

'Yes, I know you love me Ed as much as I love you. Don't be shy, tell me the truth. You do love me, don't you?' She wrapped her arms around him.

'You know I do.'

'So, let's think about it now. Imagine it, Ed. Do you ever think about the future? I mean our future. I do, I imagine it all the time.'

'But Melly.' Ed dragged his hand over his face. 'We're only fifteen. I've never thought about getting wed before. That's years away. I

65

haven't even had a proper job yet. You know I'm going to be working down the pit.'

'So? You don't have to, you know Ed. You're clever. I haven't got a clue about maths and stuff, but you've got a really quick brain.' She could see something shift in his eyes then, a glint of disbelief, moving to pride and wonderment. As if no-one had ever told him that before.

'And what about your father?'

'What about him?'

'He's never going to allow his precious daughter to marry a pitman.'

'Oh, Ed, we'll find a way. Love always does.'

'You don't half go about with your head in the clouds.'

'But it makes me happy. Thinking about our future and getting married and all that.'

'Lasses seem to think about it more than lads, I reckon.'

'Just think, what it will be like in say, ten years' time when we're twenty-five?'

'Twenty-five?' Ed pulled a face. 'But that's yonks away.'

'Our love will never change though. We'll always be together.'
Ed ran a hand through his unruly black hair, whilst Amelia drew him closer to her.

'My favourite daydream,' she went on, 'is imagining us together on a sunlit shore, having a picnic with a huge bamboo picnic basket and running barefoot down to the water's edge, hand in hand… What's yours?'

'Aw, I dunno.'

'Oh, go on please, Ed, just think of something.' Amelia widened her eyes, knowing the effect their blueness and her nearness would be having on him. She was right, his velvety brown eyes were beginning to glaze over with passion, although he just sighed and said,

'Probably eating a slice of that pie out of the picnic basket.'

'How like you to think of your stomach.' Amelia laughed. 'Oh, and I do love to think of snuggling up to the fireside with you on a cold winter's evening…'

Ed leaned closer and she smelt the unique smell that was Ed, of warm skin and young, clean perspiration. She could hear his breathing growing faster. How she loved the deep tanned weather-beaten face, the deep-set eyes, softening like velvet. They kissed each other shyly,

66

gently at first and then with growing urgency. Amelia felt as if her heart would burst right out of her chest with pure joy. They'd left the window open allowing a gentle breeze to ripple across the room as they grew closer. She thought she would never be so happy again as she was right now, knowing she was secure in Ed's love and that he wanted her. She wanted these moments to go on forever.

Then a voice called below from the open window, and they immediately broke apart, breaking the spell.

'Oh no, where has the time gone to?' Amelia moaned, 'Bother, the gardeners are finishing for the day. You'll have to go now.' She jumped off the bed and began smoothing down her creased clothing whilst Ed frantically searched about for his shoes.

With disgruntled reluctance she bustled Ed back down the back stairs and out into the garden, thinking of how wonderful it would be when they were together for ever...

Later on, Amelia noticed Ed had left his treasured penknife, glinting on the windowsill. She immediately picked it up, spun around the room to bury it deep under her mattress for the time being. Thank goodness she found it, what on earth would her father have said if he'd spied it sitting there?

# Chapter 14

A few weeks later, Jeremy had insisted on lighting the wood burner as it had been raining and was a cool evening for the time of year. The gentle, smoky aroma of new wood burning filled the air, mingling with the lingering warmth of his cooking.

Verity had settled in and was finding it easier than she'd imagined living at Monument Cottage. Although beautifully renovated, she felt the best of its original features had been preserved, and she loved the extension of a porch and sunroom on the back complete with a sturdy tiled roof.

Old fireplaces had been retained although there were a few creaky floorboards, the noisiest one being on the landing just outside their room. And it still tended to be cool at night with its high ceilings and spacious rooms when the heating went off.

The living/dining room stretched across the width of the ground floor and had dual aspect windows, with the dining room table beside the window at the back of the house. To the right was a door leading into a small room which could be used as an extra bedroom and they'd put the sofa bed in there for the time being. It was in the oldest part of the house and chilly when the heating was off, but if anyone did happen to sleep in there, she thought they could simply leave the door open and the warmth of the fire would creep through.

Jeremy was very happy at the moment because he'd received some long-awaited royalties from a film script he'd written around six years ago. The movie had just reached the top of the 'slate' and had finally been produced and released. They were having a glass of wine to celebrate although he still needed to do some marking of essays this evening.

He was sitting at one end of the table with his laptop in front of him, reading and scribbling comments on his students' typewritten papers, pausing frequently to comment out loud. Every so often he got up and paced around the room, gesturing and talking, glass in hand. He found it very hard to keep still for long. Verity sat at the other end with her back to the monument view, with Grandad Ed's crumpled folder on her knee, her unopened laptop in front of her. It was very warm and cosy.

They both laughed at Pedro and Tom who were stretched out on the new blue diagonally patterned rug, vying for the best position in front of the fire, pretending to be asleep but keeping one eye half open in case the other moved and slyly gained an extra inch of prime floor space than the other. Tom was still getting used to the noises of the house, he would sit up on occasions and put his head on one side and twitch his ears as he listened to the particular way the boiler groaned or the radiators gurgled.

Looking around at the dancing firelight, the basket of logs against the pale lemon wall, shadows bouncing off the gleaming wooden floor tiles and strategically placed reading lamps casting pools of soft golden light around the room. Verity thought to herself that life couldn't be much better than this.

They'd just eaten, a delicious Chicken Pasta with chorizo and garlic bread to start, paired with red wine and then Caramel Apple Crumble, baked by Jeremy with apples from their very own apple tree. The red wine had made her Verity feel even more mellow. He was an excellent cook and loved experimenting, having picked up lots of ideas from his travels over the years. She caught Jeremy glancing over at her. 'Happy?' she asked.

'Blindingly so.' Jeremy smiled. 'Shall we have an early night?'

'Another one? Oh, I'd love to but I must get started on this research. You keep on with your marking.'

'Ah well, it was worth a try.'

It had turned dark early outside due as much to the sheeting rain as to the late hour and Verity had closed all the blinds and curtains against the rain swept garden and the monument, which was all lit up like a beacon against the elements.

She had been looking forward to starting her research, if a bit apprehensive but just hadn't had time due to work pressures until this evening, when she had put time aside. She strategically placed photos and newspaper cuttings in front of her, on her half of the table, unlike the sprawling mess on Jeremy's half which threatened to creep over and engulf her own pristine piles.

69

She felt optimistic and enjoyed a challenge, feeling a bit like a private detective. Maybe she should have a notice board and pin everything on there? Jeremy often began planning his scripts with a storyboard. Let's start at the beginning. She'd decided just to look through all the photographs first and try to get a feel for the task ahead before she even thought about going online.

Verity wanted to lose herself in Amelia's story. Jeremy brought her in another glass of wine, and she began to attempt to piece together what she knew so far from what Grandad Ed had told her. Heaven knows she needed some distraction tonight.

He'd met Amelia Temperly, fifteen year old daughter of the Lord of the Manor, because his mother was the housekeeper at Monument Manor back in 1946 when he was young. She was used to cooking for large numbers for the local gentry's shooting parties as well as day to day family meals.

He used to sneak into the kitchen, through the walled vegetable garden, when there was no-one else around, and fill his pockets with leftovers, such as slices of game and pigeon pie and fat scones, usually when he was on route to Penshaw Hill with his mates. Verity could just visualise his mates hanging around sheepishly at the back kitchen entrance, hiding behind the shrubbery and acting as lookouts, and then Ed emerging with his pockets (and cheeks) bulging, doling out his delicious treats and escaping over the iron gates of the manor house, away into the woods.

Amelia was born there in 1931, and her frail young mother wasn't around much. Amelia never talked about her and Ed didn't like to ask too much. Her father, Lord Temperly, a wealthy landowner, ruled the roost. Amelia, an only child, bored after school and especially if it was raining, used to sit on a kitchen stool at the scrubbed pine table and watch Ed's mother as she baked. She never offered to help, preferring to go riding when the weather was fine.

Sometimes they would talk. Ed's mother often said she should have been born a boy. 'Don't be fooled by those luscious blonde curls and porcelain complexion, she's a proper little minx that one,' she'd say to the other housekeeper. 'Spoilt rotten and a right gob on her.' Amelia only laughed if she overheard as she knew Ed's mother was fond enough of her.

Then she met Ed one day by chance, knowing him vaguely from school and started to tag along with them, tying her hair back from her face and walking miles and miles over the rural landscape and getting into all sorts of scrapes, climbing trees, falling into hedges and raiding apple orchards and best of all, scrambling up to the summit of Penshaw Monument.

'I was good looking when I was young, you know, the lasses liked me,' Grandad Ed had told her and she could imagine he was. In fact, she'd seen photos of him among the stuff he'd given her, and although small in stature, he had a kind of presence, mean and moody and angular. He was a good runner with a lean and wiry frame and always did well on Sports Days at school, with female admirers cheering him on. Verity thought that back in those days, boys were probably still tomboys at sixteen, although maybe just starting to think about girls.

Amelia and Ed fell in love and started going out together on their own. Secretly of course because her father would not have approved. Grandad Ed didn't elaborate much on their courting days, as he called it, just said that they enjoyed each other's company and she was a good match for his sharp wit and mathematical brain.

She liked her own way though, and apparently on that fateful day in 1946, they'd had a flaming row. Ed was fed up of her tantrums and told her it was all off. He'd regretted it straightaway but was too proud to admit it in front of his mates. Then of course, headstrong as ever, she'd climbed the eighteenth pillar and confronted him on the parapet of the monument, begging him to take her back with all the passion of young love. He'd told her they'd talk later but she couldn't wait.

His last memory before he fell off was that she was trying to follow him, shouting and crying, and trying to pull him away from his mates.

'What happened next?' Verity had asked.

'Well, she just sort of disappeared,' Grandad Ed's brown eyes had clouded over. 'I tried to find out of course but it was many weeks later when I recovered, before I was even able to ask anything and I was told she'd gone abroad to live with relations in Italy. I was sent away to recuperate in a clinic by the sea for a few weeks and I never saw her again. They just kept their gobs shut and my Mam lost her job, which I couldn't understand as it had nowt to do with her. It meant that I had to go and work to bring some money in as soon as I was able.'

So, Amelia was last heard of going to live in Italy. But that was way back in 1946. What had happened to her since then? Had she married? What was her married name? Where was she now and was she still alive? So many questions.

One of the photographs she was studying seemed to come to life in front of her eyes. It was a headshot of Amelia and Ed laughing happily together, then the picture seemed to blur before Verity's eyes. She blinked and looked again and instead of the grainy black and white of Amelia and Ed, she saw herself and Jeremy in the same position, laughing up at each other. Warmth spread hopefully inside her and she felt her cheeks flush.

'What are you smiling at?' Jeremy asked, glancing up from his paperwork.

Verity looked up too and their eyes met and she felt her heart sing at the love suffused in his cornflower blue eyes. She hadn't thought it was possible to ever feel as happy as this. She shook her head and when she looked back at the photograph between her fingertips, it was once again Amelia and Ed who stared back at her.

Must be the wine, she thought, shaking her head. 'Nothing,' she whispered. 'Just having a moment. And thinking how lucky I am.'

Verity began googling the Temperly family and Monument Manor. She delved further and further back in time through a riotous mix of Lords, Earls, Lord Lieutenants, politicians, musicians, and artists until she found whom she knew had to be Amelia's father. Charles Claud Temperly. Born in 1899 and died in 1961 with a twin brother, he had been a military man and a British Peer. He was also a politician as well as a landowner. Verity skimmed through the information –he was married to Lady Eliza who, after producing one daughter, Amelia Violet, was committed to a mental institution for most of her life before dying young. Poor Amelia. No wonder she'd been troubled.

Interested, she read that the heir to the manor nowadays was Samuel John Temperly, whom, she reckoned, as Charles didn't have any other children apart from Amelia, must have been a descendant of the son of Charles twin brother. He would have been Charles' great, great, great nephew? Or something like that. Samuel lived abroad and let out the family home where he had grown up to an agent who managed the estate on his behalf. He only returned on rare occasions to stay for a short while but was happy to allow the local church to hold functions twice a year to raise money.

Verity shut her tired eyes for a second, thinking they weren't keeping up with her brain. Then she came across on the same website, an advert for an 'Summer Cheese and Wine Soiree' at Monument Manor which was opening its doors to the public for one night only. The ticket price included two glasses of wine, raffle prizes and a chance to have a look around the Temperly portrait gallery. It was for the following Friday evening.

Now there's a stroke of luck, she thought, sitting up straighter and noticing the still full glass of rose wine, took a sip. If I can go and have a look around, maybe I can find something out, or maybe there will be someone there who knows the family. A great start. She must ring Grandad Ed and tell him.

She scanned through the info about Monument Manor itself, which was situated on the east edge of the vast estate and accessed by a long and winding avenue, which in springtime was furnished on both sides by carpets of golden daffodils. The whole estate had been purchased by the Temperly family way back in the 1500's and apparently there had been a manor house on that site long before that.

The grounds of the Estate incorporated a river and a lake as well as some other grand houses. It was a traditional working estate with working livery stables and many paddocks for the horses. Extensive dense woodland shrouded the house from prying eyes and diagonal belt of conifers shaded from the east and west. And it all was just down the road from here. Who knew?

And here was a colourful online photograph of the manor house she'd heard so much about. She immediately booked a ticket online.

# Chapter 15

The sound of a car pulling up outside made her sit up straight. It was unusual to hear a vehicle at this time of night as their house was at the end of the lane. Then a car door slammed and a few seconds later the doorbell rang. Pedro went berserk, running to the window and barking like crazy whilst Tom sat up and stretched skywards, bristling in every sinew.

'Pedro, shhh, be quiet,' shushed Jeremy. 'Who could that be?'

Verity shrugged and stood up but Jeremy jumped up, scattering papers everywhere. 'I'll go.' Pedro followed him, still barking although his tail wagged.

'Probably someone lost,' Verity thought, yawning but when Jeremy didn't return straightaway, she got up slowly, stretched and hastily picked up the pile of papers from the floor before padding in her fluffy mules through to the front porch. Tom, decided it wasn't worth the effort of investigating further and moved quickly over into Pedro's vacated spot.

'Oh.' Verity was surprised by the presence of a young man in the kitchen, wearing an oversized parka with the hood up, hauling a backpack off his back onto the kitchen table on which already rested a guitar and a huge keyboard. Jeremy was just coming in from the porch with another holdall.

Under his hood, Verity saw he had an angular face, and a sullen expression with a roll up cigarette hanging out of the side of his mouth. He looked very young. He slouched back out of the back door and came in again with a computer tower and a sound deck, speakers, trailing cables everywhere.

Verity watched in amazement, pulling her dressing gown cord tighter around her waist. Thoughts crowded into her head. Was this a rehearsal for a play? Was he one of his students? but she managed to say, 'Hey, what's going on? Who's this?'

Then there was a loud knock at the door. 'Is someone paying the bill?'

The young man looked at Jeremy and removing the cigarette from his mouth and shoving it into his jeans pocket, muttered, 'Have you got any cash? I'll pay you back.'

Jeremy quickly obliged and paid the taxi driver and soon the car was driving away back along the road to civilisation whilst Verity drew herself up tall and waited for an explanation. Jeremy cleared his throat.

'Verity, I'd like you to meet er… someone. This is Albie.'

Albie grunted something which might have been hello.

'Hello. Albie. Who are you exactly?' Verity asked. 'Are you one of Jeremy's students?'

Albie snorted. 'You haven't told her, have you?'.

'Told me what?'

Jeremy shifted from foot to foot. 'He's not one of my students but he erm…does belong to me.'

Albie took off his cap, revealing lots of long, dark blonde, straggly, greasy hair. Or was it wet from the rain? It looked like it could be a very similar colour to Jeremy's. Verity looked from one to the other. Uncertainty on Albie's face, trepidation on Jeremy's. Was she imagining it or did they look like each other?

A raft of emotions flooded over her, anguish, tension, shock, amazement. What did he mean, belong to me? Not another secret. No, it couldn't be. A long lost love child? Her heart plummeted. She knew things were too good to be true. Was her perfect world about to crash?

'What do you mean, he belongs to you?' she kept her voice calm but could feel the colour drain from her face.

'Not in that way.'

'Then in what way?'

Jeremy sighed. 'He's my nephew.'

Relief washed over Verity for one blissful moment, then she felt guilty for thinking such a thing. Then, reality grounded her thoughts. 'What exactly is he doing here at this time of night?'

'Uncle Jer said I could stay here.' Albie thrust both hands in his pockets, still staring at Jeremy. 'Any time at all.'

Jeremy – 'Erm, well…

'You haven't forgotten, have you?'

'No, of course not.'

75

'You mean you've just forgotten to mention it to me?' Verity folded her arms.

Jeremy nodded and pulled a face. 'Yes, something like that. I er...might have said Albie could live with us for a while.'

'What?' Verity rounded on him.

'And I'm afraid I got the date wrong.' Jeremy looked at his watch. 'I thought it was next month you were coming. I thought I had plenty time to'...he glanced at Verity, to explain things.' Albie shook his head.

'Jeremy. A word.' She was distracted by a strange gurgling noise. 'What's that?'

'It's me,' Albie admitted. 'I've been travelling all day and I haven't had much scran.'

'So where have you travelled from?'

'From the South. Hampshire. My train was delayed, that's why I'm so late.'

'Hampshire! Good heavens.' Verity's good manners immediately took over. 'Right, Albie, you must be starving. Let me take your coat and come on into the dining toom. It's cold standing in here.' She divested him of his sopping wet parka and hung it up in the porch. 'Jeremy, is there any of that pasta left?'

Jeremy nodded. 'Yes, loads, I'll heat it up.'

'We can sort this all out tomorrow,' she looked at both of them, pleased to note that Albie was taking off his muddy shoes, leaving them in the porch under where his coat was hanging. At least he had some sense.

'Do you like chicken pasta?' Jeremy asked him.

'Yay, sound. I like anything.'

Albie, clutching a smart looking mobile phone, followed her into the cosy dining room where she hastily cleared away all her papers so he could sit down whilst Jeremy heated up what was left of the pasta. Albie then proceeded to demolish it at an alarming rate, stopping only to ask if they had any hot chilli sauce, the hotter the better, which Jeremy immediately produced. Albie then began to squeeze it all over his pasta to Verity's surprised horror.

'Coca Cola?' Jeremy asked, waving a bottle at him.

'Can I get a can of lager?' Whilst he was tucking in, Verity looked around to see Jeremy hovering. 'Jeremy. A word please.'

He followed her back into the kitchen.

'Right. Explain to me what he is doing here?' she whispered, not wanting to appear rude by discussing Albie in front of him. They talked in lowered voices.

'Albie is my step-nephew.'

'Oh, so you're not even properly related?'

Jeremy went on quickly, 'I was brought up with his mum, she was fostered by my step parents. I was talking to Sandra a few weeks ago and she mentioned that Albie had asked if he could come stay with me for a while.'

'Why?'

'Because he's just left…he's between jobs and the North East is the in place for new music at the minute.'

'Heavens. He doesn't look old enough to have a job. He looks about twelve.'

'He's twenty-one and left Uni with an excellent degree, a First I may add.'

'Wow. But why he is between jobs?'

'I'll explain later.'

'But he can't stay here.' she whispered loudly.

'Can't he? It won't be for long, I promise.'

'But…but...what about…?' Verity was furious and wanted to shout at him what about our cosy love nest? Albie wandered in with his phone in hand.

'What's your Wi-Fi password?'

Verity had this written down by the television, so she stomped past him into the living room and handed it to him. 'Here. By the way, I should have asked you this before, does your mum know you're here?'

Albie nodded. 'Sort of.'

'Then, shouldn't you ring her and let her know you've arrived safely?'

'Nah, she'll be out with her new boyfriend.'

'Text her then.'

Albie rolled his eyes but gave in under Verity's glare and quickly sent a text.

'That food was lush by the way.'

'Thanks mate,' Jeremy was pleased.

What was that strange smell? Verity wondered. Then she realised it was Albie's stockinged feet. His socks must have been wet and now they were steaming in the warmth of the room and leaving damp patches on the wooden floor. The whole room stank. And he was wearing odd socks.

'Would you like a hot shower?' she asked, thinking thank goodness they had a downstairs cloakroom and he didn't have to come upstairs just yet.

'Nah, I'm all right thanks.'

Let me rephrase that, Verity thought, then spoke firmly, 'The downstairs shower room is just off the kitchen, Jeremy will show you where it is while he makes up the bed.'

'I could just sleep on the sofa?'

'No, you can't, that's where Tom sleeps. My cat.'

'You've got a cat as well?'

'Oh yes, he's somewhere around.' Tom must have sloped off upstairs out of the way.

Verity suddenly realised she felt very tired and drained. She opened the door to the right which led to the little room in the oldest part of the cottage. There's a sofa bed in there and it will be warm for a while because of the fire. I'm off to bed now.'

'I'll...er make the bed up then,' Jeremy said. 'Where do we keep the spare sheets?'

Verity hurried up the stairs to the airing cupboard and gathered up what she needed, throwing them into Jeremy's open arms at the bottom of the stairs. Sounds about right that he had no idea where the bedding was kept.

She called down to them. 'Tomorrow morning, we can all have a proper talk and sort things out. Okay?'

Albie mumbled something back.

She'd had enough of today and of Jeremy's latest surprise. From upstairs, she overhead him talking to Albie. First came Albie's mumbled tones which she couldn't quite hear, something about being 'full on' and then she heard Jeremy's voice and his low laugh.

78

'No, don't you worry about her. She'll be fine with it. It's just a bit of a surprise. She's very kind hearted and she'll do anything for me.'

Would she really? What? Who did he think he was? He obviously thought he could get away with anything.

Hurt washed over her as she thumped the pillow mercilessly into shape and flung her head down on it. |Her eyes swivelled in the direction of the doorway where Pedro was hanging about, tail swishing.

'Don't even think about it,' she said, as he trotted over to the bed. 'You are not sleeping on this bed tonight.' Pedro backtracked out of the room, making the floorboard creak before he pounded down the stairs.

Yes, Jeremy, she turned over and plumped the pillow again before flinging her head down on it, thank you for yet another surprise.

# Chapter 16

*Some scientists say there is a gene modification to blame for those who need more sleep. Although they don't know exactly why some people need 12 or more hours of sleep, there is a name for it. It's called "long sleepers," and they make up approximately 2 percent of the population.*

Verity glanced at the kitchen clock. She was on her second mug of coffee and wondering just how much longer did they have to wait until Albie surfaced? She wanted to get this chat out of the way and felt annoyed rather than nervous. She knew Jeremy was aware she could hardly bear to speak to him this morning and he was busying himself making full English breakfasts for them but Verity remained silent, not allowing him to dispel the frosty atmosphere. She hoped the delicious aroma of sizzling bacon would tempt Albie out of bed? Or rather, off the sofa bed.

'I would send Pedro in to wake him up but he's already in there.' Jeremy attempted a joke. Albie must have let him sleep on top of the bed then. Verity turned the radio up and opened the door to the living room.

Shortly afterwards Albie emerged and headed for the back door, focused on rolling a cigarette between his fingers as he moved, whilst clutching his phone at the same time, eyes squinting at the light and half closed. He dropped a Rizla paper on his way. He looked like the walking dead. Barefoot, he'd slept in a grubby, creased grey t-shirt and a pair of shorts and Pedro shadowed him closely, little tail wagging, having shown his allegiance straightaway, even though Albie didn't seem to be paying him that much attention. Verity heard the lighter click outside the kitchen window.

'Sit down mate,' Jeremy invited him as he slowly lumbered back into the kitchen.

'I don't usually do mornings, I only got up for a smoke.'

'What? Verity looked pointedly at the clock. 'It's after eleven.'

'Is that proper coffee I can smell?' he asked, slumping down at the table, trying to focus on his phone. 'Smells lush.'

Jeremy nodded and put the re-filled cafetiere on the kitchen table and Verity filled up a mug for Albie.

'Sound.'

'Sleep well, did you?' Verity asked.

'Nah, I could hear snoring. I need around twelve hours kip.'

Verity was speechless. She couldn't believe that but not that she'd had much experience with twenty year old boys, apart from her nephew 'Our Johnny' whom she'd grown up with and he'd suffered from ACD and hardly needed any sleep at all.

'Breakfast?' Jeremy placed a huge plateful of bacon, eggs, hash browns, tomato, mushrooms and two fried eggs in front of him and Albie sat up straight. 'Sound. Thanks,' before putting his head down to concentrate on tucking in, only lifting it to ask for hot chilli sauce again.

'Verity?' Jeremy looked the picture of contrite domestication, gesturing to a pan of creamy scrambled eggs off the hob, wiping his brow and standing in a patch of sunlight which illuminated his golden curls, his smile winning. Dressed in faded blue denim shorts which showed off his butterscotch tanned legs, his old blue t-shirt made his bright eyes pop.

'Scrambled eggs?'

Why did he have to be such an appealing human? 'No thanks, I've had my grapefruit and cereal.'

'I'll have them,' Albie put in.

'Made with real butter?' Jeremy tried to tempt her again but she stood up, shaking her head and topping up her mug with hot coffee. 'When you've finished, let's have a little chat in the garden.'

'Yes, boss,' said Jeremy, winking and she shot him a look. Did he have to be so flippant when she was seething inside? Hadn't he even noticed? She'd pretended she was fast asleep when he came to bed last night, curled up with her back to him, although she felt tension in her every muscle. To make things worse, she heard him snoring almost immediately. Jeremy never had any problem sleeping either.

She sat down at the little table in her favourite garden space, flicking through Twitter on her phone, Tom rubbing against her ankles. At least you're on my side, she thought. It was a bright morning with a nip in the air and a clean, blue washed sky.

The other two joined her with a scraping of garden chairs, Albie sitting opposite with another unlit roll up cigarette hanging out of the side of his mouth.

Verity got a good look at him. Tangled, tousled hair covering his forehead, which was actually a light shade of blond since being washed, but was still in dire need of a comb. Now his eyes were open, they appeared so dark blue you could almost drown in them, in fact they were almost navy. He had dark shadows underneath which looked almost like delicate bruising, a long nose, face appearing gaunt due to the hollows under the high cheekbones, sulky mouth and overall, skinny to the point of looking undernourished. Which clearly wasn't the case.

'Right, let's start at the beginning,' Verity said. 'Albie, what brings you here?'

'He…'began Jeremy.

'Let Albie speak.' Verity put in.

Albie yawned and spoke out of the corner of his mouth, due to the roll up. 'Well, I've just quit my job.'

'Who did you work for? And why did you leave?'

'It was a Fast Response Contact Centre. I couldn't stand it any longer.' He removed the rollup which was making him talk like he was a gangster and continued with vehemence, 'and I had to work night shifts which didn't suit me. I need my sleep. It was rubbish.'

'Your mum said the money was very good for your age?' Jeremy questioned.

'Suppose so.'

'Surely it was better than all those supermarket jobs?' Jeremy interjected.

'How many jobs have you had?' Verity asked.

Albie shrugged. 'Since I left Uni? Oh, a few. Not many really.''

Goodness, he must have only lasted a few weeks at each of them, Verity thought.

'He's got a really good degree though,' Jeremy chimed in, 'didn't you Albie?'

'Yeah, I got a First in Music Technology.' Verity noted a spark in Albie's voice.

'That's very good,' admitted Verity.

'Better than mine,' Jeremy stated.

Albie sat forward, his eyes lighting up. 'What I really wanted to do was set up a business and a record label for my music.'

'Now, that sounds interesting,' Jeremy said.

'Well, my Mum didn't agree, said I should be making some money. So, I stayed at the contact centre until I couldn't stand it any longer, saved up some cash and decided to come to Newcastle where there's a good music scene. And my mum said Uncle Jeremy might have some contacts as he's a writer and an actor.'

'Oh, I see,' Verity said. 'When did you speak to Jeremy about this?'

'Oh, loads of times. He said he would have plenty of room for me when he moved into his new house.'

'Right,' said Verity, turning to Jeremy. 'And you didn't think to discuss it with me?'

Jeremy looked awkward. 'Sorry, I forgot to mention it with everything that's been going on. You know what I'm like when I'm working. I'm so hopeless and I'm absent minded at the best of times.'

'I had noticed.' As if his creativity was to blame for everything?

'Do you really mind so very much?'

Verity addressed Albie. 'You do realise we're around ten miles around from the city of Newcastle? It's fifty minutes on the bus.'

Albie shrugged again. 'Where I live, it's around seventy miles on the train from London. In the middle of nowhere. It was a dead-end town and all my mates have left for London. I don't mind the bus.'

'Why the North East?' Verity was curious.

'Well, Uncle Jeremy really sold it to me. Said he loves it here. Everyone is so friendly. Not like in the South. And there's nothing for me in Hampshire.'

'How long are you planning on staying?' Verity asked.

Albie shrugged again. 'Not for long. Just until I can find a place of my own.'

'And you're sure your family is happy for you to stay here?'

'Yeah. There's only Mum. She won't mind. She thinks an awful lot of Uncle Jeremy, they were brought up together.'

'I bet she does,' Verity thought.

'To be honest, she's never in the house anyway. She'll be glad I'm out of her way.'

83

Verity thought there might be a bit more going on under the scenes but she wasn't sure what. Why didn't he just move out and get his own place with his mates? Why here? Wasn't it a bit drastic to move up North? Although, that was exactly what Jeremy and his stepdad had done.

'We've never really got on,' Albie admitted glumly. 'I used to get in the way. She used to farm me out to her mates when she went on holiday with the girls.'

Verity felt a pang at this. She too was also used to being farmed out when she was a kid and knew what loneliness felt like. And no mention of his father.

'And I could always talk to Uncle Jeremy.'

There was a pause in the conversation and Verity was aware of two pairs of eyes on her, waiting for her decision.

'I can pay my way. I've got some savings. I eat a lot,' Albie added, making her smile despite her misgivings.

'And he does mean a lot,' Jeremy explained. 'We can sort the money out later, can't we V?' glancing at Verity to see if she was happy with that.

Verity was lost in the past for a moment as she was reminded of when she first went to meet her Grandma Anna. She was fifteen. It mattered so much to her that Grandma Anna let her stay there, after a childhood of being passed from auntie to auntie whilst her dad gallivanted off with another new woman.

She remembered, exactly how she'd felt then when she first entered Grandma's house with Uncle Bobby all those years ago. It was like going back in time. The roaring heat of the fire, the homemade bread resting on the hearth, the picture of her mother on the mantlepiece, the clothes drying on an overhead pulley, the homemade chocolate eclairs glistening on the kitchen bench. Johnny, Grandma Anna's nephew lying in front of the fire toasting his stockinged feet and the banter and laughter of her cousins as they helped themselves to bread and dripping in the kitchen.

The warmth of her welcome and the sensation of feeling absolutely at home…It felt so familiar.

And not wanting to go back to her cold, sparse bedroom at Auntie Doris's house at Lilac Square, which didn't have a scrap of lilac

84

anywhere, just a square patch of stubby grass where stray dogs and even the odd horse wandered aimlessly. Please Grandma, I won't be any trouble. I promise.

'I'm staying then?' Albie's voice shook her back to the present.

'Oh, go on then. For now.' Verity said. He was obviously a bit of a lost soul, like she had been, how could she refuse? She only wished Jeremy had told her sooner, she might have had time to get used to the idea. After all, they'd just moved in here together properly. Albie staying was going to change the equation somewhat.

'Yes!' said Jeremy, punching the air.

'Sound,' said Albie. 'Okay if I go back to bed now?'

'No, it isn't,' Verity reproached him. 'It's twelve o'clock. I want that room tidied up and the sofa bed back into place.'

'How about we show you around the house?' Jeremy suggested. 'You didn't see much of it last night.'

'Yes, we need to stash your stuff somewhere.' Verity glanced at the pile of holdalls and backpacks in the corner of the kitchen, the guitar and speakers stacked against the wall.

'You can decide which room you want,' Jeremy said generously.

'How many spare rooms have you got?' Albie grimaced slightly. 'This house is way bigger than it looks from outside. It looked like a proper country cottage last night with the smoke rising from the chimney.'

'Come and see for yourself,' Jeremy jumped up from the table and led the way upstairs, followed by Albie, Pedro and Verity. Tom chose to watch from a safe distance at the bottom of the stairs, tail swishing. They each hit the creaky floorboard on the landing.

There were four bedrooms up there in total, Verity and Jeremy's was the first door on the left at the top of the stairs, then there were two smaller ones and at the end of the corridor, separated by the spacious bathroom, was the room which stretched right across the top floor.

Verity opened the door of the larger of the two smaller ones. 'I thought you might like this one?'

Albie peered in and his face dropped when he saw the single bed and small narrow window. Then he was distracted as Jeremy was moving along the landing and throwing open the door of the dual aspect room much to Verity's horror. 'What about this one?'

'No, no, I thought we agreed that one was earmarked for your indoor office?' Verity cut in.

Jeremy shrugged. Albie entered the light flooded space and his eyes lit up. 'Now, this is proper cool.' He began pacing slowly around the room.

It was light and bright, painted white, double windows with a monument view of course, at one end and a view of the greenery of the country park from the other.

Another floorboard creaked noisily under Albie's bare feet.

'There's one of those in just about every room,' Jeremy said. 'It's as if it's saying hello.'

'I need plenty of light when I'm composing. And space for the acoustics. And there's a double bed. Brilliant.' He plonked himself down on it and lay back. He put his hands behind his head and looked out at the monument. 'I can sleep in here and there's room for my equipment.'

'Make yourself at home, won't you?' Verity half smiled.

Albie bounced a few times then sat up. 'Do you know I'm nearly twenty-one years old and I've never had a double bed?' His delight was apparent.

Verity folded her arms. 'I had to wait until I was married and bought my first house before I slept in a double bed. Why would you need one?'

Albie's shoulders slumped as he sat up and Verity immediately felt bad as this was the most animated she'd seen him yet. Jeremy was probably happier working downstairs in the hub of the home anyway. And it was only for a short time…

'For all the sleeping he does,' Jeremy joked.

Verity faced him. 'Jeremy?'

'To be honest V, I'm just as happy downstairs using the dining room table. I don't need all this space.'

'Right, that's settled then.'

Albie looked like he'd already moved in as he stretched his gangly arms and legs out on the bed. 'Cool. I knew it was time I left home.'

Verity thought for a second, fine, but why did you have to come and live in mine? Then felt immediately guilty again.

'What do you think of that?' Jeremy asked, indicating the monument, where from here could be seen the western end of the structure with the arch rising to a shallow point and four angled pillars dominating underneath. 'It's a local landmark and it's all lit up at night.'

Albie pulled a face. 'I'm not into views.'

'Well, let's move your things in then, shall we?' Jeremy said.

'Sound. Then I can catch up on some sleep.'

Verity looked at him to see if he was kidding but his face was perfectly sombre.

Later, leaving him to settle in, Verity sat in silence, opposite Jeremy at the dining room table, flicking through her research info.

'Are you still mad at me?' Jeremy asked. 'He's not a bad lad you know. Just a bit...'

'Laid back?'

'Yeah, I suppose he is. It'll be all right, you know.'

'You always say that. Hadn't you thought that we might need - or want to be on our own for a while?' Verity said. 'Doesn't it matter to you? Or are you taking me for granted already and we're not even married yet?'

'No, not at all.' Jeremy pushed his chair back and came and stood behind her chair. 'I just felt sorry for the lad. He hasn't had much of a home life growing up.'

'I don't think you can even see what I'm getting at.' She felt frustration as she knew he knew her own home life hadn't been great until she was fifteen.

'He won't even make much difference to our lives,' Jeremy put both his arms around her but she pushed him away.

Something inside her snapped. 'Is this what it's going to be like for the rest of our lives together? You do something and we fall out and then I forgive you?'

'I'm so sorry. I just seem to mess everything up. But I don't mean to. I honestly love you to bits.'

'You are...exasperating. Yes, that's the word. Exasperating.'

'I'd do anything for you V.'

'Really? Then leave me in peace to look at this research.'

He moved his arms upwards and began burying his head in her neck.

The familiar smell of him, his hair soft against her cheek made her heart ache. She just wanted to lean back against his warmth. But it was all too raw and she just couldn't agree with him. And she was still annoyed at what she'd overheard last night.

'It'll all work out, you'll see.'

She so wanted to believe him.

# Chapter 17

*April 1946 – Italy*

Amelia awoke to unfamiliar surroundings. Her heart was beating very fast and her tongue felt thick in her mouth. She tried to get out of bed but found herself fighting a tangle of heavy white linen. As soon as she attempted to place both feet on the stone floor, she found that her head swam and her legs buckled beneath her. She lay back down on the bed, breathing very fast. Where was she?

Her eyes darted around the room and as thick walls and lavender and white décor swam into focus, she thought it was not unlike her own bedroom back at Monument Manor. There were two doors to the right of the huge bed in which she lay with its overhanging canopy and there was a huge picture window right opposite. But it wasn't her home.

'That's the door to your bathroom.' She heard her father's voice.

She saw that her father was standing in the open entrance to the room, dressed in a smart suit and tie. She struggled to see what was behind him but was could only see what looked like a long dark passageway, stretching away behind him. He was carrying a jug of iced water and a glass on a tray which he deposited on the bedside table to her right. She struggled to reach a sitting position and her father plumped the pillows behind her head.

She winced. 'My head hurts.'

He shut the door and gestured around the room.

'Uncle Samuel has furnished this room specially for you with your favourite colours. See, everything is lilac and white. Is it to your liking?'

'It's very nice but…'

Everything seemed to be happening in slow motion as if she was a step behind and couldn't catch up. She watched as her father, a tall straight figure, drew back the white curtains from the large picture window facing the bed. They billowed gently in a cool draught. However, the view which was revealed was not that of Penshaw Monument, standing sentinel on top of its green hill, instead formal emerald lawns sloped away to become undulating fields of gold as far as the eye could see, racing to meet the bright blue horizon. The brightness of the scene hurt her eyes.

Her father stepped away from the window. 'Just wait until you see the view from the other side of the house. Fiesole overlooks the city of Florence. We're very high up here.'

Then she remembered. She was in Italy. In Villa Rosa in Fiesole, her Uncle Samuel's Italian residence. But why couldn't she remember anything about the journey here?

'How are you feeling?'

She tried to speak but her mouth was very dry.

'Still tired? That's no problem, don't try to get up just yet.'

'I'm thirsty.'

'Here,' he handed her the glass of water.

Her hand felt shaky so she put both her hands around the glass and took a large gulp. Water had never tasted so clean and cool and she drank greedily. That was so much better.

'Welcome to your new home.'

Panic gripped Amelia as she clutched at her stomach. 'My baby? Is my baby safe?'

'Your baby is fine. The doctor confirmed that last night and he gave you something to help you sleep,' her father shook his head. 'And to calm you down.'

Calm her down? Her head throbbed. What had happened to make her need something from a doctor?

She breathed deeply. 'What are we doing here?'

'Don't try to remember. You're perfectly safe and you are to stay here for your confinement.'

'Then can I go home?'

'I'm afraid not.'

'But why not? I don't understand.' Amelia began to sob. Tumultuous emotions jostled in her brain as she strived to remember. She knew there was something troubling her deeply, something horrendous but she couldn't quite think what it was.

Her father produced a pristine handkerchief from his suit jacket pocket. 'Here. Now come on, don't upset yourself. Don't let's have another weeping episode. Everything is going to be fine.' She thought

90

she heard him mutter under his breath, 'If you do as you are told of course.'

He looked around the room, found a chair and brought it to her bedside where he sat down and gazed at her, twiddling his thumbs.

'You are a very lucky young lady, Amelia. Lucky that your Uncle Samuel, my very kind twin brother, is willing to let you stay here on his beautiful Florentine estate whilst you have your baby.'

'I am of course very grateful, father. But how long need I stay here? I love England, it's my home. Will I ever be able to go back?'

Her father stroked his moustache. 'Not for a long while. If ever.'

Horror gripped her as realisation dawned and she remembered what had happened on the monument.

'It was my fault, wasn't it? I was responsible. I killed Ed.'

'Listen to me Amelia.' His cold hand covered hers. 'You did not kill that…that boy. It was an accident waiting to happen. Those youths and their preposterous stunts. They thought they were invincible.'

'No, no, it was my fault. All my fault.' She jerked away his hand and rocked back and forward, silent tears springing again from her eyes. 'I went up there to talk to him and…'

'Forget about it. I don't want to hear it. Of course, you didn't kill him. They shouldn't have been running about on the parapet and over the pediments in the first place.'

'I killed him. And I love him. I loved him!' She began to sob again, a jerking raw sound. Goodness, was she really making that horrible grating noise?

He leaned forward and shook her shoulders. 'Rubbish! That is the last time I want to hear you say that. Listen to me – I am telling you it was not your fault. Pull yourself together or I will have to arrange to have the doctor give you another sedative.'

He waited until her sobs subsided into hiccups and took hold of her wrists, gripping them tightly. 'Listen to me. I never want to hear you speak about that boy again. Or what happened in England. Do you hear me?'

His steel grey eyes bored into hers. She tore her gaze away, shooting glances around the room, looking anywhere to avoid his gaze. 'He's gone for good Amelia. You don't need to think about him ever again. Forget him.'

91

Her eyes rested on the adjoining doorway.

'That second doorway - that's where the nurse will sleep. She will be arriving soon.'

'I don't need a nurse.'

'Oh, but you do. She will keep an eye on you when I go back to England and when your time comes. She'll make sure you don't do anything stupid.'

Amelia felt a cold shiver down her spine.

'But, but…I can't stay here. I don't even speak Italian.'

'You're a bright girl, you'll soon learn. Uncle Samuel and your Cousin Sam will teach you what you need to know.'

He let go of her wrist, sitting back and resting his elbows on his knees.' 'However, I must insist upon certain conditions.'

'What sort of conditions?'

He steepled his fingers. 'You must never talk about that boy and what happened in England. Agreed?'

Amanda bowed her head.

'You mustn't do anything rash that will affect the baby. And as mentioned before, you cannot go back.'

'But Monument Manor is my home.'

'Well, you should have thought of that before, shouldn't you?' His eyes flashed.

'It's the only place I've ever lived. I love it there.'

'You will learn to love it here.'

'But I must apologise to Ed's family for what I did. I've got to make them see that I didn't mean to do it. That I really loved him.'

'You had no part in it at all.'

'But I did. I must make them listen.'

'No, no, no!' he sat back in his chair, glaring at her, his face contorted. 'Oh, why are you are so headstrong? You're just like *her*.'

'Her? Do you mean my mother?'

'Yes. Of course. Your mother.' He got up and began pacing around the room, hands on his head. 'She was going to leave me. How could she even think of leaving when we had you, a child together? I was very, very concerned for her state of mind.'

Amelia's heart was beating so fast in her chest it hurt.

'So, I did the kindest thing. The only thing. The only option available to me.'

'What did you do to her?' Amelia sat up straighter, feeling as if her heart was going to burst clean out of her rib cage. 'Did you kill her?'

'Kill her?' He stopped and stood still. 'For goodness sake, what do you think I am? I'm not a monster. I couldn't kill anyone.'

'Then what did you do?'

'I sent her away.'

'Where to?'

'To a very special unit. Where she would have all the care and attention she needed.'

'What was this place?'

Her father moved again, coming to a standstill in front of the window. 'It was a mental institution.'

The room darkened and Amelia felt like she was going to faint. She gripped the coverlet but her fingers shook uncontrollably.

'How could you?' she shrank back against her pillows.

'It was the kindest thing for her.'

'And she died in there? You told me she died because of her health conditions.'

'That was true. She was not a well woman. She was extremely frail.'

'But you put her there. In a mental institution.' Amelia shook her head, making her headache worse. Hot tears scalded her cheeks. 'You put my mother in a mental institution.'

'I did the best thing possible for all concerned. It was the only way open to me.'

'How could what you did ever be for the best?'

'You may as well know the whole truth. Your mother was what you might call a woman with unusual urges.' He wrenched the curtain open still further.

'Anyway, I'm not going into all that. You don't need to know about her sluttish ways.' He dropped the curtain so that it billowed further.

'I don't believe it.'

'You had better believe it. She was going to leave me for another man.' He moved across the room to the door and stood with his hand on the doorknob. 'But there was no way that was ever going to happen. I did love her you see, despite her many flaws.' His hand turned the doorknob but the door didn't open. 'You've got to face this, Amelia. There's no going back. The water has flowed under this particular bridge. Your life is here now. At least until you have the baby and then, maybe we can think again about your future.'

Amelia wiped her eyes.

'From this day onward, you must promise me that you will put this whole sorry episode out of your mind and never talk or even think about it ever again.'

'How can I ever do that? It's impossible.'

'If you don't do as I say, then I won't be responsible for the consequences.'

'Are you threatening me? Your own flesh and blood?'

He laughed, but it sounded hollow. 'Don't be silly. As if I would threaten my only daughter. Especially when you are carrying my precious grandchild.'

'I do believe you are! How could you even think of such a thing?'

'I only want what's best for you. For us. As a family.' He rattled something in his pocket.

'What's best for you, you mean.'

'So, do you promise me?'

She felt the panic rise in her throat. 'I can't. I just can't.'

He sighed and opened the door. 'Fine. I suggest you try and get some rest for the remainder of the day. We will discuss this again later when you're properly rested. I'm sure you will feel differently then.'

'No, I won't. Not ever. Please, let me go home.'

She watched his shoulders shrug as he left the room, closing the door behind him. This couldn't be happening. Amelia was horrified to see the door handle shake as she heard the sound of the key turning in the lock on the other side.

# Chapter 18

Verity began walking down the country lane to Monument Manor on a beautiful warm evening in late September. It had been raining on and off for most of the day but now the grass verges sparkled under a clean blue sky.

Coming up to the black iron gates with tall stone gateposts, shady overhanging trees hiding what lay beyond, Verity felt a thrill of anticipation. Under all the foliage, she could just glimpse a long stately avenue with sheltered elms on either side leading off into the distance.

She was excited to think that she was going to visit a mansion house which wasn't usually open to the masses. Such a contrast to the hectic week she'd had at work, she was looking forward to a glass of wine or two and had decided to book a taxi home.

She had seen a few little groups of people ahead on route and the occasional car had passed her, presumably carrying guests to the house. She was taking her time and relishing the solitude of the walk. She hadn't bothered to ask Jeremy if he wanted to go with her as she knew how he enjoyed his Friday evenings at the cricket club and anyway, she was quite happy to go on her own and see what she could discover. Besides, the Albie situation was still a bit raw. Another thing she wanted to put out of her mind this evening.

It sounded quite a posh occasion this Summer Soiree, so she had relished being able to get dressed up and had taken her time getting ready. She was wearing a floaty, turquoise green midi dress left over from last year's summer hols and matching heels which gave her even more height. She still looked healthily tanned, so kept her make up natural, a slick of green eyeshadow enhanced her brownish green eyes and her straight dark hair was freshly washed and hanging loose down her back, instead of the pony tail or bun she usually wore for work. She twirled in front of the mirror and sprayed on a light spritz of fruity perfume. Jeremy and Albie had gone out so she'd had the place to herself to get ready in peace.

Now however, due to the high heels, she was walking very slowly and carrying an embroidered denim jacket as it was bound to be cool later on.

'It reminds me of Manderley in Daphne Du Maurier's novel,' she mused. She was enjoying the coolness of the air, there was a faint smell like bonfire smoke mingling with the scent of summer rain and blackbirds and thrushes were trilling in the trees.

Dreamily, she was just about to walk through the gates, when she heard a sound like heavy footsteps, running quickly behind her. There was no-one else in sight the last time she'd looked, neither behind nor in front of her, she had been the only one on this walkway. Why would anyone be running? And after her, would they be upon her any second? Was she about to be knocked out of the way? The birdsong seemed to pause for a moment.

She stopped still and turned her head around very slowly. To her surprise, hurrying towards her, grinning and panting, were Jeremy and Albie.

'Surprise. Oops sorry.' Jeremy was out of breath.

'What on earth are you two doing here?' she spun her whole body around to follow her head, too quickly on her high heels and narrowly escaped twisting her ankle.

'We're coming with you. Wow, Verity you look gorgeous,' Jeremy grabbed her in a hug and kissed her on the cheek enthusiastically, even though he'd only seen her an hour ago, whilst Albie rolled his eyes.

Jeremy was all dressed up in a light blue shirt which brought out the cornflower of his eyes and dark jeans, and a deeper blue tie, carrying his best leather jacket, the sun bleached hairs on his forearms glinting in the evening sunshine. Even Albie had made the effort and looked fairly presentable in black jeans and a dark grey hoody over a black t-shirt, carrying the inevitable backpack. Verity thought that this was the first time since the night he'd arrived that she'd seen him fully dressed.

He sat down momentarily on a fallen tree trunk beside the entrance to catch his breath, putting his head down to his knees. 'I don't do walking,' he muttered. 'Or running.'

'What's going on?' Verity asked again. 'What do you mean you're coming with me?'

'I bought two tickets for you and me and now there's one spare so Albie's joining us,' Jeremy waved the tickets in the air, 'I thought it would be a nice surprise for you.'

'Well, this is a nice surprise.' Once again, she thought. 'How, how did you know about this?'

'There are posters advertising it all over the cricket club.'

'I didn't think it was your scene, Cheese and Wine I mean.'

'Research,' Jeremy deliberated. 'I'm an author, remember? I need new experiences, new surroundings to feed the creativity and to... to fuel the imagination.'

'Same.' Albie added from the tree trunk. I was going to bring my sound recording gear but decided on my camera instead.' He indicated the backpack.

'Why do I feel like I'm the strict parent and you two are the naughty children?' Verity flicked back her hair. Oh, never mind, let's get going.' She supposed she should be pleased he wanted to be with her. Although quite what Albie would make of it, she wasn't sure.

'Looks like it's going to be busy,' Jeremy remarked as another car passed them.

Albie lagged behind them, staring at his phone and texting furiously.

'Where is he?' Verity looked behind and saw he was way behind them now, frowning, head down. He was standing still, not even attempting to keep up. 'I don't know why you bothered to bring him. Why is he always so miserable all the time?'

'I'm sure he smiled yesterday.'

Verity wasn't so certain. Just as she was beginning to think there wasn't really a manor house here at all, just a long and winding road, going on and on, they traversed a sharp bend and the house appeared before them. It was far more impressive than the photograph.

It was a warm, light red brick, welcoming, tall storeyed mansion house with inlets of sleepy picture windows with ornamental Baroque style cream fluted facades and elegant cornices, slumbering in the late evening, post summer rain sunshine.

No daffodils today of course, but beautifully maintained, lush green wrap around lawns and a garden of meandering roses leading up to the front doorway. There was a buzz in the air. Everyone looked to be dressed up and happy smiling faces were in abundance.

Verity was amazed at the thickness of the archway wall between the lobby leading into the hall, where they were at once sucked into a sea of people. There was a hubbub of voices, and ladies wearing summer dresses topped by floaty chiffon pashminas in a swirling myriad of jewel like colours. She was so pleased she'd worn her heels. She was aware of a barrel-vaulted ceiling and tables set up with raffle prizes, introductory glasses of sparkling wine and orange juice, then a makeshift bar, behind that a sweeping staircase with scrolled balustrade curving up to a galleried landing laden with ancestral paintings.

'Can I see your tickets please?' the doorman asked and explained their ticket entitled them to two free glasses of wine and entry into the big raffle. Verity noticed there were some other people wandering about selling further coloured strips of raffle tickets. 'Cloakroom to the right, buffet is in the dining room round the back.' She was immediately reminded of herself doing her introductory spiel to delegates at one of her conferences.

Albie looked mutinous and hissed loudly at Jeremy, 'You didn't tell me it was going to be full of old people. It's like a sea of silver heads. I'm off back to the cricket club .'

Verity had noticed they did seem to be the youngest ones there.

'I'm the only young person here.' Albie moaned. 'They're all well old.'

Jeremy shrugged. 'Albie wait, I didn't know. At least have your wine. And there's a buffet.'

Albie's face brightened up a touch at the mention of scran.

First of all, Verity followed a steady stream of women into the cloakroom which was delightful with more thick stone walls and a draped bed where coats and jackets were being piled.

'This was the original nursery and the nurse's quarters,' someone said at her elbow as she touched up her lip gloss. The air was thick with clashing perfumes and face powder.

There were two doorways leading off the hallway and after grabbing their first free glass of red wine, Verity led the way into the Drawing Room on the east side. The heat just hit her, probably due to the huge white Adams style fireplace with real leaping flames and the fact that there were people everywhere, mainly women. Walking sticks and walking frames propped up in gay abandon, they were crammed into every available inch of space on the pink and white rosebud sofas, squashed onto cushions in the window nooks where matching comfy chairs and billowing drapes echoed the pattern and complemented large French windows, letting in erratic wafts of fresh evening air.

The room took her breath away. It was so light, predominately white, the ceiling high with coving adorned with scrolls and decoratively shaped cut out inlets, the floor being squares of light patterned wood, yet the eye was immediately drawn to the far three walls. Here, montages of golden edged miniature portraits were lovingly displayed, and reflected in strategically placed mirrors. Light bounced from the glittering gold and white chandelier and fireside lamps, flinging shapely shadows back across the room to the huge ancestral painting above the fireplace.

The miniatures were obviously all family descendants, and Verity ached to get close enough for a good look but it was impossible because of the crowding eager guests.

Albie was right, the average age was, well quite old. Verity surmised there was a mix of locals, church goers and villagers, all dressed up. Everyone was chattering loudly to each other, their laughter tinkling out whilst they enjoyed the wine and the sumptuous surroundings.

They found a space by a marble fireplace to drink their first glass of wine and soon Albie was hemmed in by two women and a walking frame, whilst Jeremy lounged against the wall, garnering lots of attentive looks. Albie looked even more fed up than usual. 'Well, I did warn him,' Verity said to herself.

The ladies wasted no time in introducing themselves and soon they had trapped Jeremy in conversation as well. Verity cringed as one of them said,

'Oh, what a good looking, lovely family you are.' She supposed it was quite a natural assumption, being the age that they were and with Albie's height and messy fair hair mirroring Jeremy's.

Ah, let them explain themselves, she thought, and clutching her wine glass, began to navigate a path through the hordes to explore.

She wandered through another splendid reception room with a vast chimneypiece with dominating stags' heads and Temperly insignia and lots of velvet covered window seats, then into the dining room where a huge table groaned under the weight of a stupendous buffet. It wasn't just Cheese and Wine. The silver platters lined with gossamer fine doilies around the perimeter were filled with mini chocolate eclairs and tiny sculptured, white iced vanilla slices and Verity noticed they were rapidly disappearing as lots of hands reached across the table for them.

'Just a mouthful,' someone laughed.

The wallpaper was exotic, Chinese style, adorned with vivid humming birds and there were long vertical cupboards laden with china with a space underneath obviously for each of the family dogs, their names scrolled in gold lettering. She found the whole house enchanting.

Moving on, Verity caught a glimpse of the corridor leading to the long stone walled kitchen but the sign said No Entry, also access to the bedrooms was denied, so she continued on and realised she'd come full circle and was standing at the foot of the staircase.

She picked up another glass of wine and quickly made her way upstairs to the landing which to her surprise was empty, where she began to study each gilt-edged painting in turn. Now she began to feel excited. At last, a chance to study the ancestors and see if she could discover anything useful. The portraits were of various family members going back a few centuries, with their names and dates underneath. These were Amelia's people. Amelia had lived, ate and breathed in this house. Adrenalin began to pump through her veins.

She started from the left-hand side of the gallery and studied each painting from a distance until she reached the far end of the gallery. There she stood for ages, engrossed in the painting in front of her, which was a cherubic child with the most winning smile, until she nearly bumped shoulders with someone who was engrossed in the next painting from the other end. She narrowly missed spilling her wine. They both turned into each other.

'You're not allowed to take photographs of that one,' the voice said, camera swinging from his shoulder. 'That's the famous *Happy Child.*'

Verity was aware of white shirt sleeves rolled up, dark tie and floppy dark hair. Sharp dark eyes flicking this way and that.

'Oops sorry,' she said, stepping away. 'Not that I was going to.'

'Oh, it's you. Hello again,' said the voice of the journalist from the top of the monument. 'What are you doing here?'

'Oh, hello. I'm here for the Cheese and Wine party. And you?'

'I'm here to cover the event for the local paper.'

'Well, it doesn't look like you're doing much covering up here.'

'On the contrary. I've been taking action pics of the crowds down below. Amazing what you can see from up here. I'm Paul, by the way, Paul Longwood, Fellridge Advertiser.'

'Verity Raffin.'

They turned towards each other and he outstretched his hand which she took and they shook hands solemnly.

'Pleased to meet you Verity Raffin. Again.'

They both laughed together. He moved closer so that his shoulder was touching hers and looked at the painting.

'Do you like it?'

'I love it. It's adorable. Who is it?'

'Ah, well that's what makes it so fascinating. Nobody knows the story behind it. It's an enigma. All we know is that *The Happy Child* was surely the happiest and loveliest baby there ever was.'

'It makes the hairs stand up on the back of my neck,' she reflected. 'But in a good way.'

He sighed and leaned towards her slightly. 'Think what a scoop it would be for me if I could only discover the identity of *The Happy Child*. But then, I say the same thing here every year.'

Verity felt she could stand and look at it all evening but she was here for a reason. It was a wrench but she managed to tear her eyes away from *The Happy Child* to find Paul regarding her intensely. She took a deep breath. 'Do you know where I'd find a painting of Amelia Temperly?' Born 1931, daughter of Charles Claud Temperly, Earl of the County, born in 1900.'

'So why the interest?'

'Oh, it's just something I promised I'd look at for my grandad.'

'Really? You need to be over to the right somewhere,' he pointed to the rear end of the gallery. These ones are more recent. There's a big Temperly Family Tree on the wall as well which may help.'

'Thanks,' and she was off to have a look as fast as her heels would allow on the polished floor, her skirt swishing. He followed her. She was surprised as to how far back the gallery reached, its walls were absolutely crammed with artwork going back to the 1700's.

It took her a while to study each painting in the 1900 section until she found Charles Claud Temperly and Amelia Violet Temperly, the father tall with proud stance, dark hair and clothing and a handlebar moustache. She stood for a long while, studying Amelia closely. She was beautiful, with big blue eyes and flaxen curls, the mouth slightly petulant, reminding her of Albie's sullen disposition. She didn't look particularly happy.

'Look, here you are,' Paul called from the Family Tree wall. And there it was. Lady Amelia Temperly – Jack Trevalsa (Artist) – married in 1949.

Hurray! This was real progress. She had a name to go on now. Mrs Amelia Trevalsa. This could be a breakthrough.

Her heart racing, Verity began frantically googling Jack Trevalsa, Artist on her smartphone. A long list popped up, all described as artists. Fingers feeling a little shaky, she began scrolling. Her face must have shown her dismay as the hopelessness of the task as the list went on and on.

'Maybe I could help you?' Paul's voice cut into her thoughts.

'What?' she'd been totally engrossed and forgot he was still there, peering over her shoulder at her phone. She clicked off the internet, snapped the cover shut and put it back in her handbag. 'Sorry, I was miles away. You were saying?'

'My uncle knows an awful lot about their history. Colourful past some of them. I could arrange for you to talk to him if you like.'

'How does he know so much?'

'He's the agent who manages the estate. Bit of a jobsworth but he's very helpful. He lives here.'

'He's very lucky. It's a beautiful house and estate.'

'Parts of it are falling into disrepair and it's very expensive to run a place like this. He's gone into booking the place out now for meetings and events.'

'Ah, now that is interesting. I work in Events Management and I'm always looking out for new conference venues…' If she could do the two things at once, even better.

'Ah, so that's your line of work.'

'How do I make an appointment?'

'I can do that for you if you want?'

'Well, I wouldn't mind a look round the meeting rooms and kitchens. Could you wangle that?'

'Not a problem.' And Paul arranged it there and then for the next week by text.

'I could run a story for you as well. I can see the headline now,' he demonstrated with his hand still holding the wine glass – 'Grandfather searches for the lost love of his life.'

'What on earth makes you think that's the story?'

He tapped his nose. 'I can always sniff out a story. I just know when there could be something in it.'

'No thank you.' Verity said firmly. That was the last thing she wanted.

'Oh well, always worth trying. Oops, don't look now but I think we're being watched.'

Jeremy was standing at the foot of the stairs, looking up at them, a glass of wine in each hand. Then he was hurrying on his way upstairs to join them, his smile bright.

'There you are. I brought you another wine.' He handed her the new glass and she handed him back the empty one with a flourish.

'Thank you, although I'm sure I've had more than my quota.'

'Is this your husband, the videographer?' Paul nudged her arm.

'Oh, he's not my husband,' her voice tailed away.

'Not yet,' Jeremy said, smiling and putting his arm around her shoulders. 'Soon to be.'

Paul chuckled. 'Hello mate, pleased to meet you. I'm Paul – Reporter for the local rag.'

'Jeremy – Playwright and author, seeing as we're doing job titles.'

'Verity?' Paul asked. 'Come on, your turn.'

'What? Oh, me? Conference Manager – Conference-able.'

There was a pause as they all looked at the engaging painting of *The Happy Child*. Then Jeremy swigged his wine and said,

'Come and see outside. You haven't seen the gardens yet. They are superb. There's a laburnum avenue and a maze. Oh, and fountains.'

Paul pushed his business card into Verity's hand. 'Here's my card if I can help with anything else. Also, if you change your mind about that story just let me know.'

'I'm sure I won't, but thank you for your help.'

'You'd better hurry. The housekeeper turfs everyone out at ten o'clock,' Paul warned, calling after them. 'She's a regular Mrs Danvers.'

Jeremy had been right about the grounds – they were amazing and the lush lawns seemed to stretch on for ever. There was a hollow to the east of the house which Verity had read could have once been a moat.

'It's been raining again,' Verity remarked, feeling her heels begin to sink right into the sodden grass, so she took them off and carried them.

They wandered arm and arm, past the maze, and along the fountain strewn avenue, her head starting to spin a little but she didn't care. There was even a space which used to be a swimming pool.

'Well, I've had an absolutely lovely evening,' she said as, all too soon, they were making their way back along the drive. Wine fuelled and feeling slightly fuzzy around the edges but absurdly happy, like only one can feel on a star spangled, fresh end of summer evening, she put back on her shoes, not caring that the heels had lumps of grass sticking to them.

'Where's Albie, by the way?'

'Bailed out ages ago. He couldn't cope with all the adulation. Well, he was the youngest person there and males were in short supply. Do you know what he said about one of the ladies? He said she could talk a glass eye to sleep.'

They both laughed, arms around each other's waists as they continued down the lane.

She was hardly feeling the cold, maybe it was the wine. She felt euphoric at what she'd discovered so far. She felt on the brink of a discovery in her quest to find Amelia. She had her husband's name and an appointment with the agent of the Estate next week. A good start.

'I think he likes you,' Jeremy said, pulling her closer.

'Who?'

'That journo chap.'

'What? Are you jealous?' Well, that would make a change. It was usually Jeremy who garnered all the attention.

'Well, maybe just a bit.'

'No way. Don't be. He's a journalist after a scoop – he's programmed to be curious that's all.'

They were nearly back to the end of the drive when Verity realised, she'd left her coat on the nanny's bed. No matter, she'd hopefully pick it up next week.

# Chapter 19

'Greyson alert.' Sophie reported, as she sat opposite Verity in the Conference Office.

'I reckon we've got about half an hour before he gets to us.'

Verity looked at her watch. 'Well, if he doesn't hurry up, I'll miss him. I've got a venue visit this morning.'

'He'll be telling them all the same shit jokes. And laughing at them himself.'

'That's unfair Sophie,' Verity said. 'He always cheers people up. And he gave you this job remember?' Sophie, slim, young with hair (extensions) long enough to sit on, was a hard worker, but sometimes needed reining in.

'You're always on his side. I get what you mean, though.' Sophie studied her new gel nails.

Verity thought a lot of Sophie, she was a godsend at conferences, and had also become a friend and firm ally, although much younger than herself.

Shrieks of laughter filtered down the corridor, heralding the approach of Greyson Parkin, CEO and football enthusiast, a short, balding Geordie, as he swashbuckled into the room, filling it with his presence.

'Morning, good morning,' he bellowed. 'Have you had your hair done Sophie? Looks hot.' Hot? Verity hid a smile at the look on Sophie's face. Then he began,

'Hey, I must tell you what happened on the train yesterday. Just listen to this…'

The story was considerably shortened as Verity was already on her way out of the office.

'Now, Verity, how are you getting on with the urgent gig?' he asked.

'I'm on it, I'm on my way now to a venue visit,' she told him.

'Excellent. It would be good to be able to cascade some info down to the troops this afternoon?'

No pressure then, Verity thought and caught Sophie's eye as he began telling her another joke.

Driving to Fellridge, Verity was a little early for her appointment at Monument Manor, so she decided to park in the churchyard next door.

It was directly adjacent to the cricket pitch and it was easy to visualise a six being hit and a cricket ball soaring over the low stone wall and straggly hedge. Followed by a fielder haring across the grass and loping over the wall through one of the gaps to find the wayward ball.

She could see the spirelet of the red roofed club house roof rising over the greenery against a flat, grey sky. Tall shady trees sheltered the other side of the graveyard from the road, rustling in the wind.

The beautiful church building echoed the style and light red and beige brickwork of the cricket club and had an impressive arched doorway which today, was shuttered with a many spoked, black security gate. No-one was about. It was very quiet apart from the rising wind and there was a chill in the air, maybe a hint of Autumn already.

She felt a little out of place wandering about a graveyard so early in the morning, in her smart work uniform, being a dark navy linen suit with a crisp white cotton blouse underneath and navy leather heels and large handbag which housed her laptop, her long straight hair pulled back in a neat chignon. She did have a reason for being here, though.

And here it was, as viewed on the Internet. It wasn't hard to spot, as there was a huge central area dedicated to the Temperly family surrounded by well manicured lawn. It dominated the whole of the churchyard. A few steps led up to the raised stone platform of the crypt, with a monolith in the middle which must have been at least twenty feet high, crowned with a flying cherub.

There were many stone covered individual graves here, where lots of members of the Temperly family were interred, going back a few centuries. Verity counted at least fifty, all constructed in a light grey limestone with an unusual, delicate blue tint, and fairly reasonably tended with only intermittent, unruly green weeds peeping through.

She paused at the foot of the steps and looked around, directly in her line of vision a bent and slanted headstone covered in moss, leaned towards its neighbour as if departing some conspiratorial information. Then a figure monetarily blocked out that particular view, making Verity start.

'Hello, Good Morning', a lady Vicar with long black hair and polo neck jumper under her flowing robes, was fast approaching. 'Are you interested in the Temperly family? Isn't that megalith stunning?'

'Absolutely,' Verity said. 'Can I ask you something?'

'Yes of course, I'd like to help.'

'I've just moved to the area and I'm interested in local history.' Verity saw the vicar's eyes light up. 'Are all the family buried here?'

'Oh, yes, all of them. It's a solid tradition which has continued throughout the ages. And there's plenty space for lots more,' she gestured to the platform, 'even though they all live abroad, it's customary for them to come back home to this churchyard to be buried.'

'Is it okay to step up and take a look?'

'Yes of course.' Lady Vicar smiled in agreement. 'I must get on, but please don't hesitate to come and find me if you would like to ask anything else. In fact, call by the entrance on your way out and I'll give you a leaflet about our church services.'

I knew it, Verity thought, she thinks I'm going to join her congregation. She thanked her and tentatively climbed the three steps onto the solid structure. She began studying the names on the neat rows of graves which took some time as the inscriptions were quite hard to read, engraved into the stone in an unusual, swirled Celtic style script. Some letters and figures were worn away, as were the patterns of the Temperly insignia.

Eventually, having walked around three sides of the catacomb, her neck and eyes aching, she finally found the tomb belonging to Charles Claud Temperly and next to it, one for his twin brother, James Samuel. Her heart beating fast, she took a quick photo on her smartphone. There was no sign of a grave for Amelia. She breathed in and out deeply. This was a good sign. It had to mean she was still alive, didn't it? Her heart singing, she had to tear herself away as it was time to move on to Monument Manor.

Finding the gates open, she drove slowly along the drive and turned into the carpark at the rear. Getting out of the car, she could hear the sound of a lawn mower in the distance, as she walked around to the front of the house, her feet crunching on gravel underfoot. There was a red, laden wheelbarrow parked on the path outside the house. The front door was open so she rang the bell and stepped into the hallway. It looked very different to her previous visit.

A sandy haired gentleman, a bit younger than Verity had expected, wearing a padded gilet over smart dark trousers and shirt, silently appeared out of an archway to greet her.

'Hello. I'm Verity from Conference-able.'

'Good Morning Verity. I'm Kevin Longwood, Agent for the Temperly Trustees.' He had a gentle voice and a calm, old fashioned aura about him.

They shook hands. 'Come in, I've been expecting you,' and he led her through the empty hallway with its shiny wood floor, past the closed doors of the sumptuous rooms she'd seen last week. There was a smell of old-fashioned furniture polish which reminded her of the beeswax stuff Grandma Anna had used, with a hint of lavender.

She caught sight of a cleaner complete with rainbow coloured feather duster coming out of the cloakroom which prompted her to remember to ask if an embroidered denim jacket had been left on the bed last Friday evening.

She was lucky and soon, with her errant item over her arm, she was ushered into the small room under the stairs which was Kevin's office. It was immaculate, although there was only room for a dark brown walnut desk and two chairs, padded in red and the wall behind him was covered in dark wood shelves housing very olde worlde, interesting looking hard backed books with dark red marbled spines. A delicious aroma of freshly brewed ground coffee pervaded.

'Would you like some coffee? Freshly brewed.' He turned around to a gap on one of the shelves where there was the full complement of tea/coffee making facilities including a vintage teapot, a cafetiere and bone china mugs. 'Or I can make some tea if you prefer?'

'Oh, coffee would be absolutely lovely thanks.' She assembled her laptop ready to take notes.

He produced a large plate of plump choux buns, iced with thick dark chocolate and fresh, white cream oozing down the sides, as well, which he passed towards her. 'Freda's very kindly brought us some cakes as well.'

Verity thought Albie and Jeremy would have loved these.

'What sort of function are you thinking about?' Kevin began typing on a small silver laptop.

'I'm looking to book two different series of meetings. The first lot are half day brainstorming confidential meetings for our CEO and his senior managers. The second are for 121s so we would require a small, intimate room for those.'

He nodded thoughtfully. 'I think you've found just the right place.'

Verity nodded as she finished her choux bun. 'And I have to say these are absolutely scrumptious. They're just like my grandma used to make. Light as air.'

'They are delightful, aren't they? Thanks, I just needed a few details so I can work out a costing. I'll show you around the rooms first.'

'Would it be possible to see the kitchens as well?'

'Yes, of course. Come and say hello to Freda. She'll be delighted to hear your kind comments.'

He led the way to the west bay of the house where down a few stone steps and along a short thick-walled stone corridor was a long galley kitchen with light streaming in from sashed windows. Stone flagged as well, it felt cool, the kettle boiling away on the hob, however, Freda, the cook was nowhere to be seen. It felt like a room bereft without its owner, expectant like a dog awaiting the return of its master, to charge it into life.

Now here she could imagine Amelia, bored and lonely, running along the passageway and settling herself at the thick pine farmhouse table, cheekily helping herself to sweet treats and pastries, the kitchen cat purring at her feet, waiting with eager excitement for a glimpse of Ed and his mates. They'd be laughing and jumping over the garden wall, then maybe they would jump up at the kitchen window in devilment, looking behind them to see if the coast was clear...

Verity took her time and walked slowly around the kitchen, peering out at a walled kitchen garden alive with colour.

'Your bosses could take a stroll around the gardens as well if they wanted a break. Have you time for a look?'

'Oh yes, please.'

'Then we'll go back to the office and I'll print you off a quote.'

He seemed to have all the time in the world, although she guessed that wasn't the case. He showed her around the gardens which she'd only had time for a quick tour of at the Summer

110

Soiree, they were laid out in rooms with a rose garden, an apiary garden, a yew avenue, an Italian garden, with hornbeam hedging adding grandeur, or was it screening a view?

'What's over the hedge?' Verity asked, peering over it. She was just tall enough to see it was, or was once a swimming pool, or lido, very overgrown and forlorn with broken tiles and uneven paving.

'That was Lady Arabella's private swimming pool back in the day. She'd take a dip first thing every morning.'

Fascinated, Verity drank it all in. There was also a vibrant orchard and beyond it were a row of cottages, which Verity guessed must be the estate workers homes.

'I'm afraid a lot of the place needs some money spending on it. That's why we're expanding into doing events.'

'Paul says you know a lot about the history of the family?'

'Yes, my nephew has written a lot of articles about the family. There's a lot to write about. There are some, well should I say, interesting characters. You're not a writer as well as an Events Manager?'

'Oh no, I'm just interested because my grandfather used to come and visit here when he was a lad.' She didn't want to say too much about her quest, just in case information was imparted back to his journo nephew. 'I've recently moved to the area and it was good to discover all this was on my doorstep.'

Kevin led the way back past the moated area to the back of the building.

Verity took a deep breath. 'Do you happen to know if Amelia Temperly, daughter of Charles Claud Temperly is still alive? He was born in 1900 and she in 1931.'

'Ah, I'm sure there'll be a section about them in one of my tomes. I'll look it up. There's a brief description about each of the members of the family in these books.'

Business over, the quote was agreed and a contract organised.

'I am sure it will be a pleasure doing business with you,' Kevin said, as they shook hands to seal the deal. Verity liked his polite demeanour, and his old-fashioned air. He reminded her in a way of herself, she herself had been called old-fashioned quite a few times, probably due to the fact that she'd spent a lot of time with older

111

people, like her Grandma Anna and Auntie Bertha when she was a teenager. Not that she cared about people's comments, she often thought her life had just begun at fifteen when she moved in with Grandma Anna and got to know her and Uncle Bobby. And anyhow, the place was just a dream. She knew Greyson was going to love it.

'And you too. I'm looking forward to working with you. I know everyone is going to be impressed with this place. It's just perfect.'

'I'm so glad we can be of assistance. Right. Now to find your Amelia Temperly.' Kevin searched the shelves and lifted one of the heavy books out very carefully, blew off the dust and very carefully thumbed through until he found the section he wanted.

Verity found she was sitting on the edge of her seat and holding her breath.

'Ah, here we are. Amelia Temperly. Born 1931. Oh. my goodness. Oh dear.'

'What is it?' Verity asked, gripping her chair. 'Is she dead?'

'No, I don't think so. It looks like a bit of a family scandal, I believe.'

'No way,' Verity's heart was racing. 'What sort of family scandal? What happened to her?'

Kevin began reading out loud in his calm, gentle manner. 'Amelia Violet, only daughter of Charles Claud and Eliza. Brought up by her father as her mother died when Amelia was four years old.'

Oh, poor Amelia, Verity thought, no wonder she was lonely, growing up in this huge place without her mother and only a cold, severe father to look after her. 'Now according to this,' Kevin continued, 'Amelia left Monument Manor in 1946 to go and live abroad at the family seat in Fiesole, near Florence in Italy. They had a villa there.' He paused.

'Go on,' Verity said quietly.

'It goes on to say she married an older man, one of her father's friends who was an artist. A Cornishman, by the name of Jack Trevalsa who had his own art gallery. He was a much revered artist and they went on to have three children in total.'

A Cornishman. Brilliant. Verity's head was spinning. So now had the name of Amelia's husband and a place. Cornwall. That would narrow her search down somewhat. An artist from Cornwall. Ah, but how much older was he? He would most probably be dead by now.

Was Amelia still living in Cornwall and did she have anything to do with the art gallery? And what of the family scandal?

Yes, that must be when she disappeared, Verity thought, then said out loud, 'So what was the scandal? Something to do with her father, I suppose?'

'Oh no, although he did have a bit of a reputation for being a ladies' man. On this occasion it was the daughter that caused the scandal.' He looked up from the book and spoke directly to Verity. She felt like she was holding her breath. The room was very still apart from the faint ticking of a clock somewhere and Verity could vaguely hear some geese honking loudly in flight outside. Then she heard Kevin's voice again.

'She was with child apparently. And her only fifteen years old.'

The room started to spin and Verity had to put her head down to make it stop. No, no that couldn't be right. It wasn't possible. His face seemed to be swimming before her eyes.

'Are you okay, would you like another coffee? Or a glass of water?' Kevin sounded concerned.

Verity didn't want to make a fuss so she managed to compose herself and sit up straight, trying hard not to slump back in her chair. Even though she felt aghast and in turmoil. 'No, I'm fine thank you, honestly.'

Amelia was pregnant. That was the last thing she had expected to hear. 'So Amelia…she was with child?' Her voice broke slightly on the last word. 'Are you sure?'

'Well, that what it says here and, in those times, it would have been a big scandal. Reading between the lines it appears as if she was banished abroad to have the baby. Would you like to read it?'

Verity shook her head and stood up. No, she'd heard enough. So, Amelia's father had hushed it up. Even though he had a reputation himself of being a ladies' man himself? Verity was astonished and shaken to the core. What kind of father would do that? What if Amelia had thought all these years that she had killed the one she loved? What would that do to a person? She gathered together her things to leave.

'Are you sure you wouldn't like some water?'

'No, thank you, I'm absolutely fine and I must get back to work. Thank you so much for your time today and for sorting out our requirements.'

'Thank you for your booking,' Kevin showed her out but she hardly heard his final words. 'I'll be in touch before the first meeting to finalise arrangements.'

Verity's mind was a blur and she had to sit for few moments in the car before driving off.

Amelia had been expecting a baby. What a shock. Grandad Ed's baby. It had to be. Her hands felt damp on the steering wheel and she wiped them quickly on her skirt.

She was certain Grandad Ed had no idea about this at all. He said Amelia came to make it up with him that day but he didn't mention anything else. Could it be that she had something momentous to tell him but never got the chance? And then, after his accident, she simply disappeared. It didn't take much to fill in the gaps.

Amelia, aged only fifteen, was exiled abroad to have Grandad Ed's baby! And he didn't know a thing about it.

But…Amelia thought she'd killed Grandad Ed. Whilst, in actual fact he was very much alive and had another child he knew nothing about, living a life somewhere on the planet.

# Chapter 20

*1949 – Amelia – Firenze*

'May I suggest a Vin Santo to finish and to aid the digestion?' Jack Trevalsa asked Amelia as they sat at an open air restaurant in the square Piazza del Duomo, situated directly opposite the rambling, gothic complex of buildings comprising the Cathedral of Santa Maria del Fiori.

She felt overwhelmed at the nearness of the magnificent cathedral, which seemed to march off in both directions, further than the eye could comprehend with the terracotta tiled dome peeking through the middle. Oh, the intricacy of the lozenge shaped panels, the diamond outlines, the niches filled with statues, in a decorative fusion of white, green and red marble culminating at a dizzying height.

'Yes, please,' Amelia said, knowing that the amber coloured dessert wine would be a perfect finish to the huge meal Jack had treated her to after their art gallery visit. It was the first time she'd been away from the manor house in a long time and she hoped her new green polka dot A-Line shirt dress with its full skirt, white trim and thin belt was doing her justice. She'd curled and brushed back her long blonde hair as best she could, copying pictures in the glossy magazines brought to her by Uncle Samuel's latest girlfriend.

'So, what was the best part about the Uffizi?' Jack asked.

'Do you really have to ask?' Amelia dabbed at her eyes with a paper napkin, scared her eye make-up had run.

'As your art tutor, I believe I must.' Jack's lived in face creased further into an enigmatic smile.

'It has to be *The Birth of Venus* of course. It was so beautiful it made me cry. In public too.'

Jack chuckled. 'I noticed.'

'It was just so magical.' Amelia felt the tears threaten to spill over again. She would never forget her first sight of the painting of the calm and serene goddess rising from the ocean, blonde tresses flowing, luminous on a giant seashell being blown towards the shore by the rise of the sea, whilst pink roses fell softly from the heavens. And all suffused and illuminated with such a soft delicate light. 'It was like nothing I've ever seen before.'

She paused to dab at her eyes again. 'It's almost as beautiful as the portrait you painted of Eliza.'

Jack laughed. 'Ah, yes. Now that painting I call *The Happy Child,* as there is no doubt that Eliza is the happiest and bonniest child that ever was.'

Amelia felt her cheeks flush with happiness at the thought of her daughter and at his praise and felt a warmth flood throughout her body. Though that could be partly due to the Vin Santo.

'I do agree with you, but then, maybe I'm biased.' Amelia gazed around her in delight.

The darkening night air was heavy with the smell of garlic and pizza, mingling with the richness of new leather, perfume and lingering strains of coffee. The clanging of a bell tower rent the air, competing with the excited shouts of children at play in the square whilst their parents dined. Random fireworks fizzed in the purple sky towards the emerging sequins in the backdrop behind the buildings.

'Oh, I can't tell you how good it feels to be out of the house.' Amelia shook back her waved hair.

'Don't you like living in Fiesole?'

'I do love Fiesole perfectly well, but I rarely leave the estate.'

She thought fleetingly of the girl she used to be, the one that used to run over the fields and up the hill to the monument with such abandon. But she was not allowed to think back to those times. She shook herself inwardly, feeling a shiver down her spine, hearing her father's voice when he voiced his demands.

'Why is that? Is it because of your father?'

Amelia bowed her head. 'Yes. He hardly lets me out of his sight.'

'He's very protective of you, isn't he? Hasn't he any plans to go back to Monument Manor?'

'Not right now unfortunately.' Amelia sighed. 'He rather seems to have settled here for the time being.'

'Hmmm.'

'Not that I want to be away from Eliza for any amount of time, of course.' Amelia felt her face light up just at the very mention of her little daughter. Sometimes the depth of her feelings for Eliza scared her a little. 'But I did so want to visit the Uffizi Gallery.'

'And I, being your art tutor, was, of course, the perfect chaperone. So glad to be of service.'

They both laughed.

'And you have enjoyed your day out, I take it?'

'Enjoyed it? I've absolutely loved every moment. Thank you so much for showing me around and for the delicious meal too.'

Jack leaned forward and looked right into her eyes. Funny, Amelia thought she'd never really noticed what a rich chocolate brown they were, soft and kind and how they crinkled at the corners when he smiled. 'It's my pleasure. The least I could do for my best student.'

'I thought I was your only student?'

He laughed and seemed about to say something but Amelia's eyes darted across the plaza to rest on a striking octagonal structure.

'I've never seen buildings like these, that one looks just like a layer cake.'

'Ah, the Baptistery of San Giovanni. The third building in the trio.'

'It's enchanting.'

The conversation paused for a moment, then Jack spoke. 'You know, you can talk to me anytime about your father, or anything else, if you wish?'

'No, well, yes there may be something.'

Jack locked his eyes with hers again. 'Well go ahead. I'm happy to listen.'

Amelia sighed. 'It's just that my father has hinted at having Eliza sent away to boarding school as soon as she is old enough. In fact, more than hinted. He's told me it is what he wants to happen.'

'No, surely not?'

'Oh yes. He wants me to stay here and help run the estate with Uncle Samuel, in the absence of him having a wife.' Her voice cracked. 'But Jack, I can't bear the thought of being here without her.'

Jack reached for her hand across the table and patted it. 'But– he must be able to see how much you love her and how well you look after her.' He shook his head. 'Sam did mention something about him being a tyrant but I didn't think he'd go that far.'

117

'I know you're probably thinking – Amelia you're eighteen – why don't you just leave with Eliza? But the truth is, what could I do? Where could I go? I never finished my education and I've no money of my own.' And she couldn't tell Jack that her father had threatened to tell the world about her terrible secret if she even dared to think about leaving home.

'What would I do without her?' Amelia felt the hot tears ready to spring again behind her heated eyeballs.

'Would he really carry out such a threat?'

'You have no idea what he is capable of.' Amelia took a deep breath. 'There is a reason Uncle Samuel calls him his evil twin.'

'Surely, he was joking?'

'No. Father never jokes. Did you know that he had my mother committed to a mental institution?'

'What? No, I didn't know that.' A shadow fell across Jack's kindly face. 'That's dreadful. Was she mentally ill?'

'I don't believe so. I know she suffered from asthma and various other conditions and was very frail but he had her committed for no reason other than she was highly strung and a little rebellious. He couldn't control her.' Jack covered both her hands now with his own, his eyes clouded.

'Also, because she had the audacity to fall for another man and he simply couldn't bear the thought of her leaving him.'

'Is this all true?'

'Yes, he told me the whole story. You see she was going to leave him and take me with her.' Amelia's tears were falling freely now and Jack provided her with a pristine white handkerchief. 'But she never got the chance. She died in there when I was four.'

Jack's features face creased further as he frowned. 'I'm so sorry Amelia. That's shocking. I did suspect there was something, but I didn't know the full extent of it.'

Amelia blew her nose on the immaculate hanky and wiped her eyes, depositing most of her carefully applied eye make up on it. 'I'm sorry to spoil such a perfect day. Maybe I shouldn't have told you.'

'No, I'm glad you did. It's good to talk.'

'You've always been so kind to me.'

'I'm a very kind person.'

118

They both laughed again.

'I can show you a different path to a more fulfilling life.' Jack leaned closer across the table and increased the pressure on her hands.

Amelia felt as if an electric current travelled up her arm as he began to stroke the inside of her left wrist.

'How do you mean?' She didn't withdraw her hands but shifted them slightly.

Jack raised his eye to hers. 'You could always marry me.'

'Marry you?' Amelia jerked away her hands and nearly knocked her glass over, catching it just in time and attracting a waiter's attention. 'You are actually proposing to me?'

'Most certainly. Would the idea be so abhorrent to you?'

'No, no, of course not, it's just that…phew, well the last thing I expected was a proposal of marriage.'

'Is it because I am a little older than yourself? Well, maybe quite a lot older actually. Thirteen years to be precise.'

Amelia's brain was whirring and her eyes stung with crying. She knew she must look a right mess with her reddened eyes and cheeks. How could anyone possibly want to marry her? She shook her head.

'Then why should age hold us back? In my favour I'm a friend of your father's nephew. A family friend who comes from what they call a good family. And I don't believe you are totally indifferent to me, am I right?' His eyes sparkled.

'Well…'

'What I mean is we've known each other for a while now and we get along, ever since I was commissioned to paint Eliza's portrait which led to the pleasure of giving you art lessons.'

'Yes, we've spent a fair time in each other's company. But marriage?'

'We would be going into it with a shared love of art and children and books.'

'True.' Amelia was struggling to take it all in.

'I do have a little money behind me and a house. Not as grand as what you are used to but I can provide a roof over your head.'

Amelia's hand shook slightly as she removed it from his to raise her glass and take another sip. As if she was bothered about having a grand house.

119

'I honestly don't think your father would object.'

No, he'd be delighted to get me off his hands, Amelia thought.

'And I do believe you would love my home in Cornwall.'

'You would want to go back to England?' Amelia felt her heart lighten.

'Yes, it's my home. I only came here for a holiday to see Sam but I ended up doing a little bit of work and staying longer than I anticipated.'

'I've never been to Cornwall.' Amelia looked up at Jack from under her clogged eyelashes.

'Oh, you'd love it. The colours are exquisite especially in the summer– the gold of the fields, the blue of the sky, the green and turquoise waters - the light over the sea is like none other anywhere in the world. It's an artist's paradise.' His expressive face lit up as he gestured and Amelia thought how could she ever have thought he was old?

'There are plenty of fields of gold for you and Eliza to run through – right down to the sea. She would adore it.'

'She could go to a local village school?'

'Definitely. Also, I have plans to open my own art gallery and you could help me run it. You have a good eye. I also know you have a good head on your shoulders and would be a good asset. You could help me instead of your Uncle Sam.'

'But I've never worked before.'

'I could teach you. I need someone to talk to the clients and show them around the gallery, you would be very good at that.'

'So, is this really a business proposal?' The wine had gone to Amelia's head a little and she was enjoying the conversation, not really believing it would ever happen.

'Well, I wouldn't want you becoming bored.' Jack laughed. 'No, but I can see there are benefits for both of us. You escape from your controlling father and I gain a business associate as well as a wife. A beautiful wife at that. And a child who most certainly is the happiest and most beautiful child that ever was.'

'And you would be willing to take on Eliza? Another man's child?'

'Yes. Most certainly. As my own. I would consider myself very lucky.'

120

'And you don't want to ask any questions about Eliza? About her father?'

'No need.' He paused to drain his glass and set it on the table. He reached for her hand again. 'You see, I happen to love you Amelia.'

Amelia felt her cheeks redden further and her heartbeat quicken. 'But...?'

'I knew the first moment I set eyes on you when I came to paint your baby's portrait. You looked so young and scared but there was a light in your eyes – you have such spirit.'

Amelia drained her glass.

'Look. I'm not asking anything more of you than companionship at least at the moment.' His eyes twinkled, the crinkles deepening. 'However, if anything more does grow as we live and work alongside each other, then who knows?'

Amelia shifted a little in her seat, the folds of her new skirt settling around her, remembering how it had been for her and Ed. But then, Ed was lost to her for ever. She knew there was no way she could ever experience that magic again. Why not marry Jack? She certainly enjoyed his company as a friend.

'I'm offering you a way out of your present situation. You'd be free to come and go as you please. I know we could be happy together.'

Maybe I could run over the fields again like I used to? Amelia's thoughts spiralled.

'Think about it. I've set out my case. You don't have to give me an answer right now.'

It was growing darker still and the buildings were taking on a rosy glow. Amelia's eyes moved along the dazzling exterior of the cathedral with its pastel shades of green, grey, pale pink and white like meticulously worked tiers of icing sugar, set against a backdrop of darkening sky. So fragile yet she was aware of the enduring strength of the buildings. Her heart felt like it was flooding over with warmth.

'Although, please don't make me wait too long.' He touched his lips gently to her hand and Amelia felt as if an explosion had gone off in her heart.

Then he was leaping up from his seat to gently place her jacket over her shoulders, taking his time, his hand brushing her bare arm. Again, she felt that frisson of excitement. Something she never thought she'd

121

ever feel again, after Ed. No, this couldn't be happening. It must be a combination of this surreal city, the romance of the scented night air and the Vin Santo…

'It's getting cold. I'd better get you back home soon.' He took her hand and wrapped it within the warmth of his own as they strolled back to the car via the River Arno. Amelia saw lovers all around her, elegantly dressed couples promenading hand in hand, others lingering by the bridges with their arms tight about each other as they embraced, the lights of the city shining on the dark water behind them.

The one thing which was very apparent to Amelia was that there was no rush, here in Florence they had all the time in the world for each other. She envied them so much she had a pain in her chest. Florence certainly was a city made for love and romance. She glanced up at her companion, linking arms now and enjoying the unfamiliar sensations which rocked her mind and body.

She wondered if maybe the cathedral had cast a spell over her as her heart was soaring like the majestic heights of the basilica as they paused to watch another firecracker popping in the cool evening air.

# Chapter 21

Verity opened the door, recoiled and quickly shut it again. She was aware of the silkiness of Tom, her faithful shadow, attempting to wind himself around her ankles. She made to walk away but instead, tentatively opened the door again a little way and peered inside. Tom took one look and turned back immediately, disdainfully slinking off along the landing. Now she was on her own.

It was the smell that hit her first. It was like hot sweat mixed with mouldy cheese. Then the warmth of the thick air enveloped her. The computer tower glared purple in the gloom and various lights and knobs winked and blinked from the huge futuristic monstrosity which she believed to be the synthesiser. She was aware of the hum of machinery as she almost tripped over the snakes of cables and charging leads lining the floor, the geography of which was beyond her. It was so dark because the curtains were shut at both windows.

She was always extremely tidy, maybe even a bit OCD which she blamed on the fact that she'd never had any space of her own as a child, being passed from auntie to auntie and sharing bedrooms with her cousins, so she always ensured her own space was immaculate. She'd never seen anything quite like this before. Some of the households she'd lived in might have been untidy and strewn with toys but never quite like this. She was aghast.

The beautiful room with its dual aspect windows, was almost unrecognizable. How could this have happened in such a short space of time? If she didn't know better, she might have thought that the non-existent burglars had been back.

There was a mountain of clothes on the floor again, coats, jackets, socks piled on top of each other, mingling with wet towels. It was similar to the one that had been on the kitchen floor the day after he'd arrived. Now, nearly a month later here they were again. It was a veritable floordrobe. Why? There was a perfectly good wardrobe just a few steps away. Albie had seemed so pleased with the room Jeremy had willingly given up for him that she just couldn't believe that he'd let it get in such a state.

All surfaces were covered with an assortment of filthy mugs, cups with decomposing teabags in them, and smeared glasses with varying amounts of liquid which could have been coffee dregs or cola. There were plates sticking out from under the bed with half eaten pizza crusts and a whole bacon sandwich which was looked so hard that it looked like it would shatter in a million crumbs if touched. The one that got away.

Rizla papers littered the floor, mixed up with discarded chocolate bar wrappers and pot noodle cartons. There was even what looked suspiciously like a chocolate Jaffa cake squashed face down into the carpet. And there was her favourite cafetiere with mouldy coffee grains like thick soil clogging up in the glass.

With great difficulty she began to pick her way to the far window, noticing how the curtains were bulging with cutlery sticking out of the gap where they met in the middle, the protrusions meaning that something was on the ledge. She was right. Three half-eaten bowls of cereal with spoons sticking out of them adorned the windowsills.

'So that's where all the spoons went.'

Jeremy's head appeared around the door with the sound of frantic barking behind him.

Pedro shot past her and immediately dived under the bed.

'No, Pedro,' she quickly fished him out and picked him up. 'Don't want you eating something and poisoning yourself.' She passed him to Jeremy who put him down in the hallway and shut the door on him. He began scratching at the door and whining.

'Don't let him back in,' she hissed at him.

Jeremy entered the room fully, his face a picture of disbelief and Verity rounded on him, her arms folded. She felt her cheeks burning in anger.

'Where is he?' she spat out the words.

'He's out.'

'I know he's out, but where is he? Because, believe me, I'm going to kill him when I see him.'

'He's gone to record a track with his mates at that recording studio I told you about.' Jeremy looked slowly around the room, then went on tentatively, ''He's been working very hard on his music.'

124

'What to the detriment of all else? That is no excuse for this stinking hell hole.'

Verity had been astounded at the way Albie had settled in so quickly. He'd made friends already, some being young cricketers from the club. He'd also been helping Jeremy out with his creative writing classes at Uni, handing out papers and making tea, just to keep him busy whilst he settled in. How had this happened? Had she been so engrossed in her research for Amelia that she'd missed how much his room was a tip? He obviously hadn't been doing any washing. But plenty eating by the looks of it.

They'd only really had one blip since Albie moved in which had occurred when Jeremy and Verity had had a night away in a plush hotel to celebrate Jeremy's birthday. When they came back later the next day, everything had seemed to be in order until Verity noticed that the pictures in the dining room and living room didn't match. And then in the conservatory, the glass was missing from the glass topped bamboo table.

Albie had had a party with some cricketer mates and they'd moved everything breakable just in case they got smashed. Apparently, there'd been a houseful as the few mates Albie knew had asked the visiting cricket team as well. Albie admitted to it straightaway and when Verity asked what on earth did they think they were going to be doing that warranted moving pictures and he said just lots of leaping about dancing and practising bowling with an imaginary ball. Verity couldn't imagine him leaping about dancing as it took him half an hour for him to walk downstairs to the back garden for a cigarette each morning.

However, there was no damage at all, everything was clean and tidy, it was just that they'd put things back in the wrong places. At least they'd had the sense to think about moving stuff, Verity had told him and the three of them had ended up having a laugh about it.

'Don't worry, I won't be doing it again, it was too much hard work.' Albie said. 'We had to lug all the bin liners full of empty booze bottles all the way down the lane so you wouldn't spot them in the bin. I'm surprised that man in the nearest cottage hasn't told you because he did come along and ask us to turn the music down.'

But this was a totally different scenario.

125

'I thought you said you were keeping an eye on him?' Verity took a couple of steps towards Jeremy and nearly fell over the detritus littering the floor.

Jeremy put out a hand to steady her. 'I was, I have been, but...but I've been working as well. I've been away for a few days touring the play as you know.'

'You promised me he'd keep his room tidy. This wasn't part of the deal.'

'I know, but I think he just lost sense of time and everything when this recording studio chance came up. He loses himself in his work.'

Amelia snorted. 'That's no excuse. You're a creative person but you don't live like this.'

'I know its messy but it's all superficial, isn't it?'

'That's not the point. He's not even a teenager.'

Verity held her temper and picked her way up to the other window which had the monument view. She flung back the curtains, and welcome light flooded into the room. Then she threw open the window, letting in some much-needed fresh air and revealing the side view of the

monument. As she did so, she knocked over a bowl of half-eaten ice cream which had solidified, so when the bowl bounced off the carpet, all the contents stayed put.

However, the bowl had been hiding something. Two distinctive long, brown marks on the brand new, bright white, PVC windowsill. Looked like dirt or chocolate or something else.

'Jeremy, just come and look at this.' She could hardly speak. 'Just look at it.'

They were burn marks. She saw the red mist rising before her eyes and her throat felt choked.

Jeremy came and looked. 'Oh no. He must have been smoking out of the window.'

They looked at each other and Verity felt her smoldering anger rise and rise. This was the last straw.

'Can't we just cover them up with an ornament or something?' Jeremy dared to suggest.

'No, we cannot. Those windowsills are brand new.' She took a deep breath which wasn't a good idea as she inhaled some fumes from the bottle of Jeremy's homemade extra spicy chilli sauce which was also perched on the window ledge, minus its top. It made her catch her breath and cough a little.

'Right,' she recovered herself and picked up the sticky bottle without thinking and replaced it again.

'Tell him this has to stop. Or he goes.'

'But V - isn't that a bit harsh?'

'He's not a flipping kid. He's twenty years old. And he's *your* nephew. Tell him, Jeremy.' She strode past him to the door as best as she could, ungainly stepping over the obstacles in her path.

'I will. I'll talk to him. I promise.'

'I mean it. You've got until tomorrow morning to sort this mess…and him out.'

She turned with her sticky hand on the doorknob. 'Or I will.'

She opened the door and nearly knocked Pedro over who was on his hind legs and still scratching on the other side of it.

# Chapter 22

To take her mind off her present turmoil, Verity shut herself away in the little room downstairs, away from the rest of the house, with her laptop and a cafetiere of coffee (obviously not the one with the mouldy coffee dregs in it from Albie's room). Tucking herself up on the sofa with the only sound in the room being Tom purring contentedly beside her, she logged on, took a deep breath and began by googling Jack Trevalsa – Cornish Artist. She found a website easily enough which was dedicated to his collections and immediately recognized one picture.

'Ouch,' Verity was distracted by the pain in her right hand. Annoyingly, she had to get up to run it under the cold tap in the kitchen. There must have been some raw chilli peppers in that homemade sauce on Albie's window ledge and the backs of her fingers and the palm of her right hand were burning a little from when she'd picked up the sticky jar. Goodness knows how he and Jeremy actually ate that stuff.

She couldn't wait to get back to the sofa where Tom had rolled over into her vacated space, and the painting of the child with the engaging smile on the screen which seemed to reach out and gather her in and make her want to smile back, despite her churning thoughts. It was of course, *The Happy Child,* with whom she had been so taken with at Monument Manor. She was delighted to see the painting again, although it was a much smaller version on screen. It lifted her heart just looking at it. Just what was it about it which made it so special? she mused.

It was just a child sat on a bench against a plain dark green background which highlighted the radiance of the skin. A heavy golden frame bordered the painting. She zoomed in and studied more closely the chubby face which simply glowed with glee, the dimpled hands and the intermittent tufts of fine, fair hair.

The large, deep, dark eyes gleamed with more than a hint of mischief. How could it be possible that a painting could make your heart sing? She didn't know, but she knew she loved it and at this moment she wished she knew more about art.

It was hard to tell how old the child was, not much more than a baby, maybe at the toddling stage so probably around eighteen months at the time of the picture? She couldn't help but wonder what kind of a person had this charming little baby grown up to be?

The text advised that this artist had died in Cornwall in 2000, aged 82, leaving a wife, Amelia and three daughters, Violetta May, Gloria and Cornelia. Verity reckoned that Jack must have been around thirteen years older than Amelia. So, Amelia and Jack had three daughters. Had he accepted Amelia's first child as his own? Was the first named, Grandad Ed's child? Or was it possible that the three daughters were all Jack's, in which case, what had happened to the baby Amelia had given birth to in Italy in 1947? Where was he or she now?

Aha! Further information about the artwork could be found over on the Jack Trevalsa Facebook page. Verity headed over there and discovered that some of Jack's paintings were displayed in an art studio in Fowey, Cornwall which was run by close members of his family who lived there. So, Amelia wasn't mentioned in person, but surely, she was one of those close family members?

Excited by this information, she shook off the pain in her burning hand and clicked on the 'Contact Us' icon, disappointed to find it was just a standard form and not giving any information away. She searched a bit further and eventually discovered an address, telephone number and generic email address.

There was also a picture of the studio, which looked like it was in a quiet, slanting side street, halfway up a hill, facing pastel coloured buildings leading down to the glittering estuary on which coloured boats bobbed under an azure sky. She'd never been to Cornwall but it looked gorgeous.

Verity had a dilemma now and her mind was racing. How was she to get in touch with Amelia? She couldn't put what she wanted to say in a letter. She needed to meet her face to face. Or should she maybe telephone the gallery and ask to speak to Amelia and tell her over the phone? No, there was a chance Amelia would think she was a fraudster or off her head. Or refuse to speak to her at all. Well, how could she put it?

I just rang because I wanted to see if you were alive and inform you that you didn't kill my Grandad?

No, she had to be subtle about it and it had to be done in person. She had to go to Fowey. She felt excitement rising in her gut at the thought.

An idea struck her, making her sit up straighter. She knew nothing about art, just what she'd read in books when she was growing up and she'd once had a memorable trip to London with Grandma Anna when she was eighteen and visited the National Portrait Gallery. But she enjoyed looking at art and knew what she liked and she'd been thinking about buying some artwork to hang here in their new home, Monument Cottage. What better opportunity than to buy one from Amelia's art shop in Cornwall? She knew exactly which one she would like to buy.

A noise in another part of the house brought her back to the present in an instant. She got up to stretch her legs, opened the door a crack and was vaguely aware of activity, legs going up and down the stairs, the clink of cutlery and the chink of glasses and cups going into the dishwasher, the hum of the washing machine. She even heard the hiss and the click of the floor steamer, the thumping noise that it made when it was switched on to heat up and hadn't had enough water put in it.

She ignored it all, let them get on with it. Well, he'd been warned. She meant what she'd said.

She rejoined Tom on the sofa and clicked on Shop Now, beginning to browse through the artwork for sale. She eagerly skimmed through his art collections – beautiful, intense paintings of seascapes and shipwrecks at Cornwall, of Monument Manor surrounded by golden daffodils and of a stunning white villa in Italy covered in pink bougainvillea.

Then, she found there was a whole section dedicated to *The Happy Child* with lots of different versions of paintings in varying shapes and sizes, all reproductions of course of the original oil on wood painting, right down to ceramic mugs and tea towels with the enticing child's face on everything. Lots of *Happy Childs*, so obviously a very popular range which wasn't surprising. In fact, it was the sort of smile she could imagine Jeremy having when he was little…

130

She clicked on her favourite sized version of the painting which was one of the largest on offer, and looked at the price. Whew, it wasn't cheap, but wouldn't it look good in the living room above the wood burner? It would cheer up everyone who looked at it. Oh no, it was out of stock, but customers were advised to reserve a copy. Brilliant. Now she had an excuse to ring the shop.

Should she do it now? Yes, there's no time like the present she told herself. It was an 01700 number.

She flicked onto the keypad of her smartphone and tapped in the number, pausing to take a swig from her coffee cup. Ugh, it was stone cold.

As if on cue, the door opened and Jeremy appeared, looking apologetic yet smiley with a fresh mug of coffee which he set down for her. 'Thought you might be ready for a brew.'

'Shhh,' Verity remonstrated, pointing to the phone so he knew she was just about to make a call, handing him in return the cafetiere of cold coffee and her untouched mug.

'Are you okay?' he asked tentatively, hovering beside her. 'You've been in here for ages.'

Was he trying to say she was so engrossed in her research she was forgetting about him? How dare he? Hadn't he got enough to do in sorting his nephew out? Then she thought, just how many hours had she been sitting here? 'I'm fine,' she mouthed back.

'What have you done to your hand?'

'Oh, it's nothing, just your hot chilli sauce.'

He immediately went off to dump her crockery and came straight back with a damp handkerchief which he wrapped gently around her sore fingers. 'It won't sting for long.'

'Thanks', she said, wanting to press on and pointed to the phone. She dialled the number and waited, her heart racing, whilst Jeremy, after hesitating and hovering for a few seconds, practically tiptoed out of the room. She couldn't bear to ask him about Albie just yet.

The phone rang at the other end for around six times and she was just about to give up, disappointment and relief flooding her brain in equal measures, when a female voice answered, sounding a little flustered at first. It definitely didn't sound like an older person's voice.

'Good afternoon. This is the Trevalsa Arts Collective. How can I help you?'

Verity took a deep breath before speaking. She was so aware that she could be speaking to one of Amelia's descendants that her heart was throbbing so hard in her ribcage it hurt.

'Good afternoon,' she managed to reply as brightly as possible. 'I've been browsing on your website and I'm looking to order a copy of *The Happy Child?* It's showing as out of stock and says to ring this number to purchase?'

'Yes, of course.'

The voice was warm with a lovely Cornish lilt to it. Surely too youthful though to be one of the daughters? Verity supplied her details and tried to keep the conversation going as long as possible which was made easy as the girl was very interested in Verity's accent and wanted to know which part of Scotland she was from.

The ice was well and truly broken when Verity explained she was a Geordie from the North East of England and they had a bit of a laugh about it. Verity felt like her nerves were stretched to breaking point as she valiantly searched her brain as to how to find out if Amelia still worked there. Maybe she should have asked her journalist friend Paul for some tips.

'Do you know how long it will take before it's available?'

'Oh, I'm not sure. You see, the lady in charge is away at the moment. I'm only helping out temporarily. I'm a student you see.'

'Oh, right. Where does one go on holiday when they live and work in such a beautiful place?' Verity was glad she'd invested some effort into the conversation when the reply came.

'Mrs Trevalsa always visits her youngest daughter for a few months at this time of year in Turkey.'

'Oh, how lovely. What a wonderful country Turkey is,' Verity gushed. 'I've been there myself a few times. Er, whereabouts does her daughter live?'

'She runs a bar in Dalyan. a little town on the South West coast of Turkey. Do you know it?'

'Do I know it? Yes, I know nowhere better. Oh, Dalyan is absolutely amazing.' Verity thought quickly. 'I've been loads of times. I love it.' Well, she was sure it was amazing as she'd heard lots about it from Jeremy, so she wasn't totally lying.

'Same. And you should see the bar. It's proper cool. It's called the Artisan Cafébar. Café by day and bar by night.'

Bingo! Her heart leapt. She now had exactly what she wanted. But what was she to do with this information? She helped the friendly young lady profusely for her assistance in placing her order and ended the call. She hugged the information to herself. Not only had she ordered a piece of artwork which she was really excited about, but she felt buzzing because she knew where Amelia lived and worked. Only trouble was, she wasn't there at the moment.

What to do next? Sleep on it maybe. But that was easier said than done. She was restless and couldn't drop off that night. Jeremy was snoring lightly beside her and Pedro was wheezing from his basket which was placed near Jeremy's side of the bed. Funny thing was, in the mornings Pedro was always on top of their bed, cuddling in between the pair of them, or hogging the pillow, although she never had any recollection of him jumping up throughout the night. Then she'd just managed to drift off when she awoke and sat up bold upright with an idea that had been forming in her subconscious.

Of course. Well, why not? her inner voice said. Why not indeed? Excitement rose in her heart. 'Yes,' she said out loud, making Pedro twitch in his sleep. This could work.

She got out of bed and went to the landing window, carefully avoiding the creaky floorboard pulling back the curtain and revealing the illuminated west view of Penshaw Monument. A few stars shimmered in the dark backdrop of the night sky through the pillars. She replaced the curtain and turned around to see through the open door, Pedro sitting up in her space of the bed, wide awake and staring at her, ears cocked. She could hear a very faint strain of music from Albie's room along the landing. He obviously hadn't started his twelve-hour sleep stint yet. Let's hope for his sake the room was back to normal. No, no, she wasn't going to think about that now.

She had something else to think about. She hadn't had a summer holiday this year, in fact she'd been so busy with events and conferences she'd only managed to snatch a week back in June. It was now late October and she felt some time off was overdue.

133

She guided Pedro over to Jeremy's side of the bed and the little dog, delighted he wasn't being moved off the bed altogether, gave a contented little groan and went back to sleep.

She lay back on the pillows, still wide eyed and stared up at the decorative plaster ceiling. She had decided. She was going to go on holiday. Only she wouldn't be going to be Fowey after all. Why wait? She was going to Turkey.

# Chapter 23

Verity rang Sophie's number from her mobile. 'Hi.'

'Hi Verity,' said Sophie.

'Sorry to disturb your time off, but I need to ask you a favour.'

'Yeah, no probs. What is it?'

'Well, I'm going on holiday - this Saturday.'

'Wowzers. That soon? Lucky you.'

'And I need you to look after things at work.'

'Me? Lush!'

'You don't mind?'

'Are you kidding? I'll love it. So, where are you going?'

'Turkey. I'll explain all later.'

'Sound. For how long?'

'Just for a week that's all.'

'You really think I could do your job?' Pride sounded in her voice.

'No doubt about it. Only it's not really doing my job, just sort of keeping things moving whilst I'm away.'

'I'd be in charge though?'

'If you want to put it like that.'

'I would.'

'You'd be the only one in the office, but yes I suppose you'd be in charge.'

'Would I have to work late?'

'Not if you work hard during the day.'

'What about vape breaks?'

'Not as many as usual.'

'What about Greyson?'

'You can handle Greyson.'

'Yes, I can, can't I?' Sophie giggled. 'As long as I laugh at his shit jokes.'

'And listen to his stories.'

'Can't Jeremy come back and help me out?'

'No, sorry he's a bit busy at the moment.'

'Shame. I like Jeremy, he's sound. He was a laugh to work with. Especially at first when he kept getting things wrong. Remember when he lost twenty teachers because he was chasing the tea trolley?'

Verity couldn't help chuckling. 'And when he got battered with envelopes from that Stuff and Go Machine?'

'The best laugh was when he went and bought flapjacks for that Scottish Chairwoman - she asked him for flipcharts but he couldn't understand her accent.'

'When he managed to concentrate on the job, he was a great asset.'

'Yeah, all the older women at work lusting after him did cause a bit of a distraction.'

'Less of the old thank you.'

'I didn't mean you. He's old enough to be my dad though, he reminds me of him sometimes.'

'So, you're up for it?'

'Yeah, course I am.'

'Great. Much appreciated.' I love it when a plan comes together.

'Happy to help.'

'Just do exactly what you're doing now, any problems let Greyson know. We've no conferences on next week so it's just a matter of running the office.'

'Not a problem.'

'Phew, that's a huge relief for me.'

'I promise I'll keep texting you with updates.'

'That'll be great.'

'I'll be sound though.'

'Of that I have no doubt.'

'And cheers for the opportunity.'

'It's my pleasure.'

# Chapter 24

'Jeremy. Jeremy. Hi. I've got something to tell you.' Verity hurried in from work into the warmth of a Thai curry scented kitchen, dumping her laptop and handbag in one movement on the low window seat. Jeremy was stirring a large pan on the cooker, wooden spoon in one hand and a jar of spices held aloft in the other. He dumped the jar and moved forward to kiss her. 'Hello.'

His cheek felt warm. 'That smells amazing by the way. I could smell it before I even opened the front door. Can you leave that and sit down for a minute?'

'Um, sounds serious? Should I be worried?' Jeremy sat down at the kitchen table, brushing his lion's mane of hair away from his sweating forehead with the back of his hand, his face flushed.

'No, not at all. I'm really excited about it.'

'Good. What is it?'

'Well, I've got a week off work and I'm going on holiday.'

Jeremy's eyes widened.

'For research purposes. To Turkey.'

His face fell.

'Well, don't look so happy for me.'

'I am, it's just that…well, I thought you might have asked me to go with you.'

'I did think about it, but you've got that play on next week in Newcastle. Besides, I wouldn't have any spare time to spend with you. It's a working holiday.'

'You're going as soon as next week?' His blue eyes widened.

'Yes. It has to be then or not at all. Our next lot of conferences start in November.'

'When do you leave?'

'Saturday.'

'Wow. Saturday as in two days away?'

'Afraid so.' She couldn't help smiling. She was so looking forward to it.

'So, you're hoping to find Amelia?'

'Yes, that's my focus.'

Jeremy moved his head to one side. 'You're not still annoyed with me, are you? I did sort Albie out.'

'I should think so too, but no, I'm not annoyed with you.'

She had to admit that Jeremy had taken control, helped Albie to clean up his room and laid down a few ground rules which Albie had promised to stick by. Okay, so the burn marks were going to have to stay for a bit longer until they could get the windowsill replaced, but as Jeremy had remarked, with an ornament on the ledge, or a speaker as in Albie's case, no-one could see the damage.

'He's assured me he'll keep it tidy in future, no matter what song he's working on. And he's slightly scared of you, so he'll keep on your right side.'

'I'm not scary at all.' She looked up at Jeremy. 'Am I?'

'Ask your work mates,' Jeremy grinned. 'I was scared of you at first. When you stropped along that corridor past Watercooler No 1, they used to say, 'Stand by your beds. Here she comes. Boss lady.'

'Rubbish. And Albie's another reason I couldn't ask you to come along. I need you here to keep an eye on him.'

'He's twenty years old V.'

'Well, you wouldn't think so. Look what happened when we went away for one night.'

'Suppose you're right. Whereabouts in Turkey?' he caught the look in Verity's eye. 'What? No, you're not going to Dalyan?'

'I'm afraid so.' She pulled a wry face. 'That's where Amelia's going to be, at her daughter's bar.'

'No way. No flipping way.' Jeremy shook his head. 'I didn't imagine for one moment when you said Turkey that you would be going there. You're really going without me?'

She felt rather disconcerted because Jeremy had lived and worked in the river town of Dalyan on the coast of Southwest Turkey for several summer seasons around twenty years ago and he absolutely loved the place. Quite apart from the fact that he met and married the exotic girl from the Café Yummy when he was a tour guide there with Adem's Amazing Adventures. It seemed like a good idea at the time, a whirlwind romance followed by a wedding and a divorce after only a year.

In fact, all he had managed to salvage from that disastrous relationship was Pedro No 2 (son of Pedro). Still, that was a long time ago and another story. He'd been back to Dalyan several times since on holiday and still felt the pull of the place.

She supposed it was a coincidence but then again, it was a popular holiday destination, although one of the smaller, less commercial resorts. She could tell how disappointed he was.

'I could have helped you with your Amelia search,' he went on. 'You are so lucky. I absolutely love the place.'

'I know and I really, really wish you were coming with me.'

'To be there with you would have been just...just brilliant.'

'It's only for a week.' His distress was palpable and she hated being the cause of it. 'And I'm going there for a reason, not to go sightseeing.'

'Well, anyhow, let me help and book you a place to stay. I know just the place.' Abandoning the steaming pan of curry again, he dashed off and came back with his laptop where he showed her a picture of a pastel peach and white painted villa complete with glorious gardens and glistening pool.

'Looks lovely.'

'Middle Orange House. Gorgeous villa. You'd love it. From the front balcony it looks as if you can reach out your hand and touch the river tombs...You trip out of the front door and you find yourself at a crossroads.' His eyes lit up in reverie and he gestured with his hands. 'The beauty of it is that each path leads to the town via a totally different route.'

'Interesting.'

'Yes,' his eyes sparkled, 'one path leads past the bakers where they work all night long to create the most exquisite cakes. You can buy a big bag full of delicious pastries for almost nothing...'

Trust Jeremy to think of his stomach.

'Middle Orange House it is then. What will the temperature be like in October?'

'Around 25 degrees during the day, so you will need sun cream, then cool in the evenings. Mind, it's the start of the rainy season and when it rains in Dalyan, man, it rains.'

'So, I'll pack an umbrella and a rain mac.'

'What's Amelia's daughter's place called?'

'The Artisan Cafébar.'

'Hmm, haven't heard of it. Must be a new one.'

'Oh, it's so warm in here.' Verity shrugged off her navy suit jacket and went to hang it up in the porch. Jeremy caught hold of her on the way back and she felt the heat of his body under his faded t-shirt.

'And it's getting hotter by the minute,' he kissed her.

She leant closer and breathed in the warm, heady smell of him, mingled with a faint tang of perspiration from the heat of the oven.

'I love you Verity. Oh, I just can't believe I'm not coming with you. I could have shown you the best places like Turtle Beach and the Turtle Sanctuary...'

'One day we'll go together, I promise.'

'I can't wait.'

They kissed again and held on to each other tightly, not noticing Albie as he came downstairs, rubbing his eyes. 'Smells lush. Is tea ready?' He opened his eyes. 'Ugh, carry on. Or get a room.'

'We've already got several,' Jeremy winked.

'Albie, have you been out for any fresh air today?' Verity asked, trying to pull away from Jeremy who still had his arms wrapped around her.

'Fresh air? Nah. I had some last Saturday.' Albie headed for the back door.

'So, what have you been up to today?' Jeremy asked, still holding her close.

'I've been working on a track.'

Verity had begun to recognise that this was a standard Albie statement which covered the majority of questions. She heard a sizzling sound in the background.

'I think the curry's about to boil over.'

Jeremy kissed Verity on the cheek with a flourish, released her and hurried back to stirring the curry again. 'Tea won't be long.'

Albie dripped back off upstairs.

'Don't put your headphones on for five minutes or you won't hear me call you,'

Jeremy shouted after him.

Goodness, Verity thought, we sound like proper parents. Like a married couple with our own kid. Not that that would be such a bad thing.

She shook herself inwardly. Had she really thought that? She sat back down as Jeremy placed a mug of tea in front of her.

'This Amelia research has certainly drawn you in, hasn't it?'

'Now you know how I feel when you're writing. It's like you're on another planet.'

He looked chagrined. 'Really? I never knew you felt like that.'

'Oh, I don't mind, it gives me some space.'

'Do you need space from me?' Concern clouded his eyes a darker shade of blue.

'No, don't be so paranoid. You know me, I like my own company.'

'I'll miss you so much.'

'It's only seven days.'

'Can I help you pack?' his voice was wistful.

'I think I can manage.'

'You're so self-sufficient. I have to admit I might not have exactly had packing in mind…'

'Oh, I see,' Verity smiled. 'We can't though, Albie's just next door.'

'He's right along the landing. And he'll have his headphones on so he won't hear a thing.'

'He wants his scran. And so do I.'

'Of course, I need to feed you. Never mind, can't blame a guy for trying.' He smiled conspiratorially. 'Packing it is then.'

'Later on.'

'What did Greyson say by the way?'

'Oh, the usual Greyson stuff. He was standing looking at his train set when I went along to ask him.' Greyson had a full-scale railway model in his room, he said that watching the train rattle along the track was therapeutic in between back-to-back stressful meetings.

'Deserting the sinking ship etc. Can't get the staff.'

'I can just imagine,' Jeremy had worked alongside Verity and knew what Greyson was like. Basically, a big, whirlwind bear of a Geordie boss with a heart and a bit of a soft spot for Verity. Not surprising, considering how hard she'd worked for him over the last few years.

142

'Then he said, everyone knows you're the boss Verity, so if you've made your mind up, you're going on holiday, then what can I say?'

Thank heavens for Sophie. She was shaping up to her role very nicely. Also, Verity didn't have many proper friends, but she'd grown quite close to Sophie even though she was a lot younger. Sophie was fearless and said what she thought, a bit like Verity had been at her age. She was a godsend, but she was very young and inexperienced in lots of ways. Still, as she kept saying, it was only a week.

She was aware of how Jeremy felt about not being able to go with her, although he said he understood. He'd made a few comments about how she was totally engrossed in all this Amelia research and she thought maybe he did feel a little left out?

There was nothing much she could do about it though, he had Albie to keep an eye on, he'd invited him to stay after all. And he had his own work commitments. She didn't want to wait any longer to start on her quest. This was something she had to do on her own. She could make it up to Jeremy later. And she felt in a way, just couldn't shake off the feeling that maybe there wasn't a lot of time to lose, given the situation and Grandad Ed's age and Amelia's.

The next couple of days seemed endless at work then at last she was at the airport, loving the Duty-Free Shop and wandering about losing herself in trying out lots of different perfumes until she couldn't distinguish between any of them. She browsed the colourful kaftans, bikinis and sunhats in the open fronted shops, feeling in a proper holiday mode, despite the situation.

Then she sat and had a coffee in front of the glass fronted windows, watching planes arrive and depart, surrounded by total strangers and the hub of their chatter, all the while keeping an eye on the departure board for her flight to Dalaman. She felt nervous, yet excited.

Then everyone was taking their seats on the plane for the flight which was just over four hours from Newcastle to Dalaman. The click of seatbelts and the bustle for the overhead lockers. It was the first time Verity had flown alone and she had a few butterflies in her stomach. She wasn't what one could call a seasoned traveller, unlike Jeremy who had travelled extensively and worked abroad.

In fact, she was a home bird and was usually ready for home after a week away and found it hard to relax lying by the pool. But this time it would be different because she was on a mission.

Then it was the time when the plane was beginning to taxi down the runway and it seemed to take for ever. She had a window seat and was around six rows from the front of the plane. She craned her neck to see as much as she could, the grass verges trundling past, the airport terminal building getting smaller behind her. They were hopefully leaving the grey Newcastle sky behind them.

She did feel excited though and as if she was on the brink of a big adventure. And she had to admit she was looking forward to doing this on her own for her Grandad.

'Would you like a sweet love?'

'What? Oh, thanks very much.'

She accepted the lozenge from the older man sitting next to her, reminding her of Grandad Ed. He loved his sweets.

She'd managed to squeeze in a quick visit to Sand Steps before she travelled.

'Now lass, don't forget to send me lots of photos on the phone. One every hour if you can.'

He was proud to have a mobile phone now and she had been surprised at the way he had mastered texting and WhatsApp. Aged eighty-six, he still had a sharp mind. He was especially fascinated by the one of her on top of the monument which had been in the local paper.

She could hear his voice in her head now.

'I had a good brain yer knows in school. I was always the fastest at mental arithmetic in my class and the best runner an all.' As he refilled his pipe with the scented baccy. 'I think you might take after me, bonny lass. You were always asking questions as a kid.'

'Goodbye and Grandad, don't forget to keep your phone on,' Verity warned him.

He chuckled away at that. 'Eee lass, I've become like one of those folks like on the telly, them that keep their phone on.' He looked down at his Smartphone. 'What does it even mean?'

His final words were, 'Good Luck, bonny lass and I know you'll find her.' No pressure there then.

144

The plane stopped and brought her back to the present with a jolt. This was it. They were about to take off. She was really on her way now. Take off over, they were in the air, and climbing and she looked out for landmarks. St James Park, the River Tyne and all the bridges were laid out below, growing smaller and smaller. Then the pilot was doing a sharp southeast turn, the plane was at an angle and the patchwork green of the fields rose and fell diagonally as she gazed out of the window. Her stomach lurched a little as they climbed higher and higher and then levelled off, followed by the Unfasten Seatbelt sign. She gave a small sigh of relief and settled back in her seat, there wasn't much leg room but she stretched out fairly comfortably enough.

Relaxing, she sat back with her Kindle at the ready, looking out at the fluffy white clouds alongside which were all she could see now, and a gin and tonic in front of her, she felt at last her adventure had started. Although she wasn't sure she'd be able to concentrate on the latest Vera novel, maybe she'd just flick through the glossy In Flight magazine at all the exotic locations.

She felt heady anticipation of a trip to somewhere new. She really wanted to help Grandad Ed. But it wasn't just that. This was something she could do for herself. Jeremy had his writing, Albie his music. What did she have? A good job and a partner she loved to bits but she needed something else. Looking for Amelia seemed to be fitting the bill at the present time. Just what she was going to say to Amelia when she found her – if she found her - was another matter, but she'd worry about that when it happened.

The queue for the loo was long at the front of the plane, so Verity glanced behind her to see if it was worth her while making her way to the rear, when she saw something which made her do a double take.

For there, a few rows behind her, grinning and waving like two naughty schoolboys were Jeremy and Albie.

# Chapter 25

Verity nearly choked on what was left of her Fisherman's Friend. She turned back sharply to face the back of the seat in front, sitting bolt upright. No way. It couldn't possibly be. She had left them both tucked up snug in their beds at Monument Cottage a few hours ago. Things like this just didn't happen. Did they?

She took a large gulp of her gin and tonic, staring straight ahead. She felt stunned. Her companion glanced over. 'Are you all right pet?'

'Thanks,' her voice came out as no more than a croaky whisper. 'I'm fine.'

'You look like you've seen a ghost.'

I have, she thought, in a manner of speaking. Two to be precise.

Then she very slowly turned around again to see if her eyes had deceived her. They hadn't. It was definitely the pair of them. Even though Jeremy's face was slightly shaded by the fact that he was wearing a battered Crocodile Dundee style bush hat. They were both grinning. Even Albie? Yes, him too. She didn't know whether the fact that he was smiling was an even bigger shock than seeing them both sitting there. What the hell were they doing here?

People were walking about the plane by now and Jeremy was up out of his seat and up the aisle and at her side in a flash, squeezing past the drinks trolley and treating the air stewardess to a dazzling smile as he apologised.

She was aware of the admiring glances shot in Jeremy's direction by the two young girls sitting across the aisle who were nudging each other. 'Wow, he's really hot. Is it Owen Wilson?' she heard one of them whisper.

No, it isn't, she wanted to snap at them. Honestly, he looked nothing like Owen Wilson.

After the initial shock, conflicting emotions crowded into her brain. Dismay, annoyance, a burst of happiness at the sight of him. But why couldn't they leave her alone for one moment to do her own thing? Coupled with a certain longing for Jeremy which she always felt and at which she was incensed at, because he was so...so well, hot for want of a better expression. And well meaning. She loved him to pieces but

146

why the surprise?  He knew she hated them.  And yet he kept them coming.  Ooh, why did he have to be so annoying?

Of course, she couldn't make a scene here on the plane although she felt like yelling at him.  Goodness, could his smile get any bigger?  He positively glowed.  Corks swung off his hat.

'Surprise!' he greeted her, giving her a hug and a kiss on the cheek, removing his hat as the fly corks hanging off it were in the way.  He smoothed down his lion's mane of golden curls and seemed oblivious to the effect he was having on those around him.  Verity caught a giggle and, 'Nah, that's not an American accent.'

'Like the hat?' he folded it under his arm.  'I'm ready for the sun.'

'What are you doing here?' she said quietly although what she really wanted to do was yell at him.

'Aren't you pleased to see me?  Well us?' His smile drooped a little.

'Quite frankly, I'm astonished.'

'That wasn't the reaction I was hoping for.  We thought you'd be pleased.'

He gestured in Albie's direction and she looked around to see him, headphones on, being handed four little bottles of wine by the stewardess.  Tubs of Pringles followed and then a big bag of chocolate M & Ms changed hands.

'Two little bottles for the price of one,' Jeremy explained, seeing her face.  'He's organising our scran.'

'So I see.'

'I was hoping you'd be delighted to see us?'

'Oh, I am, yes I am,' she pasted on a smile, knowing that they had an audience, including the FF man sat next to her. The girls obviously still thought he was some sort of a celebrity.

'I just couldn't bear it, the thought of you going to Dalyan without me.'

'Ahhh,' one of the girls said.

'So, I pulled out all the stops and here I am.'

'I'm surprised Albie wanted to come along.'

'He's always wanted to visit Ephesus.  Besides, I couldn't exactly leave him on his own could I?'

'No way, god forbid.' Verity seethed inside. And she bet he wouldn't say no to a free holiday either. 'What about work? Your play in Newcastle?'

'I managed to get one of my writing mates to help out. This…you are more important.' Jeremy hopped from foot to foot, a bundle of exuberance.

'See, I knew he was in the acting business,' the girl on the end hissed.

'Do you think he's going to propose?' the other girl whispered loudly. 'Nah, she's already got a ring on.'

'And something else,' Jeremy leaned in closer to let someone pass by. 'Albie and I are booked into Middle Orange House too. Isn't that fantastic? We're going to have such a fabulous time.'

'You might be, I'm going to be busy.'

'I know, I know but at least we're here together. Look, the trolley's coming, I'll have to move. You just sit back and relax and enjoy the flight and we'll meet up at the case carousel in Dalaman Airport. Can't wait. See you soon.' And he kissed her loudly on the cheek, smiling at the girls across the aisle and off he went back to his seat, necks craning after him.

Sit back and relax. Was that even possible?

One of the young girls leaned over from across the aisle whilst the other one continued to watch Jeremy's departing back view until he sat down. 'You're very lucky, he's lush. Really hot for an older man. We thought he was that film star.'

Verity smiled and sat very straight and stiff backed for most of the rest of the flight. Lucky, was she? The four hours seemed endless due everything that was swirling around in her brain. She tried to process the fact that once again Jeremy had surprised her and she wasn't going to be on her own in a strange country after all for this particular adventure.

Was it so very bad that the man she loved cared enough to drop everything and follow her in her quest to find Amelia? Maybe she was too used to doing things on her own, too set in her ways? Jeremy certainly managed to stir things up, whatever he did. Well, maybe it wouldn't be too bad, if him and Albie went off to do their own thing like visiting Ephesus?

She certainly hadn't planned a lot of sightseeing. In fact, all she had imagined doing was going to Amelia's daughter's bar, she hadn't thought past that.

She looked around once and saw that both Jeremy and Albie had their heads back, fast asleep. Jeremy's mouth was open. Yes, girls, you'll find he's not quite as hot when he's snoring.

Due to the hum of the engines, the warmth in the cabin and another gin and tonic, she finally managed to drift off to sleep and awoke just before they began the descent to Dalaman. She sat up with a jolt and saw Albie waiting in the queue for the loo, having an animated conversation with one of the young girls. Well, the girl was talking animatedly to him and Albie, looking skinnier than ever in long baggy shorts and a tight grey t-shirt which emphasised his ribs, was looking at his phone and nodding every now and again.

Verity's lack of sleep meant that she arrived tired and with a bit of a headache which didn't help to lift her mood. She felt drained.

Dalyan was only a short ride from the airport and both she and Jeremy had organised taxis to take them there. After arguing about which one to use, Verity's came first so she jumped in it and Jeremy and Albie followed, Jeremy talking on his mobile to cancel his. It was hot in the car as the air conditioning didn't seem to be working properly, so the driver stopped at a Minimarket and handed them each a bottle of water. They passed neat green fields and tranquil olive groves and tall mosques glinting in the sunshine. It was just after lunchtime when they arrived.

'Here we are! Middle Orange House. That's what the locals call it,' Jeremy said. 'I don't know what its real name is.'

Middle Orange House was exactly that. Bordered by two white painted villas and nestling jewel like in the centre, snuggled the peachy pink house with cream facades against which dark scrolled metalwork of the balustrades gleamed. There was a lush lawned garden spanning the pool, with a few interspersed elegant statues, half hiding behind the pomegranate bushes. The cheerful colour scheme was continued in the bright lemon and white striped sunbeds positioned around the glittering pool.

They hauled their cases up the path and over the veranda at the front of the house into the cool interior. Verity got a quick impression of a

149

beautifully tiled kitchen, luxurious open plan living and dining rooms with rugs on the polished floors, glossy green plants in tall vases and marble stairs with a gurgling water machine neatly fitted nimbly underneath.

'We need to keep it stocked up and buy the big bottles from the nearby Minimarket,' Jeremy advised.

'What's the Wi-Fi like?' asked Albie.

'Better on the patio outside because then you can pick up next door's signal.'

'Can't wait to get in the pool,' Albie said, making for the stairs. 'Which room is mine?'

'You can have the room at the back,' Jeremy told him. 'It's got a balcony overlooking the gardens.'

Verity had never seen Albie move so quickly.

'Jeremy. A word please.' Verity waited until Albie was out of earshot.

'Yes, what is it?'

'You've done it again haven't you? Surprised me. I asked you never to do that again.' She could see the light leaving his cornflower blue eyes and immediately felt like an ungrateful bitch.

'I'm sorry, I can't seem to help myself,' he said. 'I just wanted to…' They were interrupted by yelling from upstairs.

'Quick! Up here!' Come and see this.'

'Oh my god,' Jeremy said as they hurried up to the room at the back. 'What's happened?'

'It's been overtaken by Triffids.'

Someone had left the clothes airer on the balcony and the trailing creepers from the adjacent magnolia tree had stretched over the veranda like curling limbs, striving to reach the bedroom window and tap on the glass. On finding an object in their way, they had torturously encroached themselves round and round and over and under it, strangling and engulfing the wooden slats like the red weed in the *War of the Worlds*.

'What a mess,' Verity said, feeling her headache intensify. 'Doesn't anyone keep an eye on this place?'

'I think they forgot about the back balcony.'

'Wait a moment,' Albie said, snapping with his camera as Jeremy approached with some implements from the kitchen. 'It's cool.'

Jeremy then proceeded to cut the airer free.

From the balcony attached to the airy front bedroom, which was Verity and Jeremy's, as if within touching distance, could clearly be seen the weather-beaten frontages of the age old, atmospheric Lycian tombs, hewn from rock into the cliffs.

'So. Yet another house you get to show me around,' she said.

The place was beginning to work it's magic though and shortly afterwards they sat outside on the covered patio, devouring delicious Chicken Kebabs which Jeremy had gone out to purchase from a nearby café.

Verity wandered around the garden and was drawn to the statues. One was a solitary lion with an paw outstretched as if in welcome, others were cream marble ladies with gentle smiles and flowing robes and bonnets. Then there were shady palm trees, jasmine bushes, magnolia trees. Crazy paving meandered erratically along the poolside. A little cat strolled over to lap water out of the little baby pool which flowed into the deeper curved pool.

'It's sourced by a well with pure mineral water at the back of the villa,' Jeremy said. 'So, it won't do it any harm.'

'Don't feed the cats here though,' Jeremy warned. 'Or we'll never get rid of them.'

Verity was reminded of Tom back home.

'You're very quiet V,' Jeremy remarked. Luckily for him she'd decided not to say anything else that was negative. For now. She was about to tell him her headache was getting worse and she was going for a lie down when suddenly a whirlwind of fur bounded over the wall, up the garden path and threw itself wholeheartedly at Jeremy, barking and whining in excitement, sending the cat mewling and scurrying up the magnolia tree to the safety of the balcony above.

'Hello mate, I wondered how long it would be before you appeared,' Jeremy greeted him.

'Pedro? How on earth is he here as well?' Verity asked, astounded. 'I thought dogs had to be quarantined?'

'Ah, meet Shaggy, one of Pedro's relations,' Jeremy said solemnly and on closer inspection, Verity realised that this dog was older, dirtier and definitely shaggier but with bright eyes and a short stump of a tail wagging in happiness. 'He always comes to see me when I'm here.'

'He looks just like him,' Verity said.

'Who does Shaggy belong to?' Albie asked, sharing his bag of crisps with the new arrival.

'No-one. He lives on the streets of Dalyan but he's attached to one of the bars. Lives there when he feels like it. He'll be here with us until we leave.'

'He never forgets even though it's years since you've been here?'

'Never.'

'Cool.'

Verity leaned against a palm tree and stretched her neck up to see the hillsides.

'Let's go for a closer look at the rock tombs.'

'Coming Albie?' Jeremy asked.

'Nah, I'm chilling with Shaggy.'

# Chapter 26

Verity and Jeremy walked alongside the crowded, colourful array of water taxis and boats moored on the jetty, the loud, foreign voices of the captains calling to each other bouncing back and forth over their heads like Albie's surround sound system. The sweet, heady smell of jasmine streamed out intermittently from the lush green of the adjoining gardens.

Gazing across the turquoise waters of the Dalyan Channel to the other side, where the rock tombs appeared sculpted directly into the rock face, resembling golden temples, Verity thought she'd never seen so many intense, heavenly shades of green and blue all together in one place, surrounding them. Everything was so clear and bright.

'I didn't really want to do much on my first afternoon,' she said, 'but I'd love to walk along to Kaunos and see the ruins.'

'Are you sure? It's so hot to walk. We could hire a car tomorrow instead.'

'Tomorrow's another day.' she told him. 'I've only got today for sightseeing.' She pointed to the tourist boat nudging into the greenery of the reed beds directly beneath the rock tombs. 'Then, I'd like to go on that boat.'

'Okay, then let's go to the other side. We'll need to wait for the rowing boat.' He pointed to where a tiny craft was valiantly ploughing its way across, lacing the teal green waters with white foam.

They only had to wait a couple of minutes on a little rickety pier, Verity allowing the waves lapping over the quay to cool her hot feet as they waited. Then they were rowed straight over by a Turkish lady called Denise wearing huge gold earrings, who said to make sure they asked for her on the way back.

Verity was enchanted to see there was actually a restaurant called The Other Side over at, well the other side. Jeremy looked tempted by this vibrant establishment with its colourful checked red and blue tablecloths and signs advertising Gozleme, the traditional Turkish pancakes and Pomegranate Juice, but Verity pulled him away, saying they could grab some food later.

They began the arduous walk to the ancient city and passed a man sitting outside of his house with bottles of water for sale. It was very hot and Verity felt red in the face already. She bought two and handed one to Jeremy.

Kaunos was a lost town of scattered ruins where excavations were being carried out. So, it might have been a mistake to walk this far on their first afternoon but it was interesting to see where the archaeologists were working.

'It really is too hot,' she said. 'I'm so pleased I brought this beach cap with me.'

She bought more water at a little kiosk and had drunk most of it by the time they walked around and she opted to sit and rest and watch people digging, whilst Jeremy climbed up to the highest point of the ruins and took photographs of the beach which lay around eight kilometres away. Her feet in her thin summer mules were sinking into the white sandy layers of thick dust and she grew hotter and hotter, tucking her hair under her cap.

She was glad when Jeremy didn't say I told you so but led her back onto the tour boat which was gaily decorated in blue, white and red, to have a close up of the Lycian rock tombs. She was also glad of the overhanging canopy which shielded them from the still strong sun, and they both sank gratefully onto the cushioned ledge which ran around the perimeter of the boat. She wiped the sweat from her face which was running into her eyes under her sunglasses and threatening to sting.

'Oh no, just look at the colour of my feet,' she pointed at them with dismay.

They were black and on closer inspection, she realised it was sticky black oil which must have been from the jetty when they were waiting for the little rowing boat. Black oil to which the white sandy dust from the excavations of Kaunos was sticking with a vengeance. She felt an utter sight, good job she didn't have any make up on. So different to the immaculate Verity from Conference-able. She saw the funny side though and they both started giggling like kids at the state of her feet.

'How come you look so clean?' she moaned. He was totally at home, relaxing against the comfy cushions, in his cut off denim shorts,

154

his hair sun streaked already from the lessons he held outside in the sunshine and the walks he enjoyed with Pedro, his face tanned and glowing.

'I didn't paddle on the jetty,' he chuckled.

The open air boat was filling up now and people squashed against them, dressed casually in t-shirts and shorts, bringing with them the smell of different types of sun lotion mingling with sweat. Verity moved closer to Jeremy, feeling the warmth of his arm against hers.

There was another scent too, the faint, imperceptible wafting of expensive perfume. It was probably from the lady sitting opposite whom Verity idly noticed looked the epitome of cool, so different from the other passengers. Her face was shaded by an enormous floaty hat so it was impossible to see how old she was, appearing ageless, and Verity caught a flash of a bronzed neck above a beautifully embroidered kaftan, and a slender ankle encased in a silver wedge. A cool aura of faded glamour hung about her.

Verity immediately felt even more boyish and began frantically trying to rub the dirt and dust from her feet with a tissue, whilst Jeremy took up the offer from the captain of two cold bottles of beer from the fridge in the middle of the boat and a bag of crisps.

'I'd give up on that until we get back to Middle Orange House,' he grinned, as the oil
wouldn't budge.

'Oh, I'll have one of those,' she took the bottle of beer from his hand and took a long, cold, refreshing drink. 'I've had quite enough water for one afternoon.'

Oh, that really hit the spot. So, what if she did look a sight? Calm washed over her. She was so used to wearing smart suits and heels that she felt liberated in not caring for once how she looked. After all, the whole point of the trip was to find Amelia and she would start on that quest tomorrow. For now though, she was going to live for the moment and enjoy every second in this divine place.

They were now moored right in front of a group of six rock-cut tombs, including one large one which looked half finished, which all blended into the sheer, mountainous backdrop, interspersed with pockets of greenery sprouting from the greys and beiges of the hillside, reaching up to meet the azure sky. She gazed at the ancient

155

temple-like facades turned golden by the afternoon sun and wondered what they had seen over the centuries.

The captain/tour guide left the ship's wheel and began to speak, introducing himself as Murat. Verity quickly slung one of the coloured rugs over her feet to hide them and sat back to concentrate on what he was saying. Apparently, the tombs dated way back to the second quarter of the fourth century BC and the most important ones were those with the façade of a temple, behind which was an empty front chamber.

'According to legends, the rock tombs were built as high as possible to the sky because the kings and important people were expected to be near to the gods.' Murat moved along to raise a hand to a passing party boat, it's throbbing music and shrieking from the revellers from the upper deck breaking the peace of the afternoon. Then it was quiet again.

Murat continued, 'The façade had a pediment and pillars and the burial chamber was accessed through a door.'

'Pediments and pillars. What do they remind you of?' Jeremy whispered, grinning.

'They remind me of the monument,' Verity sighed. 'Can't get away from it can I?'

'No. It's your destiny. Our destiny.' He gave her a quick hug and kissed her hair. Verity caught a whiff of beer on his breath.

Murat was now telling them that these tombs weren't completed because of the invasion of Alexander the Great and the Persians.

'Another comparison,' Verity thought to herself, being reminded of the roof at the monument back home, which was never completed due to lack of funds, or so the local legend went.

Murat went on, 'The rock tombs are lit up at night,' and Verity nodded to herself, thinking of the beacon that was Penshaw Monument, guiding weary travellers safely home.

Murat and Jeremy recognised each other at that point and with cries of 'Merhaba' and 'Hello, my friend,' Murat pulled Jeremy to his feet and soon they were chattering away, mainly in Turkish. Verity flung the rug aside and moved to the other side of the boat to take a photograph of them both against the backdrop of brilliant blue sky and reed beds.

156

She sat down next to the lady with the elegant sun hat, which was the only available space, trying to hide her filthy feet as she pressed the button and took the photo.

The fabric of her the lady's kaftan brushed against Verity's arm, although Verity hadn't seen her move. Then she felt a strange sensation which she found not unpleasant, just unusual. It was just such a strong feeling of déjà vu; it chased all other thoughts totally out of her head for a second. What was even more surreal was that the sun chose that very moment to dip behind a cloud in a sky which she could have sworn was cloudless a second ago and the whole world seemed to be obscured in greyness.

It was as if the universe had stopped for a brief instant in time, but when she tried to talk about it to Jeremy later, it seemed as if it was only Verity's world which had stopped spinning on its axis. Her best description, which didn't really clarify things at all, was the strong sensation that she felt like that moment had happened before.

Then normal service was resumed, Jeremy and Murat continued talking, the cloudiness lifted and suddenly the sun reflected on the facades, brightening them to pure gold. Oohs and aahs resounded from the other passengers. Verity shook herself inwardly. Probably too much sun? Or a combination of beer and sun?

Then she felt an intense stab at her heart, a moment of pure happiness and belonging so strong it was almost painful. Belonging? But she wasn't at home. I've never been here before, she thought to herself in wonderment.

No, she was here in this magical place, with Jeremy. All of the petty discontent had dissipated. Maybe it was that wherever he was, was home? I do love it here, she mused.

She heard the rush of wings as a stork streaked overhead, then silence as it appeared to poise momentarily in mid-flight against the azure heavens. Murat moved away to resume his commentary and Jeremy gathered his arms around her to pull her back down to their original seats. He looked into her eyes and they smiled at each other like a couple of youngsters, his eyes as blue as the sky above in his tanned face.

'He knows,' she thought. 'He gets it. He feels exactly the same.' She'd never felt so content.

157

'I knew you'd love it here,' Jeremy said. 'I did tell you it was magical. I've never seen you so serene.'

And Verity knew then that she loved him.

Amelia adjusted her floppy sun hat and gazed at the pillars and pediments of the rock tombs which reminded her of things she hadn't allowed herself to think about for years. She was vaguely aware of the younger couple opposite her, giggling and clearly having a wonderful time, revelling in each other's company. It warmed her heart to see a pair so clearly in love.

A long buried memory of another time, another place flashed into her mind. A vivid picture of her running over lush landscapes and up a green hill to the spiral staircase hidden in the pillar and flinging herself into the secret chamber without a care in the world...It was all such a long time ago but the memory was so intense. Goodness, she couldn't run anywhere now and needed to use a stick at times. Oh, but she'd had such a lovely time today, enjoying the peace and quiet of the river.

The pillars and facades suddenly disappeared as she closed her eyes for a second, seeing another temple, one with eighteen blackened golden pillars and a space where the roof should have been, a parapet which was open to the elements.

Then the young woman opposite with the wide smile and charming beach cap, moved over to sit in the space next to her to take a photograph of her partner and his Turkish friend. Amelia wanted to offer to take a picture of the three of them but just as she was about to offer the sun disappeared behind a cloud and the brilliance of the sky was diminished.

Feeling slightly dizzy, she blinked hard and sat very still until her world righted itself and then the sun was shining again, brightening the facades to liquid gold.

She felt a stab in the heart as she remembered a night, long ago in another time and place. An intense longing for home as it was when she was a young girl at Monument Manor, before her life changed for ever, a feeling she hadn't felt for such a long time.

She'd seen a kingfisher earlier, a flash of bright blue streaking along the reed bed, so fast it was hard to see it clearly and that jogged another memory of a walk by the river, where Ed had been chuffed to bits to catch sight of the very same. Ed knew about birds, he loved to see the rooks grazing on the fields and flying back to the rookery on

Penshaw Hill at dusk, calling to each other. Amelia imagined the look of wonderment on his face if he'd seen the stork, seemingly poised in mid-flight overhead. Why was she thinking about Ed after all these years?

Yet Amelia felt contentment and peace wash over her and knew that they had loved each other.

# Chapter 27

That evening, Verity fell asleep almost instantly to the backdrop of crickets from the trees outside the open windows and the hum of early evening mosquitos. Drifting into delicious slumber, she smelt the unusual aroma of sweet, heady jasmine, the scent unleashed as the sun set and darkness fell, filtering up from the gardens below. She dreamt of finding Amelia.

Early next morning, Verity felt so much better and stronger, her headache gone. She hadn't expected to sleep so soundly in a strange bed. She quickly pulled on some trainer socks as the tiled floor felt cool underfoot and wandered out onto the sunny balcony where the pool sparkled below. Shaggy was snoozing on the patio in the shade.

The villa was quiet as Jeremy had gone out early to the market to buy fresh fruit and vegetables before it got too busy, with the promise of cooking them a full English breakfast later on. He'd told her to enjoy her lie in and left her with a mug of tea, sun flooding in through the light curtains. Albie of course, was still in his pit.

She couldn't wait to get dressed and outside to explore her surroundings. The villa was certainly in an ideal location overseeing a crossroads and as Jeremy had said, each road led to the town centre. One lead past the bakery whose chimney smoked all night long, producing pide bread and crumbling sweet pastries, of which you could buy a huge paper bag full for a few Turkish lire. Another lane ambled past the cobblers, another the barbers and the Acaler where they could buy bottles of Turkish bira and refills for the water machine.

'Wherever you are in Dalyan, I reckon you're only seven minutes away from the river,' Jeremy had told her. In normal circumstances she would have loved to have strolled down to the river and boarded a boat to Turtle Beach, navigating through the tall reeds and maze-like passages of the Dalyan Delta. He'd told her about it so many times, the glorious Iztuzu Beach or Turtle Beach as it was also known, which was home to the endangered species of the loggerhead turtles.

Instead, on her first morning she was focused on going to find the Artisan Cafébar so she turned her back on the crossroads and headed for the hills, armed with a home-made map which Jeremy had drawn for her. She felt nervous, yet excited. This was a situation she'd never been in before. Would Amelia be there? Her plan was to go and have something to eat there and for the present, simply observe. She just wanted to take her time and drink it all in. And she mustn't forget to take lots of pics for Grandad Ed and WhatsApp them to him.

Shaggy awoke and joined her for so long, trotting happily along in front as if he was her guide, but lost interest when he saw one of his doggy mates scampering out of an olive tree lined street.

She passed green fields complete with grazing cattle and a backdrop of rolling peaks, layered in the hazy morning sunshine. There were lots of pomegranate trees, with their sculptured, twisted bark and multiple spiny branches, ready for harvesting as well as banana trees and olive groves. It wasn't too far according to the map and the temperature was just right for walking, but the air was growing warmer and Verity was glad of the bottle of water she'd brought with her. Crickets pulsated in the background.

Then she was standing in front of the Artisan Cafébar. It was hard to see what the building was made from because of all the palm fronds and greenery into which it nestled, she glimpsed light wood fronted balconies peeping out and there was a long, spacious, shady tea garden in front decked out with rows of cheerful blue and white checked tables and umbrellas.

As she approached via the long pathway, an older Turkish lady wearing traditional garb was putting ceramic vases of colourful flowers on the tables outside.

Verity thought she heard squabbling voices which were at odds with the beautiful tea gardens. Then two people emerged together by a side door, a handsome Turkish man who was just starting to run to fat with a double chin and a bleached, brassy blonde woman wearing lots of gold jewellery. Arguing all the while, they flounced past Verity without giving her a second glance, the woman turning around to bark out instructions to the older lady who was obviously left behind to look after things.

Verity seemed to be the only customer at the moment. She stood still in their wake and took a photo for Grandad Ed, trying to get as much in the frame of the building as she could. She added it to WhatsApp and sent it quickly, then remembered that they were two hours ahead here. He was an early riser though and wouldn't mind if the ping of a notification woke him up.

'Merhaba! Would you like to eat something?' the smiling Turkish lady approached Verity with a menu, shaking her head as if in apology for the departing pair. 'A Turkish breakfast maybe? It is very good. Or maybe Menemen? Or some English tea?'

She spoke very good English but with a strong accent and Verity saw she was much younger than she'd originally thought closer up, her oval face framed by her richly coloured headscarf, or hijab which entirely covered her hair with the loose ends covering her neck as well.

Verity's mouth felt dry. 'I think I'll have a look around first if you don't mind?'

'Of course, take your time,' she indicated the entrance with a graceful arm movement.

Inside the cool interior there were two staircases, each one leading up and meeting in the middle on a landing with a room on each side filled with artefacts and jewellery. There was no-one else around. Definitely no Amelia. And there was an empty seat behind the cash desk in the right hand room. Maybe she'd gone to the market too?

She was alone in the right-hand room and the only sound was the calming click of the fan in the background.

Verity felt she ought to buy something, she'd been in there engrossed in her browsing for so long, but what to choose? It was all so tasteful and very expensive. Scouting around for something suitable, she eventually picked an embroidered lavender bag and matching jasmine scented soap for Sophie and a set of traditional Turkish tulip shaped teacups as a souvenir to take back to Monument Cottage.

The Turkish lady came upstairs with two of the glass cups filled with a golden liquid on a lace lined tray.

'You like to drink some Apple Tea?'

'Oh, yes please, thank you very much,' Verity took one with a friendly smile and winced slightly as the glass was hot. The lady gestured she sit on the balcony, overlooking the street. There were comfortable brightly coloured cushions and a tiny wooden table for the hot apple tea. She seemed to want to talk, maybe she was bored. It was still very early.

163

'Sorry I've taken so long. There are so much beautiful things to choose from here.'

The lady seemed pleased. 'I am very pleased you like them. My name is Aylin.'

'Mine is Verity. Have you worked here for long?'

'A few years, now, I love this place. I am very good friends with the owners, Violetta and Ahmed. They were here earlier.'

Violetta! That was the name of Amelia's daughter. The bleached blonde she'd seen on her way in was Amelia's daughter. Her heart began to thump awkwardly against her ribcage.

She spoke cautiously, trying to sound casual although the reply could be so important. 'Is there another lady that works here sometimes? An older lady?'

'Ah, yes, that would be the mother of Violetta. You have seen her here? A very how do you say it? Very smart old lady. You know her?'

Verity shook her head. 'No, I don't know her exactly. Is she here?'
Now she felt like her heart was going to jump clean out of her chest.

Her glass was still warm but not too hot to pick up now, so she sipped
at the deliciously tart concoction which seemed to have just a hint of
apple, whilst waiting with bated breath for the reply.

'Oh no. She has gone.'

Oh no, Amelia wasn't here. 'She's not here?' Verity's heart sank.

'No.'

'Gone where? Home to England?' Verity was shocked, she had been
fully expecting Aylin to say, oh, she's just popped out to the market or
to the bakers. She replaced her tea glass rather more heavily than
she'd meant to. This wasn't meant to happen. She'd been quite
unprepared for the dark cloud of disappointment which descended
upon her. That would teach her to be impulsive and come over here
on a whim. She'd been so sure that Amelia would be here.

Aylin shook her head, her draped scarf bobbing. 'I do not know. I
don't think so. She travels a lot, too much for her age I am thinking. I
tell her but she does not listen. She comes every year but she never
stays here for long.'

'Why is that? It's so gorgeous here.'

'I think she does not how do you say it? Approve of her daughter
and her boyfriend.'

As the crushing disappointment and realization that Amelia wasn't
here, continued to press down upon her chest, Verity realised what she
meant. Ahmet was obviously a lot younger than Violetta and they
both appeared volatile. She felt deflated. She'd come all this way for
nothing.

'They will be back soon. You should stay and talk to them?'

'Oh, no, thanks but I must be getting back.' Verity drained her drink;
it had become much sweeter towards the bottom.

'You are staying in a hotel?'

'No, in a villa near the crossroads. It's called Middle Orange House.
Jeremy, my partner is cooking breakfast.'

'Why don't you bring him back tonight when the bar opens? Ahmet,
he makes how you say, the most amazing cocktails. And the music is
very good. You would like very much.'

165

'I'm sure I would.' Verity noticed that the tray on which her glass of apple tea rested boasted a picture of Ephesus. 'Oh, is that the temple of Ephesus? Ah, my partner and his nephew want to visit there because it looks like the Greek temple near where we live.'

'It is a very good excursion and around four hours away from here. It is, how do you say it, worth a visit. You say there is a temple near where you live in England?'

Verity reached into her beach bag and brought out a picture of Penshaw Monument atop of its green hill. 'This is near where I live.'

'You live near this temple? It looks very nice. Can I keep?'

'Yes, yes, you can, of course.' She had plenty more.

'It looks the same as one of the temples at Ephesus. The Temple of Diana. What is this one called?'

'It is called Penshaw Monument.'

She left with her purchases and a heavy heart, waving goodbye to Aylin who pleaded with her once again to try and come back in the evening for music and cocktails.

Back at the villa, she could hardly bear to recount her findings to Jeremy who was sitting on the patio in the shade doing some writing. 'Oh, I'm so sorry V. I know you had your heart set on finding Amelia. Never mind, we're here now and we can make the most of the rest of our stay. Including a night out on the town.

'I don't know, I don't think I'd be very good company at the moment. I'd be just as happy staying in.' The last thing she felt like doing was going out. How could she have been so impulsive? Amelia could be anywhere in the world.

'Oh, Verity please, just wait until you've had some food at Ismet's Place. You'll love it.' Jeremy's hair was still wet from the pool, for once it was flat and brushed back from his face, his skin turning the colour of burnished gold already.

'I...' then she caught sight of his face and he looked so crestfallen that she felt bad and agreed, although her heart wasn't in it. She just wanted to be by herself and plan what to do next. 'Although, maybe we could have a look in the Artisan Cafébar? Apparently, it turns into a cocktail bar at night.'

She was glad she had brought a couple of evening outfits, barely worn since last year's summer holiday and they posed beside the pool for a photo before they went out. Jeremy in his faded blue denim shorts and t-shirt, his tan intensifying the blue of his eyes.

'It's turning dark already, you'll need the flash on,' she told Albie.

'The days are short here in October,' Jeremy remarked.

Verity draped a glittery pashmina around her shoulders.

'Wait,' Jeremy said, 'you need some Sinkov and luckily there's always a bottle in the kitchen cupboard.' He dashed back in and began spraying both her and Albie liberally with it.

'This is in case of mozzies,' he told her.

'Waste of time putting my perfume on,' she said.

'It's better than getting bitten,' as he doused his feet in his flat leather sandals.

Albie was going off to the Jazz Music Bar with the two girls from the plane who were staying at Marmaris but were having an overnight trip to Dalyan to visit the mud baths. Apparently, they'd exchanged numbers in the loo queue.

'Are you sure you can find your way back to Middle Orange House?' Jeremy asked. 'These streets look different in the dark.'

'I'll be sound,' Albie told him.

She did feel better for making the effort and getting dressed up, although her heart was heavy. They stood at the crossroads and followed the road past the bakers which led them down to the river.

The town was absolutely buzzing with people promenading up and down the main drag, in a warm, star-spangled night, some dressed up, others straight from the beach in shorts and flip flops. The shops full of bright beachwear and flowing kaftans draped around models, spilling out onto the street space. One shop had a basket full of colourful scarves with a kitten fast asleep in the middle. There were still a lot of people about even though it was October and she noticed lots of the bars had fires going and were providing patio heaters and coverlets.

'Look at this.' Jeremy laughed at a quote on a blackboard at one of the bars: 'Alcohol is the answer! After all, what great story was every written after eating a salad?'

'That could have been written just for you,' Verity told him.

Arms draped around each other, they strolled along the lanes scented with jasmine (the smell of captured sunlight as Jeremy put it) to the

Artisan Cafébar which she was surprised to see looked very different at night with brightly coloured lights strewn up above and among the trees and lively music playing. The blue checked tablecloths were gone and a glossy cocktail menu was displayed on each table. Verity immediately took another pic for Grandad Ed.

'The cocktails look amazing,' Jeremy exclaimed, looking around as they were shown to a secluded table surrounded by greenery and handed the evening drinks menu.

'What's your Wi-Fi code please?' Verity asked, thinking she was starting to sound like Albie.

'Wow,' Verity thought. Homemade lemonade by day and Angry Pirates by night. The owners were definitely onto a winner here, the shady, idyllic afternoon tea gardens had morphed into a vibrant haze of throbbing music and chatter and the place was buzzing with atmosphere. Shaggy had come along too and sat companionably on Jeremy's feet.

'Can't wait to try this,' Jeremy said, like the big kid that he was. He had of course, gone for the Angry Pirate which was the cocktail of the day. He picked up the laden glass with both hands and the ice-cubes tinkled, which was a feat in itself, considering there were so many other elements in there all elbowing for space. Apart from the alcohol, a colourful combination including wedges of pineapple and melon, fancy straws, cocktail umbrellas, cocktail sticks jostled and there was even a tiny skull and crossbones flag.

'Whoa, that's strong,' Jeremy took a long gulp and pulled a face.

Verity chose a fresh Pomegranate Juice. She was trying hard to put a brave face on things for Jeremy's sake, but the truth was she was bitterly disappointed by the turn of events and didn't really feel in holiday mode. If only she felt she could relax and really enjoy herself, but there was too much going on in her head.

She shivered a little. 'Apparently they catch the cooling sea breezes here in this garden, even though its nine km away from the ocean,' Verity recounted what Aylin had told her this morning.

Jeremy got up to go to the loo and Verity immediately began WhatsApp Ing Grandad Ed. She remembered the conversation they'd had when he found out the fact that she could send pics to him from a foreign country.

'Eee, by that's clever lass.'

'As long as I can sign into the Wi-Fi, of course,' she'd told him. Which led to an explanation about Wi-Fi which she wasn't sure was totally understood.

She felt a stirring of emotion at the thought of Grandad Ed and how she was going to tell him that she hadn't found Amelia?

There was no sign of Aylin or Violetta or her husband although Verity went to the loo upstairs several times to check if they were anywhere inside. She studied the cocktail menu and decided she may as well join Jeremy. She was on holiday after all.

A couple of Rum Punches later, she felt a bit more mellow and forgot about the heavy weight which seemed to be bearing down on her chest and when Jeremy pulled her to her feet, they both danced and swayed in a space next to the foliage.

On the way back, Jeremy laughed as her phone pinged as it picked up the different Wi-Fi codes from each bar they'd visited and they floated into Middle Orange House much later. Downstairs in the villa was cool and quiet.

'No Albie?'

'No, if he was back,' Jeremy said, 'the kitchen cupboards would be open. He'll probably just crash out on the sofa under the water machine when he comes in,' he poured two glasses of water from said machine and began hurrying upstairs.

'Nightcap on the balcony?' he called over his shoulder.

Verity had forgotten all about Albie. 'Shouldn't we be worried in case he gets lost on the way home?' she gulped down the cool liquid thankfully.

'I told him to text if he needs us.'

They watched the bright pathways in the sky of the planes coming and going into the nearby airport and listened to the crickets. It had been a magical evening in its way. Hazy from the cocktails, and with no mozzie bites at all, thanks to the Sinkov, Verity felt it was a shame it wasn't a proper holiday.

'What's that noise?' she said. 'Sounds like someone laughing.'
It was coming from Albie's room. Jeremy rapped on the door. 'Albie – are you back?'

The door opened slowly just a crack, and Albie's head appeared around it, his hair tousled.

A stifled giggle came from further back in the room.

'Who else is in there?' Jeremy asked and pushed the door open more fully to reveal one of the girls from the plane sitting on the bed wrapped in a bed sheet, hair all over the place and waving.

'Hi,' she beamed. 'I'm Esme.'

'Er, hi yourself,' said Jeremy and shut the door quickly, leaning back against it. Verity gave him a look, feeling shock and then relief. 'I know, I know, he's twenty years old.'

'At least he's back,' he said, and Verity drew breath, feeling a wave of relief flooding over her. Maybe this was what parenthood felt like?

# Chapter 28

Reality set in the next morning when the first thing that popped into Verity's head was the fact that Amelia wasn't here in Dalyan. What was she to do next? Then she heard the faint sound of snoring through the wall from Albie's room.

'How about spending the day by the pool?' Jeremy asked.

'Fine by me, I need to think about what I'm going to do next,' she told him, feeling preoccupied and more than a little disjointed. 'I can't think past today.'

He whipped up a delicious Turkish breakfast of ham, hard-boiled eggs, olives, sliced tomatoes and crusty bread which they ate on the patio. 'We'll do absolutely nothing today but chill by the pool.'

Jeremy just wasn't the type to do nothing for long though and he was soon back on the patio in the shade, typing ideas for a new play on his iPad. It was still warm and sunny, although he said the rain clouds were gathering and there may be a storm later.

Tired and with a slight hangover, Verity dozed a little as she tried to settle by the pool. She gazed at a translucent dragonfly resting its red wings by the pool in the dappling sunshine. Looking up, she saw a glittering line up of dragonflies on the telegraph wires, as if awaiting their turn to join in. Another snap for Grandad Ed to wing its way across the ocean to Sand Steps. No Amelia but at least she could keep sending him pictures.

The lagoon blue pool tiles with their white marble frosted layer edging looked like iced slabs of Kendal Mint Cake shimmering in the sleepy heat.

Despite herself, Verity gloriously anticipated a tranquil day to plan her next move. She hadn't slept very well despite the Rum Punches and Angry Pirates and everything seemed to be turning over and over in her brain. She stretched out, muted strains of music from a nearby hotel drifting over on the slight breeze. The air was blissfully warm and sunbeams danced like prisms behind her eyes. Hens clucked calmly from a nearby hen coup and a lot of cooing and wooing was going on overhead from abundant wood pigeons. The occasional baaing and mooing of cows could be heard in the distance from the surrounding fields. The villa really was in an ideal location. Then all was silent as Verity drowsed. Her last conscious thought was how could she find out where Amelia had gone?

She was awoken by a strange sound like the slow clicking sound of knitting needles and lifted her head to see what it was. Over the low villa wall, she saw two women, one a very old Turkish lady in traditional dark patterned clothing and with her head covered, emerging from one of the lanes at the crossroads. She was leaning heavily on sticks and walking very laboriously, the clicking of the sticks growing louder. It took the woman a long time but eventually she stopped at the wall of the garden opposite.

The other woman who accompanied her looked very different. She was short and plump, but wearing a beautiful, long, white linen kaftan and gold sandals, her head covered with a matching scarf. Verity could see from here that she had lots of dark eyeliner around her eyes.

The older lady then began poking at the fruit in the branches of the fig tree with the stick in her right hand until the figs rained down and she caught them, placing them in the front pockets of her gown, the other lady helping her.

Verity turned away as she felt like she was staring. She could feel the sweat begin to trickle down her face and reached for her beach towel. A golden heat haze seemed to be lying over the garden. She was really enjoying the rest, as relaxing was something she never had a lot of time for in her normal life. Time for a dip maybe. Jeremy had disappeared inside, probably in search of another cooling drink.

Then, just as she rose from her sunbed, smoothing down her bikini, an horrendous noise broke the languid silence. What on earth?

It was the sound of frenzied zapping as Shaggy leapt over the wall into the street and began circling backwards and forwards, baring his teeth and growling as the woman picked up her sticks and prepared to walk away.

'Shaggy!' Verity was horrified. She slung her beach robe over her shoulders and thrusting her arms inside, hurried over to the wall to retrieve the normally good-natured little dog.

'I'm so sorry,' she gasped, her bare feet disturbing the dust of the back lane. She picked up Shaggy who wriggled and turned his head back to face the woman, still baring his teeth. 'I can't imagine what's

172

got into him.' He's not even mine, she thought to herself as he continued growling.

The older lady turned around and faced Verity, who noticed that she was wearing dark glasses. She then began to spout forth a torrent of Turkish, very loud and angry and brandishing one of her sticks.

Verity stepped backwards, the stony ground digging into her bare foot. 'Ouch,' she cried out.

'Fatma, Fatma!' the other lady put her arm around the older lady in an attempt to calm her down but she continued her torrent, shaking her stick. She turned her back to walk off in the direction she'd come, seemingly quicker than before, whilst the second lady stood still. Pedro gave another groan, escaped from Verity's arms and leapt back over the wall of Middle Orange House where he ran inside.

She noticed that close up, this lady was deeply tanned and her face crinkled into lines as she frowned at Verity without the trace of a smile. Verity pulled her beach robe more tightly around her body, fastening the belt.

'I'm sorry,' she said again,' I can't imagine what's got into Shaggy.'

The second lady smiled a smile which didn't reach her eyes. 'I can.' So glamorous from across the street, close up she had skin deeply lined to the consistency of leather and too much red lipstick, the strands of visible hair brassy.

'You're English?' Verity was surprised.

At that point, Aunt Fatma turned at the crossroads and repeated a few sentences, waving her stick.

'What is she saying?' Verity asked.

Shaggy was emitting a low growling noise from the safety of the patio.

Her laughter cackled out. 'I don't think you really would like to know. It's for the best.'

'Oh, but I would.' Verity said. 'Was she swearing in Turkish? It seems to be the same sentence over and over again. Please tell me.' It suddenly felt very important that she knew. Oh, where was Jeremy when he might have been useful? Oblivious to the pandemonium out here that was for sure.

The lady sighed, a rushing sound. 'If you must know, she said, 'hasn't your dog ever come across a witch before?''

Verity smiled back then the enormity of her words struck home. No, that couldn't be right. It must be the sun. She was sure she'd heard wrong. She was hearing things, she must be.

'Sorry,' she said, 'would you mind repeating that?'

Cackling laughter rang out again. 'Well, I did warn you dear. She said, 'hasn't your dog ever come across a witch before?''

Verity immediately felt a cold shiver down her back and the afternoon seemed to darken.

'A witch? She's a witch?' she asked.

The woman laughed. 'I didn't mean her.'

'You?'

The lady shrugged. 'Was this your photo?'

Verity looked down and saw the woman had the picture of Penshaw Monument in her hand.

Wait a moment. Was this Violetta standing in front of her? How could she not have recognised her? Well, she did only pass her very quickly yesterday. Verity's heart felt like it was about to jump out of her chest. She managed a nod. 'Well, yes it was.'

'You are the one that was snooping around, asking questions?'

'I wouldn't call it snooping exactly.'

'I knew it. You were looking for my mother.'

'Yes, I may have been but...'

Violetta leaned closer so Verity could smell smoke on her breath. 'Don't come near me again asking questions. Go back home to England and forget about my mother. Leave well alone, I am warning you.'

'Or what? You'll put a spell on me? Look, I didn't mean any harm. I only wanted to...'

'She doesn't need you coming here and bringing up the past. It's all forgotten about. She's gone home and doesn't need you disrupting her life. So don't even think about doing anything else, do you hear me?'

Then the man in the Mosque began to sing, his voice taking precedence over everything, the whole world that was this little back street, as his voice echoed eerily across the town, reverberating around the nearby valleys.

The world seemed to stop turning and it seemed irreverent to speak any more words but Verity was in turmoil inside, the blood seemingly singing in her veins. The older lady stopped in her tracks and stood very still.

Then the singing stopped, and the spell was broken. The lady turned abruptly and stalked back off up the lane, followed by Violetta who hadn't waited for a reply.

'Wait, please.' Verity started after her but the older lady brandished her sticks once more and Shaggy's growling intensified. Verity turned back towards the villa and when she turned around again, the lane was empty.

# Chapter 29

'Would you like some iced tea? Peach flavour?' Jeremy emerged on the patio, beaming and oblivious, carrying a tray with drinks overloaded with ice and fruit. 'What's going on? What's up with Shaggy?'

Verity slowly recounted the events of the last few minutes. Was that really all it was? Had that really just happened? Now she was telling the tale it sounded unreal and a bit ridiculous.

'A witch?' Jeremy shook his head. 'Can't believe I've missed all the excitement.'

'I don't know if I would call it that. She was very vindictive.'

He put down his load and handed a glass over, the ice cubes tinkling.

'Why would she want to warn me off meeting her mother? What is she hiding?' Verity took the glass, her hand shaking a little. 'I don't understand. And why was Shaggy so scared? He lives here. Surely, she wasn't really a witch?'

'Sounds strange, I admit.' Jeremy said. 'It could be the head gear. Shaggy hates some hats. I've never known him to growl at anyone before though.'

Feeling suddenly cooler still, she entered the villa and sat down heavily on the sofa, making the cushions bounce.

Jeremy followed her in, sat down next to her and made a sound which sounded like a low chuckle.

'Well, thanks a lot,' she bristled. 'I didn't find it particularly funny you know, being ranted and raved at in a foreign language in the back street by a Turkish matriarch who was with a witch who was most probably putting a life-threatening curse on me.'

'I'm so sorry. I didn't mean to mock.' Jeremy rubbed his eyes and put both his arms around her. 'I was actually chuckling at the colour of your feet.'

Verity looked down and saw that her feet were once more, absolutely black, with ripples of dust splaying up and around her ankles.

'Not again.

'This is becoming a habit.'

'Goodness! I need a shower.'

Jeremy went on. 'I think I might know the older woman with the sticks.'

'You've seen her before?'

'Yes, a lady of her description lives in the Villa Duranne just round the corner. It could be that Shaggy was barking because she brandished her sticks at me once when I took a short cut through her garden.'

Verity was only slightly mollified. 'He was barking at the other woman. His hackles were up and like you said, you've never, ever heard him growl before at anyone.'

'Still, could be the combination of headgear and sticks. A perfectly reasonable explanation. No need to worry.'

Verity drained her drink and went to find some headache tablets in the kitchen. 'Shaggy lives here. He should be used to headgear.'

'Maybe the sun's been too much for you today, it's been really hot.'

'I haven't had too much sun if that's what you think.' Verity felt annoyed with him. 'I haven't had the chance. Too much going on out there.'

She was sure she hadn't imagined the dark sense of ominous gloom but was beginning to feel rather silly so after washing the dust off her she went back out to try and chill out for the rest of the afternoon. She heard a sound like the loud banging of drums filling the air and horns hooting as a wedding car packed with people drove along past the villa, banging what sounded like tin lids accompanied by lots of shouting and waving.

Jeremy waved as its occupants who whooped as they passed. As the noise subsided, Jeremy advised, 'the wedding celebrations go on for four days. They drive up and down every street in town, making a lot of noise.

Verity gave up. 'I'm going for a lie down. I'm sorry. I seem to have had a bad head ever since I arrived here for one reason or another.'

'I'm coming with you.'

Much later, upstairs, in the bedroom above the gardens, Verity finally drifted off to sleep again to the strains of a piece of haunting piano music coming from the school beside the river. The same piece of signature music rippled over the village several times daily, to call the children to and from school as well as signifying playtimes and lunchtimes.

The afternoon wore on and she heard a resounding cock a doodle doo. And another. And another as the afternoon chorus gathered momentum from various locations across the town, like having sets of music speakers blasting in different directions.

All this was played out against the constant clicking of the crickets which seemed to grow louder at regular intervals and then fade again to being part of the background.

Then her phone signalled a text from Sophie.

*'Hi. Greyson says he's sinking without you.'*

*'Tough.'*

*'He had no-one to wind his train set up - ha ha - only joking! He's fine.'*

*'Glad to hear it.'*

*'By the way, you didn't tell me I had to take proper notes at the Thursday meeting.'*

*'Sorry, I might have forgotten to mention that...'*

*'Thanks a lot.'*

*'I knew you'd cope.'*

*'It wasn't too bad I suppose. He talked about football for 15 mins first. Then he told everyone at the meeting I was his temporary carer.'*

*'Typical Greyson. Bye Sophie. Thanks for the update.'*

*'And I had to make the coffee.'*

Verity chuckled to herself. *'Bye Sophie.'* Whilst texting, and in normal conversation as well come to think of it, Sophie always had to have the last word.

She abandoned trying to rest and joined Jeremy who was back at work downstairs on the patio. The noises had subsided, apart from a tractor trundling along the crossroads, preparing to spray the meadows with mosquito repellent. Soon all was quiet. It was the time of day when the sun was fading, and the mosquitos were starting to rise dizzily out of the grass as the temperature fell. The heady, yet cloying, sweet smell of jasmine began to gather momentum.

'She's gone home.' Words were ringing in Verity's ears, now that the shock of the encounter had sunk in. 'She's gone home.' Rather than, 'Hasn't your dog ever seen a witch before?'

178

That was it! Amelia had gone home. All Verity had to do now was to follow her. And it would take more than a marauding witch to put her off.

# Chapter 30

*The demonstration of ordinary soundscapes as music – there are different ways to listen to our world...*

Verity had an awful lot on her mind. Today was Sunday and tomorrow her first day back at work and she was already planning to ask Greyson for more time off. A weekend just wasn't long enough to drive to Cornwall and back – unless she flew to Exeter and hired a car from there to drive the seventy-four miles to Cornwall? She was frantically googling options at the kitchen table under the window when Albie and Jeremy came in. Albie looked as if he was going out and she wondered how Jeremy had managed to prise him out of his room.

'But you promised you'd help me today?' Albie dumped a huge backpack at the other
end of the table.

'I'm really sorry mate, but I've just been called in to an impromptu pitch meeting at Newcastle, I can't miss it. He's a producer and he's only in town for the weekend.'

'What about my research? I've been looking forward to it.' Albie turned his back on Jeremy to open the biscuit cupboard.

'Hey, I've had a thought. Verity could maybe help you out, couldn't you V?' Jeremy's tone was pleading.

'What?' Verity didn't look up. 'Me?'

'You're not doing anything much are you?'

Verity raised her head to see two pairs of eyes staring in her direction.

'Well, I am kind of in the middle of something important...'

'Oh crap.' Albie said.

They both looked so crestfallen she closed the laptop lid with a snap. She supposed she would have time to check it out later. And it wasn't often Jeremy asked for her help.

'All right, all right, I'll do it.'

'Sound.' Albie perked up.

'What is it you want me to help you with?'

180

'Field Recording.'

Jeremy said, 'Which roughly translated, means standing very still, keeping very quiet and holding the cables.'

'So where are we going?'

'On location,' Albie opened the fridge and added a couple of cans of coke and some packets of crisps and biscuits into the side pockets of his backpack. 'You'd better take some water.'

'Looks like we're out for the duration. So, it's up to the monument I presume?'

Albie pulled on a padded outdoor coat and then began to carefully lever the enormous backpack in place over his shoulders and hunched it further up on his back. It looked as big as him, he was so thin. He shook his head.

'To the Sub Station.'

They headed out along the still country lane in where Albie seemed oblivious to the fact that although the trees had not yet lost all their greenery, there was a gilded carpet of burnished copper, gold and yellow autumn leaves underfoot. The air was full of the pungent scent of wet foliage drying out in the sun and starlings chattered away on the telegraph wires, their outlines black against the azure sky.

'What exactly is field recording?' Verity broke the silence.

Albie sighed. 'Well, I'm a producer of electronic music, right?'

'Yes?'

'I'm carrying out some research because music producers relate to sound in their environment and in its widest sense, field recording refers to the process of capturing sound outside the measured confines of a studio.'

'I see', Verity said. That must be the longest sentence she'd ever heard Albie utter. 'Sounds very technical.'

Much later, after helping to hold cables and keep quiet at an eerie place which resembled a space village set in the middle of graceful parkland, where a chaotic mass of robotic transformers and switchgear crisscrossed and interconnected, sunshine glinting over single angles, they ended up sitting on the stone base of the monument to finish off.

'Ouch, I've been stung,' she said, 'must have been those nettles we ran through to get away from all those kids.'

Albie giggled. 'They thought we were off the telly.'

181

Verity was surprised now that the monument didn't fill her with quite as much discordant dread as it used to. It was since her talk with Grandad Ed. Maybe she was getting used to it?

She surveyed the view whilst Albie began munching on crisps.

'A productive session so far?' she asked.

Albie cracked open a can of coke, shaking his head. 'Nah, it's crap. I need more material. Talk about the peace and quiet of the countryside.'

Verity laughed. 'I never realised it was so noisy.'

'Next time,' Albie said thoughtfully, 'maybe we'd better go in the early hours of the morning when there's no-one else about. What about at three in the morning? Put your alarm on for half past two and then you can wake me up with a bacon sandwich.'

Verity looked at him in horror, then saw his eyes crinkling into the surrounding dark circles.

'Did you just make a joke?' She grabbed a bag of crisps from his lap. 'Here, give me some. All this walking about has made me hungry.'

Albie dangled his skinny, jean clad legs over the edge.

From here, looking through the pillars towards the east, where, past the twirling wind turbines and silver factory roofs, Verity could just make out the sea in the distance. She laughed to herself.

'What?'

'You're actually smiling.'

'I do smile. Sometimes.'

'You seem to be grumpy most of the time.' Their newly gained status of friendly banter was making Verity more forthright.

He handed Verity a can of coke. 'Suppose you're right. But what have I got to be happy and smile about?'

She declined the can of coke and reached for the bottle of water instead. She couldn't believe what she was hearing. 'From where I'm standing – or sitting - you seem to have a lovely life. Scran on demand. And you've got to admit, you eat an awful lot. In fact, that's an understatement.' Albie shrugged, his ribs showing through his faded t-shirt. Verity continued, 'the best room in the house to play your music in, a comfy bed to sleep in, people who care about you. Need I go on?'

Albie shook his head, but she continued on. 'Well, listen to this. Has this ever happened to you? When I was at school I was once the only child in the class who couldn't go on a school trip. I had to stay behind all day in the classroom all on my own, apart from one teacher who kept an eye on me and let me read books all day.'

She paused for a sip of water. And would you like to know why I couldn't go on the trip? Because I was living with an auntie who simply didn't have any money to pay for me to go.

My dad was off living with his new woman, and she had three kids and so he couldn't spare any either. Can you imagine how that felt?'

Albie shook his head again, an expression of horror on his face. 'That must have been proper crap.'

'It was. I remember saying to myself many times, Oh, not another Auntie. I just wanted to cry but I learnt early on that crying didn't help. I only felt worse afterwards and it made my eyes sore.'

'No wonder you're a bit weird about marrying Uncle Jer.'

'What do you mean? I'm not weird.'

'I only meant that – after such a rubbish childhood it must be hard to trust people.'

'That's very true.'

'He really wants to marry you, you know. He tries very hard.'

Verity was lost for words. Was it that obvious? She was a bit shaken by Albie's words; she didn't think he'd taken much notice. There was a long silence, then Albie broke it.

'Anyhow, I can't stay here forever. I've got to go home sometime.'

'What's so bad about going home?'

'That just it. People don't care about me.'

'I'm sure that's not true. Jeremy does and so…so do I.'

'I meant my mother. She's not bothered.'

'I doubt that very much.'

He snorted. 'It's a fact.'

'What makes you think that? Have you tried talking to her?'

'She wasn't interested. Why do you think I'm here?'

'To see your uncle? While you look for a job?'

'That's another thing I haven't got. I've got a 2:1 degree in Music Technology and no job.'

'You've hardly looked. If you get a job in Newcastle, you could get a flat there and you wouldn't have to go home.'

'Do you want rid of me?'

'Course not. Stop changing the subject.'

'I'm not. My mum's only bothered about her next boyfriend. Not about me.'

'At least you've got one.'

'What do you mean?'

'Your mum. Mine died when I was a baby.'

'Soz. I didn't know that. What about your dad?'

'My dad didn't want to be bothered with me, so he passed me around a succession of aunties. When one auntie got fed up with me, I stayed with another one and another, sharing bedrooms with loads of other kids.'

Albie shifted his position and looked up from where he was staring at the graffiti high up on the one of the blackened pillars.

'Really?'

'Yes. Really. My dad fell out with just about all of the family. Then when I was fifteen, I was lucky enough to meet my Uncle Bobby who introduced me to my lovely Grandma Anna. I moved in with her and my life began.'

She noticed a look in his deep brown eyes which was the nearest she'd seen to respect.

'Uncle Jer says you've got a really good job.'

'I've worked very hard for it. I think you're a hard worker too. I've seen that today.'

'Thanks.'

She was curious. 'What about your dad?'

Albie opened his mouth to speak but then shook his head, stood up and began gathering up all the gear. 'Can we get on? If we move over to the other side and I can try the spoon test out on the stone over there where it's quieter?'

Verity stood up and began brushing away crisp crumbs. Enough soul bearing for one day. Let him digest what she'd told him. There didn't seem to be a rift between them anymore, however now she was keen to know more about his family situation and he didn't want to talk about his father. Give it time, she told herself, we've made some progress today. That must have been the longest conversation they'd had yet.

She trailed after Albie, laden with coats and coke cans and bottles of water.

'Here, can you hold the mike for a minute?'

She grabbed the mike as well and watched him unravel cables again, when she heard a voice say, 'What's going on here?'

Paul, her journo friend was eyeing the pair of them with amusement, especially the large fluffy mike. 'Are you with the BBC?'

'Field Recording,' Albie muttered, looking up only briefly.

Paul laughed. 'I see you have a glamorous assistant. Hello Verity. Fancy bumping into you again.'

'Hi there. This is Albie.'

'Is Albie, er, yours?'

'He's Jeremy's nephew. Albie is a Music Producer.'

'Ah, I see, pleased to meet you Albie. I'm Paul, Reporter, Fellridge Advertiser.'

Albie muttered a greeting, his arms full of cables. Paul turned to Verity.

'How's it's going?'

'Good thanks. Are you taking photos again for the evening edition?'

'For my sins. Finished for the day now though.' He indicated the pillar second from the end where the doorway was now being closed, the white, hard hats stacked away for the day.

'Actually, Albie would you mind?' Paul whipped out his camera.

Albie nodded his head to show his agreement and posed while Paul took a shot of him in between two of the most easterly blackened stone pillars, his angular features brooding, and holding out the fluffy microphone in front of him. There was a neat view in the background of green fields and the lighter ribbon of the road and the cars going around the roundabout below as if in slow motion, captured in the gap between pillars.

'Thanks a lot. Most interesting shot I've had all day.' He turned back to Verity. 'I thought you might have been in touch?'

Verity must have looked blank. 'Me? Why would I?'

'About that story we discussed?'

'Oh. No, I haven't changed my mind.'

185

Paul whipped out a business card and handed it to Verity.

'I've already got one, thanks.'

'Have another, just in case.'

'Thanks, but I won't change my mind.' Verity took it without looking and shoved it in her coat pocket.

'Hope to bump into you again soon,' Paul called after them.

'He so likes you,' Albie smirked as they packed up.

'He's a pushy journalist that's all, trying to sniff out a scoop. Any scoop. You'll probably be in tonight's paper. Famous Music Producer spotted on Penshaw Monument.'

Albie shrugged and led the way back down the front of the hill.

# Chapter 31

Verity felt hot and exhausted when they finally got back home. She peeled off her padded jacket, scarf and gloves and strung them over the kitchen table for once without bothering to hang them up. She wasn't hungry having eaten her body weight in crisps so she decided to go straight up for a bath with some of her Mindful Bath Salts which worked wonders after stressful days at work. Albie had already dripped off to his room to listen to his recordings with a Chinese takeaway he'd picked up on the way back.

She heard Jeremy come in later and shout from the kitchen, 'Hi, I'm back.'

She'd noticed his precious notebook lying open on his bedside table and knew he'd been awake since five, probably with ideas crowding into his subconscious for a new play. She'd felt him reach for the notebook, which he always kept to hand in case of such lightbulb moments, as quietly as he could so as he didn't disturb her and also and Pedro who was lying on his feet and heard him frantically scribbling. He always said if he didn't get his thoughts down on paper, they'd be gone by morning. He was never so happy as when he was creating ideas. They didn't always come to fruition, but then, that was a writer's lot apparently.

'Hi, you're back, how did it go?' Verity yawned as she padded downstairs into the kitchen in her robe and slippers. 'I can't wait to tell you all about today.'

'It went okay. Just a waiting game now for funding. As usual.'

She saw that Jeremy had picked up her jacket from where it had fallen to the floor in the porch. 'I can smell your sweetshop candy perfume.' As he draped it over the hook in the porch, something fluttered down to the floor. It was a business card. He picked it up and attempted to put it back in the pocket but he dislodged another card which fell out as well. He bent down to pick both items up to hand to her.

'Oops, aren't things just awkward,' he said, then looked down to see what was in the palm of his hand.

Two business cards rested there with the same name on them. One had scribbled on it 'To Verity. Love from Paul Longwood, Reporter, Fellridge Advertiser. X

Verity took them absentmindedly and wandered into the living room where she flopped down on the sofa, dropping the cards on the coffee table and gazing up at the empty space above the warmth of the wood burner. This was where *The Happy Child* painting was going to be and she thought how good it was going to look hanging there. Then an idea struck her.

What if she went to collect the painting in person from Amelia's Art Gallery in Fowey? If she rang up and found out when it was likely to be ready, instead of shipping it to her here in Penshaw, she could actually go and pick it up herself? Brilliant, she had decided to go to Cornwall anyway but now had a legitimate excuse. It may mean she needed to drive there instead of flying to Exeter. Fine. That was one less thing to arrange. She would ring up first thing tomorrow morning. What a brainwave.

She was surprised when Jeremy stood in front of her, looking edgy. 'Is there something I should know?'

'Like what?'

Jeremy sighed. 'About this Paul Longwood or whatever his name is?' He indicated the discarded cards.

Albie was on his way downstairs minus the hoodies and backpack and dipped into the conversation.

'He proper likes Verity.'

'I see.'

'What? No. Of course not.'

Verity was distracted from her train of thought. 'Don't be ridiculous.'

'He keeps bumping into her,' Albie went on.

'Rubbish. He's only out for a story for his paper, that's all.' Verity hardly bothered to glance at the offending cards. 'Which he isn't going to get.'

'Then why have you kept two of his business cards?' his tone was jokey but with just a hint of concern.

'Just because I was so disinterested in them that I never got round to throwing them away. Put them in the bin, tear them up I don't care.'

She was surprised, she'd never known Jeremy to even be the slightest bit jealous before. He was usually so laid back.

'It's just that you've been rather well, quiet lately,' Jeremy said later when Albie had gone into the kitchen. 'Thought you might have gone off me?'

'No way.' Verity was indignant but managed to convince him that was all it was. How could he possibly think that of her? She was nothing if not loyal. It was just so unlike him.

'You see, I'm a bloke, right?' he continued with his train of thought.

'Right, I'm with you on that one.' Verity put her arms around him.

'And I know that a bloke doesn't bother to help you, I mean like getting you an appointment with his uncle at the Manor, unless he's after something.'

Verity wound her arms upwards around his neck. 'I told you, all he's after is his next big scoop.'

'Hmm, okay, no worries,' Jeremy hugged her back.

'You have absolutely nothing to worry about. I'll make it up to you I promise, once this is all sorted and I've found Amelia.'

'That'll be good,' he said, 'seeing as we didn't quite manage that romantic time in Turkey I'd hoped for.'

Then, after dropping the cards into the flames of the log burner, she proceeded to ring Grandad Ed to keep him up to date with events, while Jeremy tried very hard to concentrate on his marking.

189

# Chapter 32

Verity sat at a window table in the pub so she could see the eye-catching view straight opposite, a vista of bright, shiny, ruby red ivy which completely covered the wall. Stunning she thought. If she moved her head just slightly, she could also glimpse an angled view of the monument, dominating above the rooftops. Sophie set down two glasses on the table and looked around her, long hair swinging.

'So, this is your local?'

'Yes.' Verity picked up her glass. 'But you know I haven't really got time for this.'

'Course you have. You promised me a girls' night out.'

'Yes, but I didn't know I was going to Cornwall then.'

'You're not going until the weekend.'

'We've both got to be up for work tomorrow.'

'I could stay at yours and we can stagger in late together.'

'You're welcome to stay if you want.'

'So am I just doing the same at work as the last time?'

'Yes, hold the fort as Greyson would say.'

'Ha-ha. Keep an eye on the watercooler whisperers, they're proper worse when you're away.'

'What is this anyway?' Verity swirled her cocktail stick around the golden liquid in her glass and took a sip and then another.

'It's an aperol spritz cocktail, I knew you'd like it.' Sophie clinked her glass against Verity's, the packed ice cubes tinkling. 'Next time it's defo cocktails on the Newcastle quayside.'

Verity glanced at her phone for the time. 'I need to see Jeremy and Albie for a few minutes before tomorrow comes.'

'Okay, we'll go back soon. I would like to see Jeremy too. You're very lucky you know.'

'What makes you say that?'

'Because Jeremy is seriously hot – for an old guy.'

Verity shot her a look.

'Sorry. Ha-ha, he's old enough to be my dad. Only joking V.'

'I know.'

'Anyhow, I was telling you about Lesley who works in HR.'

'What about her?'

'She's just split up with her husband.'

'Has she really?'

'Yeah. Apparently, she's off on the sick because she's depressed.'

'I can imagine. Poor thing, maybe we should have invited her tonight.'

'It's not like you to be so empathetic.'

Verity shrugged. 'I'm not that bad. I just believe in getting on with life.'

Sophie twirled her straw. 'What happened with your marriage? You've never told me.'

'Oh, I don't talk about it much.' Verity swirled the ice around her glass. 'Probably because it felt like…like a bereavement.'

'As bad as that?'

'Oh yes. I felt such a failure. In fact, at the time I felt so down that I thought it would have been easier if it had been. A bereavement I mean.' Verity shook her head and took a large swig from her glass. 'Sorry, that was a terrible thing to say.'

'No, it's not.'

'It would have been easier not to have to see him every day. We worked at the same place.' She took another long drink. 'I still don't like talking about it.'

'Well maybe you should. Have you ever told Jeremy what you've just told me?'

Verity shook her head. 'I try to forget it ever happened.'

'So, is that why you're stalling on marriage plans?'

'I'm not.' Verity shuffled in her seat. 'Am I?'

Sophie shrugged. 'Maybe.'

'You know, I don't feel like that now. I'm very happy with Jeremy.'

Sophie jumped up. 'That's good. Time for one more and then you can show me your lush new home.' She tossed her hair over her shoulder. 'And I can meet Albie. Oh, and I don't care if the dog sleeps on my bed.'

# Chapter 33

Verity opened the door in the middle of the slanting, sun shadowed street and stepped inside the Trevalsa Art Gallery. Her action caused a bell to tinkle which sent a ripple around the shop. An aura of calm immediately folded around her.

Cream walls showcased a variety of beautiful modern seascapes, some stormy, some summery, and there was a desk at the far end of the long room. A sign indicated that there were more pictures up a steep flight of stairs, which Verity surmised would lead to a showroom in the attics of the more traditional paintings. There were also cabinets lining one wall full of *Happy Child* paraphernalia, mugs, cups, tea towels and smaller pictures.

For a brief moment she was totally alone, her heart beating fast, and then a lady appeared from behind a beaded curtain and leaning on a walking stick, moved to greet her with a wide, generous smile. Time seemed to stand still within this oasis which seemed far removed from the bustling street and Verity had her first sighting of Amelia Trevalsa, formerly Lady Amelia Temperly.

Amelia! At last. This was her. She'd found her. She knew it. Surely Amelia would be able to hear her heart banging so hard against her rib cage as she moved closer and held out her hand.

Tall, frail yet slightly querulous looking, Amelia had white hair swept up into an elegant chignon which highlighted her high cheekbones. Her skin was lightly tanned and although there were some lines on her face, Verity thought she probably had less wrinkles than her daughter. She was very smartly dressed and reminded Verity of a long, lean, weeping willow tree.

'Good morning. How may I help you?' her wide smile lit up her whole face and her accent was cut glass. What a lovely voice she had. In that second Verity could imagine how vibrant she must have looked when she was younger.

'Good morning,' Verity managed to smile back. To her horror she felt tears pricking her eyelids. How pleased Grandad Ed was going to be but she couldn't give the game away just yet, she had to be composed. 'I've...I've come to collect a painting.'

'Ah, then you must be Ms Raffin? We've been expecting you.' She also had a very firm handshake which was surprising as she looked so frail. 'Thank you so much, my dear, for buying *The Happy Child.* Such a good choice.'

'Call me Verity please. I absolutely adore this painting,' Verity gushed, 'it's to go over the fireplace in the living room in my new home.'

'I'm so pleased you like it. It's always been our best seller.' Amelia rang a little bell on the desk and as if by magic, a young lady appeared, carrying Verity's wrapped painting very carefully.

'I sort of fell in love with it as soon as I saw it.' Verity knew she was gabbling. 'I would simply call it the happiest and loveliest baby that ever was.'

'I totally agree.'

They smiled at one another then Amelia took her by surprise.

'Wait a minute dear…have we met before?'

Verity immediately felt guilty. Was her plan to be discovered before it had even begun?

'No, I don't think so.'

'Strange. I never forget a face. Never mind dear, it will come to me.'

'Now, dear.' Amelia moved back to the desk and flicked open a diary. 'I need to book you an appointment for our consultation.'

'Consultation?'

'Oh yes, I always have a little post purchase meeting with my important clients when they buy one of our paintings. All part of the service, especially as they're spending so much of their money.'

'Yes, of course,' Verity couldn't believe her luck. Things were actually going her way for once. She wouldn't have to explain all here in the Art Gallery. Amelia obviously was treating her as an important client, probably because the painting was so expensive. Wouldn't she get a shock however, when she found out the real reason behind Verity being here?

'I feel that it's only courtesy. And after all, who knows you may wish to buy another painting in the future?'

'Indeed, I might.' Verity winced a bit inside, feeling a pang of discomfort because that really wasn't her intention at all.

'Could we make it tomorrow?' Amelia looked up from the gold edged diary, an elegant pen poised in her delicate white hand. Her wrists were very slender.

Tomorrow. Perfect. 'Yes, I leave here the day after tomorrow so that would be ideal.'

'Where are you staying, dear?'

'In Charleston, the hotel on the water's edge.'

'Ah, an admirable choice. I often go there for morning coffee. I'll come to you. I can be there for 10.00 am sharp, if that suits?'

Even better! A private consultation. Amelia didn't mess about. Verity knew just the spot in the Pier House she would have to make sure was available for their meeting.

'That would be perfect if you don't mind travelling to Charlestown,' Verity smiled and they shook hands again. Oh, the strength behind that handshake.

'Oh, not at all dear. It's only a few miles away in my little car. Where are you from?'

'I'm from the North East near Newcastle upon Tyne.'

Was there a tiny flicker of something, like a gleam of interest in those pale blue eyes? No, it was gone as quickly as she had imagined it, and Amelia turned opened the door for her.

'Very nice dear. Do you need a hand to your car with your painting, er Verity?'

'Oh no, thanks. I'm fine,' Verity remembered that parking had been a nightmare, in fact there just didn't seem to be any, eventually she'd found a high level car park and walked down past the sparkling turquoise waters of the estuary, hearing the chug chug of brightly coloured boats and even catching a glimpse of a cruise liner hiding just around the curve of the bay.

She wouldn't have cared if the painting was heavy, her heart felt so light. She'd bought it without a frame which as well as keeping the cost down, had made it reasonably light and easy to carry. All she could think of was what a brilliant piece of luck she'd had today and she was meeting Amelia again tomorrow.

Verity was enchanted by the unspoilt, historic Georgian harbour of Charlestown on the south coast of Cornwall where she was staying. It was the port where Poldark and many other films were made. She'd chosen it purely because of the location, not too close to Amelia's art gallery and also because of the glorious photographs she'd seen online.

Part of the harbour and docks were now a base for an array of square rigged, sailing ships with dizzyingly tall masts and a plethora of fishermen's' creels, nets and twisted ropes and she noticed there was a tiny bridge over the impounded harbour.  It was quiet because it was out of season although it looked as if quite a lot of the local businesses, cafes, restaurants etc. had remained open all year around.

She loved her room, which had a sea view and two windows, right in the middle of the front of the building.  The outdoor terrace under her window also overlooked the harbour.  How she wished she had more time and was staying longer to have time to properly explore.

The receptionist had been very helpful when she'd asked if she could reserve the table under the window in the enclosed almost secret little room just off the hallway.  She'd discovered it earlier whilst exploring the hotel and it was ideal for her morning coffee meeting the next day.

A reserved sign was immediately placed in the middle of the table. 'We serve morning coffee from ten am onwards,' she was informed.

Then she rang Grandad Ed from the stone-built terrace with its light wood tables, slatted chairs and huge beige umbrellas like ship's sails, shivering in her coat and scarf and gloves, but loving the darkened view.  She'd already sent him some pics of the historic quay with its array of sailing ships which he'd replied to with a thumbs up sign. She was the only one sitting outside.

'Good news Grandad!  I've found her.'  She heard his sharp intake of breath.

'Really?  Oh lass, that's champion. I'm so glad.'

'And I'm meeting with her tomorrow.'

'Ah, bonny lass, I just knew you'd do it.'  Verity was perturbed to hear harsh coughing on the other end. 'Have you told her yet?'

'No, not yet.  I'm waiting until tomorrow.  That sounds like a bad cough, Grandad, are you okay?'

'Aye, I'm grand, nowt wrong with me lass.  It's just a tickle.'  He coughed again.

'Are you taking anything for it?'

'I've got some throat lozenges.  Don't worry about me.'

'I'll let you know how I go on tomorrow.'

'Get yourself away in. Sleep tight lass.' Verity pondered on how they'd become closer over the last few months. 'Blood is thicker than water,' he'd told her once. It wasn't true in every case though.

As it grew darker, she watched the boats dance on the water beyond the piers and the tiny winking lights which belonged to the fishermen fishing from the quay itself.

There was no moon here but the sky was clear and star speckled and it was growing colder. She stayed out as long as she could but even the new tin cloth, winter's coat she'd bought on a whim in Fowey, wasn't quite keeping out the chill.

Back in her room she couldn't sleep so she rang Jeremy and talked to him as she lay looking out over the harbour, watching the lights play on the sea. She felt nervous at the thought of her forthcoming conversation with Amelia tomorrow. What if she blew it and said the wrong thing? Or what if her witch of a daughter found out and came storming in before she had a chance to explain? Maybe it would upset her so perhaps it would be best to leave things alone? But she'd promised Grandad Ed, she couldn't let him down at this late stage. She had liked Amelia straight away and guessed that she was a very honest, upfront type of person.

All Verity had to do was deliver a simple message from the past...

# Chapter 34

She was woken the next morning by the sound of sea birds shrieking and the rush of the ocean, lashing against the rugged bedrock walls. The tide was in.

She was down early to claim her table. The little room was ideally situated for their post painting consultation, being a small space just off the hallway, housing a couple of tables only. The one Verity had booked was directly under the window. There was a direct picture postcard view, almost like a framed portrait of the two curving piers and the mouth of the inner harbour and rugged quays leading out to the open sea.

Verity studied the room in an attempt to study her nerves. The theme was very much ships, from the pale wallpaper adorned with intricate drawings of historic tall galleons, down to the model of the boat with its flowing golden sails on the window ledge. The sails matched the shade of the lamp which was attached to the tiniest plug socket Verity had ever seen. A gorgeous smell of fresh, rich roasted coffee pervaded the air. She found she was sitting stiffly, on the edge of her seat.

'Ah, there you are dear.' Amelia had arrived. Verity's heart pounded as she rose to greet her, the older lady leaning heavily on her stick and smiling her approval.

'This is my favourite spot in the whole hotel, well done dear.'

'I thought it might be too cold outside on the terrace,' Verity said, although she noted that Amelia was well wrapped up, wearing a long, grey, stylish wool coat under her padded outdoor coat, topped off with a scarf, gloves and carrying a roomy leather handbag. It took her what seemed an age to divest herself of all her outdoor clothing, revealing a Chanel style trouser suit, and finally sit down opposite Verity.

They were seated so as they could both look straight out onto the harbour and Amelia insisted on ordering them scones with jam and cream to go with their white coffees and she asked especially for a large jug of hot water with which to top up their drinks.

'It's so very warm and cosy in here,' Verity said, wanting to stall the inevitable conversation until their order arrived.

197

'I do so feel the cold nowadays,' Amelia said, re-arranging the floaty chiffon around her swan like neck. 'Have you had breakfast?'

'Yes, I've had a huge plateful of delicious smoked salmon and scrambled eggs. I tried to go for the lightest thing on the menu.'

'I eat very little at breakfast time. I've had a few rich tea biscuits and several cups of tea.'

Their scones arrived and the steaming coffee in thick ceramic cups smelt delicious.

Verity's throat felt very dry. She'd gone through it all in her head so many times but now she was here she was finding it hard to get her words out. How would Amelia react?

Amelia produced a glossy catalogue from the Gallery. 'I brought you one of our catalogues.'

Verity thanked her and cleared her throat, not having the heart to tell her that she'd looked at it online so many times.

Amelia looked out at the view. 'Just look out there.'

Verity looked. 'It's so unspoilt and it's certainly got atmosphere,' she agreed.

'Artists say it's something to do with the quality of light here in the west. We have such strong sun, clean air and powerful colours.'

Verity nodded and took a deep breath 'Er, there's something I need to talk to you about. 'I'm afraid I may have got you here on false pretences.'

'I see.' Amelia frowned. 'You mean you don't want to buy another painting?'

'Not at the moment. Although I love the one I've bought and I wouldn't rule it out for the future.'

'I guessed as much.'

'You did?'

'Don't look so worried, Verity dear. So, before you tell me what exactly your intentions are, can I ask you a question?'

Verity was taken aback. 'Yes of course, ask anything you like.' This wasn't exactly how she'd expected the conversation to go.

'Can I ask you where you first saw *The Happy Child?*'

'Yes, of course.' Did Amelia suspect something? 'I first saw it and fell in love with it in a picture gallery in Monument Manor. In the North East village of Penshaw.'

Amelia sipped her morning coffee and topped it up from the jug of hot water she'd requested. Her white hand shook a little.

'You're from Penshaw village?'

'Not exactly from there. I moved a couple of months ago.' She put down her coffee cup and looked directly into Amelia's light eyes. 'But my grandfather is from Penshaw. Ed Turnbull.'

Amelia's hand shot out and she grabbed Verity's arm across the table. The best way Verity could describe it was that a fire seemed to have been lit in her eyes, although her fair skin had paled a little.

'Ed Turnbull was your grandad?' Verity felt Amelia's hand tremble.

'Yes. Is my grandad.'

Amelia's eyes filled with moisture and her face crumpled.

'That's the real reason I'm here. He sent me here to find you to deliver a message.'

'Oh!'

'Yes. To tell you that he's still alive.'

Silence fell and Amelia lifted her eyes, which looked huge in her gaunt face, to fix Verity with her burning gaze.

'Ed's still alive?' Amelia gripped the edge of the table with her other hand. 'You're telling me Ed Turnbull is still alive?'

Verity nodded.

'But he can't be…oh my.'

'He is.'

Amelia got up abruptly, picked up her handbag and with a muttered, 'Excuse me,' walked out of the room leaving Verity staring after her in discomfort. Oh, what had she done? Had the shock been too much for her? What if she didn't come back? Oh, what was she to do now? But Amelia wouldn't leave her coat and other items behind her. She'd just gone to the Ladies Room probably to compose herself, hadn't she?

After what seemed like an age, she returned and sat back down in front of Verity. She dabbed at her eyes, which looked slightly red-rimmed, with a handkerchief which had an embroidered 'A' in the corner.

'Please, please forgive me,' Verity leaned towards her across the table. 'I honestly didn't mean to upset you.' But in such an emotional situation, what else had she really expected to happen?

199

'It was just the initial shock, dear.' Amelia picked up her coffee cup and took a long drink before continuing, 'you see, I was there when he fell off the edge of the monument. He was only sixteen. And I'll never forget the way he screamed as he fell…' She wiped her nose. 'I still have nightmares.'

'He did fall. But he survived. Amelia, he's alive and well.'

'Oh.' Amelia opened her ample handbag, threw in the sodden handkerchief and rummaged about until she produced a pack of tissues, which she opened with shaking fingers. It seemed to take her ages and then she wiped her eyes again. Silence fell upon the table as Verity waited for her to speak.

'Oh, my word. I can't believe it. After all this time.'

'Please, don't be upset Amelia, that wasn't my intention at all. Or his.' Verity reached for her slim white hand, which felt cool.

'I'm not upset. This is the most wonderful news I've ever heard. And to think you've come all this way to find me.'

'He begged me to come and find you.'

'What happened to him after he fell?' Amelia offered the pack of tissues to Verity, as her eyes were full of moisture as yet unspilled. 'You see my father…I was led to believe that he had suffered fatal injuries…'

Her voice tailed off so Verity tried to answer her question. 'Lots of broken bones and a back injury. But he made a remarkable recovery and although he couldn't work down the pit, he worked in the Lamp Cabin until he retired.'

Amelia drained her cup, her hand visibly shaking now. 'I just wish I'd known. I would have been spared so many very dark days and…'

Verity was longing to know what had happened to Amelia after that day and the events which had led her to live in Italy and have the baby there but something stopped her. And was the baby Grandad Ed's? What had happened to the child? It seemed so very personal. Maybe Amelia would never talk about it. Verity knew she couldn't mention it.

'I still have such vivid dreams about it all.'

'I'm so sorry to have distressed you.' Verity patted her arm across the table. 'I've had dreams about the monument as well, all my life.'

'I'm not distressed dear. In fact, I've never felt happier in my entire life.'

200

'Really?'

'Can you imagine what it's like to live with the fact that someone you loved has died and it was you that caused it?'

'But it wasn't your fault.'

'I believed it was.'

'But it wasn't.'

'We argued and...'

'He knew the risks he was taking just being up there.' Verity shuddered.

Amelia's eyes were soft and she suddenly looked so much younger. 'He was just a young lad, full of devilment and vigour. I remember how much I loved him. How we loved each other.'

Verity smiled and wiped away a tear from the corner of her eye.

Amelia gripped her coffee cup handle. 'And how...how is he now?'

'He's very well.'

'And...and where is he living? And with whom?'

'He lives at Sand Steps. In an independent living flat in the North East. It's right by the sea. He lives alone.'

Verity poured more coffee, trying to steady her hand.

'Would you like to see some photographs?'

'Oh, I would, yes, please.'

Verity produced a few black and white photos from her bag. They were of Amelia and Grandad Ed when they were younger, some of them in the woods and by the stream in the grounds of Monument Manor and some with the monument pillars in the background and one from the actual parapet itself. She hesitated for a moment and kept the ones of the monument back. Maybe the sight of the ancient Greek temple would upset Amelia further. She knew how distraught she used to be when she caught sight of it.

'Would it upset you to see photos with the monument on?'

Amelia shook her head so Verity handed them over.

'He kept them?' Amelia devoured them with her eyes and then dabbed at her eyes again. 'I can't believe he kept them all these years.'

'He had them hidden in a chocolate tin under his bed. Along with his packets of sweets and Fisherman's Friends.'

201

'I remember that day so vividly.' Amelia gazed at the photo of herself and Ed, poised against a monument pillar, smoothing the photo with one elegant finger. 'I can't believe you're his grandchild.' Amelia scrutinised Verity's face. 'You do have a look of him.'

'He's a wonderful person and a lovely grandad to have.'

Amelia was still looking closely at the photos and tears were flowing freely now. Verity felt a tear slip down her cheek also and was glad they were cut off from prying eyes from the rest of the hotel, people might have thought she was upsetting the elder lady. Which she was in a way, but Amelia seemed really happy about it. In an emotional way.

'This is a most happy day for me.'

'I'm so, so glad.' Verity tried to blow her nose quietly.

'So, he asked you to come and find me?'

'Oh yes, he asked me several times before I agreed to it. I just didn't want to give you a shock.'

'Why now?'

'Well, his wife died a few years ago and he said he's been plucking up the courage to do something since then. He's never forgotten you and wondered what had happened to you.'

'I can see why he asked you to help him. You're a blood relation of course. Blood is thicker than water.'

'He's always saying that.'

'And I can see that you have a kind heart.' Amelia's cheeks were now tinged with a flush of pink.

'I wanted to help him.'

'Life can be very cruel my dear,' Amelia shook her head. 'So, tell me who did Ed marry?'

'She was called Lilian, Lily for short but he called her Red most of the time.'

'And he, they were happy?'

'Oh yes, they argued all the time apparently, like cat and dog but they had a very happy marriage.'

'Good. I'm so glad. And they obviously had children?'

'Just one. My father.'

'And?'

'Not a lot to tell. We don't get on.'

'Why's that dear?'

'Mainly because he wasn't bothered about me when I was younger.' Verity paused and sipped at her coffee. Maybe Amelia was changing the subject because she was finding it hard to process all that Verity had told her?

Or maybe she was only interested in her because of her links to her long lost love, Ed?

'Go on.'

'My mother died when I was a baby and he spent all of my childhood chasing after other women. I lived with his aunties most of the time, never had a proper home until I was fifteen and went to live with my Grandma Anna. That was when my life really began.'

'And I can see you've made a good life for yourself. I'm sad to think that you didn't have a better childhood.'

'It taught me to look after myself, I suppose. And now I've got Jeremy.'

'Who is Jeremy?'

'He's my partner.' Verity showed her a recent picture on her mobile phone.

'Well, what a good looking young man, dear. Like a film star. And you look very happy together.'

'We are. Well, most of the time.'

'Nothing is ever perfect.'

Verity asked tentatively, 'Have you had a good life, Amelia?'

'Oh yes, dear, I have. I really have. I didn't think I would ever be happy again after Ed but…When I was nearly eighteen and living in Fiesole, I met Jack. He was an artist. And a very good one.'

She paused to take a sip of coffee and Verity willed her to continue, her eyes never leaving Amelia's face.

Amelia played with her napkin. 'At first I only allowed him to escort me places because it annoyed my father. You see, he was thirteen years older than me. He was one of my uncle's acquaintances. And I liked him. He was very kind and tolerant of me and my tantrums.' Her smile broadened. 'I knew I'd never feel for him what I'd felt for Ed. I'd never feel that again. He was a wonderful painter and he taught me the basics about art. I dabbled in water colours but I was never in his league of course.'

203

'So, how old were you when you married him?'

'I was nineteen. And we went on to have three daughters.'

Verity wondered about the first baby and longed to ask but Amelia was forging ahead.

'I had Violetta first but not until I was twenty-three. We didn't think it was going to happen then Gloria was born two years later and Cornelia in yet another two. Violetta runs a bar in Turkey, Gloria is a lawyer and lives in London and Cornelia helps me in the art gallery in Cornwall.'

'Is Violetta really a witch?'

Amelia laughed, a gentle, tinkling sound, then looked surprised. 'Ah, what makes you ask that? Have you met my daughter?'

'Well, I…'

'Yes, yes that's it.' Amelia leaned forward.

Verity was surprised again. 'Pardon?'

'I have just remembered where I've seen you before.'

'Really?' Verity felt hot.

'In Dalyan.'

'You were there. I saw you. On the tourist boat.'

'Yes, that's right, I was.'

You were with a young man. I remembered his lovely curly hair.'

'Wait a second…were you the lady with the gorgeous floaty sunhat?'

Amelia tinkled with laughter again. 'Yes, that was I.'

'I remembered thinking how beautiful your outfit was.'

'Oh, thank you dear.'

'Isn't that amazing?'

'No way. I don't believe it. I went all that way to Turkey to find you, thought I'd missed you completely and now I discover that you were there all along.' Verity felt her eyes mist over. 'Our worlds collided.'

Amelia patted her hand. 'Isn't that just the way? Never mind. We found each other in the end. Anyway, back to my daughter. You were saying?'

'I went to the Artisan Cafébar and talked to Alyin. Then the next day Violetta turned up at Middle Orange House.'

'And she told you she was a witch?'

'Yes. She was very convincing.'

'I can imagine.'

'She warned me off and told me not to try to contact you again or it would be the worse for me.'

Amelia sighed. 'Oh, dear me. In her favour, she was only trying to protect me.' She lifted her cup to drink. 'In answer to your question, I'm afraid the answer is yes.'

Verity drew a short breath.

Amelia leaned forward. 'However, knowing Violetta as I do, I suppose she omitted to tell you that she is actually a white witch?'

'Is there a difference?'

'Oh yes, dear, there's a huge difference.'

'Shall we have some more coffee?' Amelia waved over a waitress who was passing the open doorway and ordered two fresh coffees and more hot water and she also asked if they had any of those round wafer biscuits they'd had the other week?

Verity's head was reeling but she was glad to see Amelia was obviously regaining her composure. Or was she simply stalling until she decided what to do next? Would she make her exit and Verity would never see her again? Her heart baulked at the thought, a strange sharp unexplained pain filled her chest.

'You do know what a white witch, is I take it?' Their drinks replenished, Amelia picked up her second, full cup of frothy white coffee which was so full it almost threatened to overflow.

'No, I don't exactly.' Verity shook her head. 'I've never really needed to know.'

Amelia sipped at her coffee. 'Well, basically white witches are those who practice goodness and benevolence in all that they do.'

'Really?'

Amelia laughed again, a tinkling sound. 'I know. Violetta can be intimidating. My daughter is very protective of me.'

'How did she become a white witch?'

'Growing up in Cornwall, she and a couple of friends grew very interested in Cornish folklore and tales of magic. Did you know there are around sixteen stone circles in the county?'

Verity shook her head. 'No, I didn't. I don't really know much about Cornwall to be truthful.'

'Such a lot of folklore.' Amelia went on to say that Cornwall had a fascinating history of myths and legends including King Arthur and

Tintagel and that Violetta and her friends had visited all the stone circles, formed a group and did lots of research. They were very interested in an old legend which was about a white witch and a healer and went on to teach themselves and others about such things.' Amelia paused to sip her cooling beverage then continued.

'Since she moved to Turkey and married Ahmed she has become increasingly under the spell, for wont of a better word, of his Aunt Fatma who believes in all that…that supernatural stuff. It's often referred to as natural magic.' Amelia sighed. 'Violetta could have been a very good painter you know, but she didn't choose to take that route.'

Verity caught the feeling that Amelia didn't really approve. 'Ah, Aunt Fatma. I've met her as well.'

'She can be perceived as the very opposite of a white witch.' They both laughed.

'Those sticks.'

'And that voice. You should hear her when someone tries to take a short cut through her garden.'

Verity thought of Jeremy.

'You don't need to worry about either of them. White witches do not cast spells to harm others.'

'I'm very pleased to hear it.'

'Most of the Turkish women in Dalyan stick to playing Pishti in the evenings but I do believe Aunt Fatma dabbles in fortune telling.'

'I was so sure she was going to burst in here and put a spell on me before I could give you Grandad Ed's message.'

Amelia's laugh jingled again. 'Enough of Violetta.' She glanced at her watch. 'I must go soon; I need to look after the gallery this afternoon. Cornelia, another of my daughters is away until tomorrow.'

Verity looked at the ship's clock on the wall. 'It's after twelve o'clock. Our morning coffee has lasted two hours. Must you go now?'

'Yes. However, can I invite you to dinner this evening? It's your last evening, isn't it?'

'It is, that would be lovely, thank you so very much.' Verity felt relieved. There was so much more to say.

Then Amelia asked her a question. 'Do you think Ed would like to see me?'

Verity nearly spluttered on her coffee. He'd never mentioned actually meeting up, just was so insistent that Amelia got the message that he was still alive. Things were going even better than she'd hoped for.

'Do you think he'd like to have a visit from me?' Amelia repeated her question. 'If you only knew how I've longed to see that part of the world again.'

Verity recovered her composure. 'I do. I really do. I think he would love to see you.'

'Then, let's arrange it, shall we?'

'You could stay with us at Monument Cottage.' Verity felt no hesitation in inviting her. 'What about coming in the Christmas holidays?'

'Thank you so much for your kind invitation, and I would certainly like come to visit one day and see *The Happy Child* in its place in your home. But I shall be staying at Monument Manor.'

# Chapter 35

Verity's mobile phone ring tone broke the sleepy silence in the back of the car and Sophie's gabbling voice broke forth.

'Verity. Can you talk?'

'Yes. What's up, has something happened?'

'No. Yes. It has. Something…really huge…lol.'

'More gossip around the watercooler? I'm worried now. What's going on?'

'One of the fly zappers have disappeared.'

'What?'

'Seriously V. Well, apparently the Personal Assistants had ordered two, one for each of the Director's rooms. And one has gone missing.'

'Has there been a fly epidemic or something?'

'Yeah, they were coming out of the heating vents. Such a crap old building.' One Director moved out of his room it was so bad. They sprayed the inner sanctum with fly spray which drifted out into the main office and just about asphyxiated everyone.'

'Nothing much I can do about it now. Sounds like it's under control.'

'It's chaos. When did you say you're coming back?

'Soon.' Verity rang off, her head buzzing. Almost immediately a text pinged.

'Breaking news! The missing fly zapper has turned up. Hiding under the blind.

Verity's thoughts were whirling around her brain. Wasn't life strange? Being here in a life changing situation and getting texts about fly zappers? Unbelievable. She didn't know whether to laugh or cry.

Another text pinged. 'When you back?'

# Chapter 36

Verity was sitting on the terrace again on her last evening, reflecting on the conversation she and Amelia had had. They'd had a lovely evening meal at the Estuary Hotel, which wasn't far from where Amelia lived and also near her art gallery.

They'd had a good vantage point, sitting in the window upstairs overlooking the shifting waters looking across to Polruan and enjoying watching the paddle boarders and children bobbing about in brightly coloured little boats, having sailing lessons.

They'd made plans to meet up at Christmas which was only a few weeks away and Amelia had promised to ring to finalise arrangements in a couple of days. Verity felt as if she'd known her for years. Please don't let Violetta talk her out of it and scupper all our plans, Verity prayed inwardly.

She was trying to ring Grandad Ed to tell him the wonderful news but he wasn't answering, which wasn't like him. He always kept his phone on now and he didn't go to bed until very late, he liked to sit in the armchair in his room and watch television or sit re-reading one of his western books. He'd read all the westerns in the visiting library.

She'd sent him several pics which Amelia had allowed her to take and Perdita had even offered to take a photo of them together, with a backdrop of the piers and inner harbour through the window. Strange, he hadn't replied with his usual thumbs up gif either. She could hardly wait to tell him how well things had turned out.

She was getting ready for bed when her mobile rang. She pounced on it, thinking it must be Grandad Ed but saw it was Jeremy again. She'd just spoken to him not long since and filled him in on her meeting with Amelia.

'Hi again,' she said, jumping into bed and turning the TV down with the remote. 'You must be missing me?'

'Always. Unfortunately, that's not why I'm ringing.' She noted the downbeat vibe in his voice sounded which wasn't like Jeremy at all.

'Are you okay?' she asked.

'I'm fine, it's not me.' There was a pause. 'Verity, I must tell you something.'

'What is it?'

'It's Grandad Ed. And it's not good news I'm afraid.'

'Oh no. What's happened?'

'Sand Steps rang our house phone. He's not well. They think it's pneumonia but he's refusing to go to hospital so at the moment he's being treated at Sand Steps until they can persuade him.'

'Oh, poor Grandad. I thought he had a nasty cough yesterday when I spoke to him.'

'He's been asking when you'll be back.'

'I'll be home tomorrow.'

'I know it's difficult but please don't be tempted to rush. Be careful when you're driving tomorrow.'

'I know, I will.'

'They've been trying to contact your dad but no luck so far. They're going to keep trying.'

'So, it's that bad.'

The warm glow of the day was quickly evaporating. Her brain was working really fast. Should she tell Amelia? Was Christmas going to be too late, God forbid? She picked up her phone to ring Amelia but decided it was best not to worry her at the moment and put it down again.

However, early next morning when she was loading her cases into her car at the side of the hotel, hardly hearing the shouts of the fishermen on the quays and the plaintive call of the gulls up above, she was very surprised to see Amelia's little car pull up.

'You left your scarf dear.' Amelia's smile was wide. 'I thought I'd deliver it in person.'

'Oh, that's so very kind of you.' Verity tried to smile.

'What's wrong?'

'It's Grandad Ed. He's very ill. It's pneumonia apparently.'

Amelia gave a sharp intake of breath and gripped Verity's hand. 'Oh no, that's terrible news. And you've got such a long drive home.'

'I know, that's why I'm leaving a bit earlier. You're lucky you caught me.'

'You should have rung me.'

'I was going to but I didn't want to worry you.'

'I don't think you should be travelling all that way on your own, with that worry hanging over you.'

'I have no choice. I'll be fine, don't worry about me.'

'You should have someone to navigate and to talk to you. Right. I've decided. Don't try to stop me. I'm coming with you.'

Verity was astounded. 'But what about the Gallery?'

'My daughter can cope. Don't argue. Drive me home to Fowey first and I'll pick up a few things and we can get on the road. How long is the journey?'

'Around seven and a half hours.'

'Good job I'm used to travelling. I will keep you company on the drive. Are you ready dear?'

'Yes, but are you sure?'

'Stop arguing and let's get on the road.'

They were nearing Bristol when Amelia's mobile rang. 'Hello', she answered in her calm voice.

Amelia moved the phone to her left ear and Verity pretended to concentrate on her driving, but the gabbling tirade didn't cease. She recognised that loud voice and it made her heart sink. She could hear everything so clearly; Amelia may as well have had her phone on loudspeaker mode.

'Mother, what the hell do you think you're playing at?'

'Calm down Vi. I can hardly hear you. Speak more slowly. You know my hearing isn't what it used to be.'

'I've been to the gallery and Cornelia told me where you are. Taking off like that on a whim. Whatever are you thinking of? You can't just…just take off when you feel like it.'

'I usually do.'

'She didn't listen to me. How dare she? I tried to warn her. Has she kidnapped you?'

'No, Violetta she hasn't kidnapped me.'

Verity's eyes widened at this.

'Where are you?'

'Now? Er, where are we Verity dear?'

'Oh, nearing Bristol.'

Amelia turned back to the phone. 'Did you hear that dear? We're near…'

211

'I heard her. Mother, tell her to turn around at once and bring you back home to Cornwall.'

'I'll do no such thing. I'm going to visit an old friend in the North East and that's all there is to it.'

'I'm going to get the next flight to England.'

'Don't be silly. You've got a business to run.'

'So have you.'

'Cornelia is perfectly capable of looking after the place for a little while.'

'A little while? How long is a little while? How long are you thinking of staying away?'

'I'm not sure, it's such a long way that I'm going to need a few days at least to recover from the journey.'

'When have you ever needed to recover from a journey? You're the most energetic person I know. I'm booking that flight now.'

'Oh, don't be so silly Violetta. I am taking a little vacation that's all. I shall be perfectly safe.'

'I'm not being silly, I'm…'

What's that dear? You're breaking up. Sorry. I have to go now. Goodbye.'

'Mother don't you dare hang up on me. I'm booking the next flight. I'll be there before you know it.' Verity's heart plummeted at this.

'Goodbye dear.' Amelia switched off her phone.

Verity was aghast and found it hard to negotiate the next roundabout. 'That's all I need – the White Witch turning up and storming in to curse me and have me arrested for kidnapping her mother,' she thought.

'Sorry about that Verity.' Amelia sounded not at all perturbed.

'She was rather upset.'

'She's always upset. Oh, the drama! And she has a temper. I'm ashamed to say, in lots of ways, she takes after me.'

Verity doubted that. 'Aren't you worried that she'll turn up and drag you away and have me arrested for kidnapping?'

'Now who's being dramatic?' Amelia laughed. 'Not at all. She is very wearing sometimes but she means well. Anyway, she wouldn't leave the country without her husband and he wouldn't leave his business unattended.'

Verity still wasn't convinced.

They were approximately two and a half hours into their journey when the red warning light came on and the engine began to make a spluttering sound. They were lucky they were passing through a little country village called Alveston, so Verity pulled into the car park at the village hotel.

'I don't believe it,' she exclaimed, parking up in a safe spot. 'Just when we were making such good time.'

She got out of the car and wandered around the car park, which was overlooking a cricket ground, as she talked on the phone to the AA and discovered to her horror that they were inundated with call outs and wouldn't be able to get there until late that evening. She'd tried explaining that it was a matter of life and death but to no avail.

She rang Jeremy, explained her predicament to see if she could tap in to his breakdown provider instead in the hope that they could reach them sooner.

'I'm sorry V, I, er forgot to renew it. It was on my list.'

'Great.' Why did that not surprise her. 'Typical, we were making such good time. I need to think what to do.'

'Where are you?'

'We're near Bristol, car park of the Village Inn in Alveston. Around 286 miles away from home.'

'Right. I'm on my way.'

'Don't be ridiculous. Are you mad? It's a four- and half-hour drive and the same back home again.'

'I insist. My car's pretty zippy and the traffic should be light today as it's a Sunday.'

'But…'

'No buts. Listen, I don't want to worry you, but I've just had another phone call. Grandad Ed has been taken into hospital this morning. He didn't want to go in but the pneumonia was getting worse. They're worried about his condition.'

'Oh no, no.'

'I reckon I'm your best bet of getting you there quicker.'

He rang back five minutes later for the post code. 'Where am I going again? What's the postcode?'

Verity went to join Amelia in the car and explained the situation.

'What? He's just dropped everything and he is coming to get us? What a marvellous young man.'

'Not that he'll have many commitments on a Sunday, but still...' Verity thought.

'It will take him around four hours to get here.'

'Oh dear. Then he has to drive us back.'

Verity's mobile rang again. It was Jeremy, ringing from his car phone. 'Did you say we?'

'Yes, Amelia is with me.'

'How is Ed?' Amelia asked. 'Shall we get out and stretch our legs?'

They wandered to the edge of the car park and looked over the cricket field where a lone youth was practicing bowling shots monotonously against the club house wall.

Jeremy hadn't said too much about Grandad Ed's condition but Verity was seriously worried, trying to convey the information diplomatically to Amelia. He was eighty-six after all and despite his protestations that he was as strong as an ox, Verity did know that he had health conditions, being a duodenal ulcer for which he took regular tablets and he only had one kidney. What if they didn't make it in time?

'Seeing as we've got a few hours to kill,' Amelia said, 'and there's nothing we can do but wait, we may as well have a little meal.'

Verity didn't really feel hungry but thought that Amelia had probably only had a few Rich Tea biscuits for breakfast several hours ago and was bound to be ravenous and come to think of it, she was really thirsty herself, having only had sips of water all morning as she was driving, concentrating fiercely on the unfamiliar roads.

There was an annex in the form of a whitewashed pub right next door to the hotel rooms, where the hotel meals were served and Amelia was delighted to see that there was a special offer meal deal on. Verity found this strange as she knew Amelia wasn't short of money, maybe it was an age thing.

So, they managed to find what Amelia called a nice spot by the window, overlooking the green of the cricket ground and next to a warm radiator and studied the menu.

'If we both have a main course, we can have a dessert free,' Amelia said. 'I'll ask if I can have a children's portion because I don't eat much. I'll explain.'

They ended up passing the time by eating steak pie made with a water-based pastry, chips and vegetables. And Verity was amazed that she managed to eat some of it, not wanting to tell Amelia her worries about Grandad Ed and that they might not make it in time, as it might spoil Amelia's appetite as well.

The choice of free desserts sounded sublime, being either Sweet Bakewell Tart with almonds, raspberry coulis, thick clotted cream and dusted with icing sugar or Strawberry & Prosecco Eclairs, followed by coffee and a luxury chocolate. Amelia devoured everything, saying it was her treat and she wasn't taking no for an answer, as Verity tried to pay with her bank card.

Then she thought she'd better order something for Jeremy as he'd most definitely be starving by the time he arrived here.

'What a charming young man he must be. Not many would do what he's doing for you,' Amelia mused. 'He's a keeper, my dear.' Verity felt a pang as she thought of Jeremy, maybe she had neglected him a bit too much lately without realising it?

At last, he arrived. He unfolded his long legs out of his car and wrapped Verity in a hug. Then he turned to Amelia with a bright smile and held out his hand. 'I'm very pleased to meet you, Amelia. I've heard so much about you. I'm sorry it isn't in happier circumstances.' As his bright eyes crinkled and his smile intensified, Verity could tell Amelia approved of him immediately.

'Won't you be too tired to drive back? Amelia said.'

'No way, I've got bags of energy, Verity knows what I'm like. All I need is some scran and a quick walk about to stretch my legs and we'll be on our way.'

As they neared the North East, during what seemed an endless journey, it was beginning to get dark and Verity's nerves deepened. Amelia had been dozing but Verity was sat straight backed and wide awake the whole time, fidgeting with her nails, her brain overwhelmed with one emotion after another, stress, anticipation, fear. Also, her neck was aching with sitting in the same position for so long.

215

'Are you okay Amelia?' Verity turned her painful neck to address Amelia in the back. 'You must be very tired.'

'I'm absolutely fine, dear.'

Unexpected traffic jams on the way back delayed their expected time of arrival somewhat and it was growing dark when Verity, who had just managed to finally doze off for a few minutes, was jolted awake by Amelia's animated voice.

'Now there's a sight to behold. Won't you just look at that?'

'Where are we?' Verity asked sleepily, the drone of the engine and the warmth must have finally made her doze off and she was loath to relinquish it straightaway.

'Still on the A1 and nearing County Durham,' Jeremy advised.

'Nearly home,' Verity thought, butterflies of unease beginning to stir in her stomach.

'Can you see it?' Amelia said again.

'What are we looking at?' Verity stretched, roused from the fitful snooze which hadn't helped to alleviate the tiredness she felt. Probably because she wasn't used to being driven about, sitting doing nothing with time for worrying thoughts to envelop her.

'Over there,' Amelia pointed, her voice hushed.

A silence fell over the car as they glimpsed their first sighting of Penshaw Monument, the temple tiny and elevated in the distance, floodlit and welcoming against a star flecked, dark navy blue sky.

'It's a guiding light.' Amelia half whispered.

Verity thought this must be such an emotional moment for her. How on earth must she be feeling? She could only imagine at the mixed distress and delight. Such memories would be surfacing.

'It's been a long time,' she said so quietly, that Verity had to strain to hear the words.

'You know, it must be sixty odd years ago since I've seen that sight…It can be seen for miles around, fifty miles away on a sunny day.'

'It's like the Acropolis of the North,' Jeremy said. 'Or the Temple of Diana.'

'When I was a little girl,' Amelia's voice gained strength again,' travelling home from family holidays, I always knew I was near home when I had my first sighting of Penshaw Monument.' She chuckled.

216

'Or Penshaw Ornament as I used to call it. How my mother used to laugh when I called it that.'

She laughed quietly, half to herself. 'Travel stained, hungry and weary, it was a beacon of hope and a symbol of home. Don't you feel the same?'

A sign of home. Verity felt choked up. She'd never before thought of it like that. For as much of her life as she could remember she had felt a shiver whenever she thought about the monument because of what had happened to her Grandad. Now she was living practically underneath it, at its very base, could she see and feel differently about it? She'd tolerated it but now she was seeing it through different eyes. It was her home with Jeremy after all. She felt Jeremy reach over and squeeze her hand where it rested on her knee and her heart lifted a little.

'I'm originally from Hampshire, so I didn't know about it until I became a local,' Jeremy said. 'I agree though, it's a very welcome sight.'

'What about you Verity, coming back from childhood holidays?'

'I didn't go on holidays when I was a child,' Verity admitted.

'Oh, I didn't mean…sorry dear.' Amelia said.

'Don't be,' Verity said, shrugging her aching shoulders. 'It is what it is.'

Darkening, low-lying clouds obscured the view of the Greek temple on the hill as they sped along, nearing their destination. Verity picked at her nail varnish and wondered if Grandad Ed would ever get to find out that Amelia was pregnant when he fell off the monument? That he'd had another child? Would it be too much of a shock for him? There was so much of the story that Verity didn't yet know herself. What would they find?

She hoped against hope that all would be well when they arrived. Please, please, after all this time, don't let the fates be against them.

Verity didn't want to wait, she wanted to go straight there, to the hospital, to see Grandad Ed, so she rang to say they were on their way and they were sorry it was so late and she was sure visiting times were long over, but was there any chance of seeing Ed Turnbull? The girl asked her to hold on the line when she went to check and Verity's

217

heart began to thump. Was this a bad sign? She seemed to be away for ages. Jeremy and Amelia waited in anticipation.

She was expecting her to come back and say, sorry, come back tomorrow. She was surprised though with some good news.

'Oh, that's amazing news. Thank you so much,' her heart began to sing. It turned out he hadn't actually been admitted to hospital after all. He'd gone in to A&E and they'd managed to treat him and send him back home. The pneumonia hadn't taken hold after all and could be treated with medication and a care package had been put in place. Relief flooded over her.

'Then we'll go straight to Sand Steps.' she announced to the car.

However, with no reply from his mobile (he mustn't have had his phone on which was unusual) on ringing Sand Steps Reception, she was advised he was in bed now and it was much too late to disturb him. They were under strict instructions from the nurse that he needed to rest. He would be available to see them the following morning after ten. No sooner. They needn't have rushed. At least the panic was over and they would see him tomorrow.

'Can you drop me off at Monument Manor, please?' Amelia directed.

'Are they expecting you?' Jeremy asked. 'Because you know you're welcome to stay with us.'

'Oh yes. They've been expecting me to stay for years. They always make Temperly relations very welcome. Even ancient ones like me.'

'Oh well, if you're sure.'

'Thank you for your kind offer but I shall be staying in The Lavender Room. I requested it specially because it used to be my room.'

'It sounds lovely,' Verity said.

'It is. There's a four-poster bed and the bath is divine. It's supposed to be haunted but a ghost won't bother me. I shall be very comfortable in there.'

The car crunched up the long drive to Monument Manor, and Verity heard Amelia exclaim as the lovely red brick manor house swung into view, cream pillars and porticoes basking in the glow of the welcoming lights burning brightly in the front windows.

'Oh. Oh, it looks just the same.' Verity could only guess at how Amelia was feeling right now. Seeing her former home in front of her, after all these years of exile was bound to be bringing back so many

218

memories. However, Amelia seemed calm enough as her welcoming committee, in the form of Paul the journo's uncle, Kevin Longwood, emerged from the lighted hallway to greet her and take her bag.

Back home, Verity flopped into her favourite chair opposite the fire and looked at the empty space above it. And Tom was delighted to see her, making a big show of brushing against her legs and sitting on her feet.

The relief Verity felt was overwhelming. Like a great heavy weight had been lifted from her chest. She didn't know how she was going to sleep though that night. She was so happy she felt she would burst. Grandad Ed was going to make a full recovery and he and Amelia would be reunited after all these years. They would have such a lot to talk about.

'Are you hungry?' Jeremy asked, bending down to stroke Pedro who was dancing around his feet in joy.

'No, we had loads to eat at the Village Inn. I'm just tired. How's Albie? I see there was no welcoming committee.'

'Working on a track?'

They both laughed. 'Don't worry, he'll be down for some scran before long.'

'No doubt. Oh, I nearly forgot. The painting is still in the boot of your car.'

'I'll go and get it. Come on boy.' And off he went with Pedro skittering at his heels.

Jeremy laid the painting on the dining room table. 'Do you mind if I take a look? Don't worry if you're too tired.'

'No, I'd love you to see it,' Verity pulled herself to her feet and they unwrapped it together under the window with the side view of Penshaw Monument and its age-old pillars and blackened stone, up above the darkened shrubbery of the slope, lighting up the sky for miles around.

Jeremy was silent as the picture was revealed and laid out on the dining room table in all its glory.

'What do you think?' she asked him.

Jeremy studied the painting, cosy lamplight illuminating the child's face for a long time. 'I have no words.' His face was solemn.

219

'You don't like it?' Verity felt her face fell. Even though she'd picked it herself for the prime position in their new home, and come to think of it, he'd picked the house himself which was a whole bigger picture, she'd still wanted him to like it as much as she did.

'It wasn't what I was expecting. When you said you'd bought a painting, I imagined a seascape.'

Her heart sunk a little, then he looked up at her and she saw the beginnings of a smile twitching.

'I love it.' Jeremy's smile grew and was soon as proportionally bright as *The Happy Child's*.

Verity flung her arms around his neck. 'I'm so glad. And I'm glad to be home.'

And it was good to be back in her own home. She glanced up at the monument and it's illuminated pillars and thought that tomorrow maybe it was time for one of its biggest secrets to be revealed.

# Chapter 37

The three of them stood poised at the entrance to the rooftop garden at Sand Steps. This really was a prime spot, perched on a rugged headland looking directly out to sea where foam edged, swirling waves were throwing themselves onto the shore. The winter sky was a washed clean cerulean blue, and the wind was crisp. Verity could taste salt on her lips and hear the roar of the surf. There was silence until Amelia broke it.

'How enchanting. It's almost as if we're surrounded by the sea. And the sky. I'd forgotten how vast the skies are in Northumberland.'

How could she sound so calm? Verity thought this is the culmination of my quest. She still couldn't quite believe it and thought, what if Violetta, the White Witch burst in and stopped the reunion taking place? There was still time. She could imagine her stotting about into Reception, ranting and raving and casting spells over everyone. They'd survived the other obstacles yesterday, what with the car breaking down and the traffic jams. It had been exhausting. But they'd made it here to this moment in time, to this place.

Then Amelia's fingers reached out for Verity's. In front of them, Verity could see the back of the figure that was Grandad Ed, sitting on his bench in his favourite spot in the sunken garden overlooking the sea, the bench flanked at either side with trellises acting as windbreakers, with no doubt, his little dog at his side. She could hear the powerful waves crashing onto the rocks below like the first time she visited.

Her legs felt a little weak but she couldn't stop a smile forming, and a bubble of excitement rose in her stomach. Then it turned to worry. What if it was too much of a shock for him seeing Amelia again after all that had happened? Had she done the right thing?

'Well, V, this is nearly it.' Jeremy puffed out his cheeks. 'The moment you've been waiting for.'

Verity turned to them. 'Would you both mind waiting here for just a minute?' she said, and disentangling her fingers from Amelia's, she patted her arm and started to hurry on ahead to Grandad Ed's bench, leaving the others sheltering from the wind against the wall of the building.

And there he was, pipe hanging out of the corner of his mouth, tweed cap balanced on his head and a fleecy red rug half wrapped around his legs and the other half draped on the seat for Tiny to lie on. His wizened face lit up with a smile as she approached him and he removed his pipe. Verity got a quick glimpse of a bright blue baggy pullover under a thick winter jacket and tartan scarf.

'Hello there, bonny lass.' He stood up awkwardly, shaking off the blanket and disrupting the little dog who shook himself vigorously and looked up at her, the intruder, his head angled.

'You don't need to get up Grandad.' Too late. Verity towered over him and bent down to wrap her arms around him.

'I'm so pleased to see you. Thank goodness you're okay.' She hugged him, feeling the bristles on his cheek grazing hers, and breathing in that sweet tobacco smell mingled with old-fashioned hair cream. Tiny began pawing at her ankles.

'He remembers you lass.' He extricated himself quickly and sat back down again, re-arranging his blanket. Verity guessed he wasn't one for great shows of emotion -or fuss as he called it. He was what you called the strong, silent type.

'You look well.' Although maybe not quite as ruddy cheeked as she remembered.

'Strong as an ox, me lass, didn't I tell you?'

'You did. You still had us all worried Grandad.'

'No need to worry about me.'

'So, tell me what happened?'

'Nowt. I fainted that's all. And I had a bit of a cough.'

'I thought it was pneumonia?'

'Just a bit of a cold. I wasn't going into no hospital. I didn't want any fuss. Such a to do about nowt. Do you know lass, they wanted me to stay in bed for a couple of days? I told them, not bloody likely, the sea air out here is the best cure there is.'

'I've brought some treats for Tiny.' Verity rummaged in her handbag for the paper bag of dog treats she'd pinched from Pedro's cupboard.

'I hope that they're the smelly ones?' Grandad Ed chuckled. 'He likes them the best.'

222

She took one out and passed over the paper bag of treats to Grandad Ed. 'Phew, they are quite whiffy.' Tiny was sniffing and pawing at her lap now in excitement and made a show of trying to do a little jump for the treat.

'And these are for you.' Verity handed Grandad Ed a bumper packet of Fisherman's Friends. 'Present from Cornwall.'

'FFs. These are A1. Thanks, bonny lass.' He put them in his copious inner coat pocket and fixed her with his deep brown stare. 'Now then. Did you give her my message?'

'I certainly did.'

'That's such a relief.' He shifted his pipe. 'What did she say?'

'Why don't you ask her yourself?'

'What?' the pipe dropped and hung precariously out of the side of his mouth.

'I've brought Amelia to see you Grandad.'

'She's here?' His mouth dropped further open and the pipe fell onto the bench. 'How the bloody hell did you manage that?'

Verity nodded. 'I'll tell you later. It was her idea.' She stood up, turned around and gestured to Amelia. She could see Jeremy offering her his arm and they both began to walk the short distance towards the bench, Amelia leaning lightly on her stick for support as well.

Jeremy stopped a few yards short of the bench, saying farewell, he had already decided beforehand to go and have a walk along the jetty and onto the beach, so as to leave them in peace. Amelia thanked him and walked the last few steps towards them.

'Ed?' she moved in front of him.

'Amelia – is it really you?' His eyes squinted in the bright light. He unwrapped the blanket, stood up again very slowly, the little dog whimpered, and they faced each other, Amelia was a head taller but was stooped over, discarding her stick onto the bench.

She bent towards him very slowly and gracefully, reminding Verity of the stem of a flower, her long wool overcoat wrapped around her. They hugged each other, Amelia was crying and Grandad Ed sniffing. He produced an enormous white handkerchief from his inside jacket pocket with a curly blue E embroidered in the corner and dabbed at his eyes.

'Oh Ed, I thought I'd killed you.' Amelia's voice was choked. 'I really did.'

'Don't be so daft. Eee lass, I never thought this day would come.'

'Nor I. It's been sixty-seven years.' Amelia said later it was as if the years just peeled away.

Verity spied a single tear rolling slowly down Grandad Ed's weather beaten, bristly cheek. He dashed it away. Amelia's tears were flowing freely now and she accepted the use of the hanky when he offered it to her, rather than fish about in her handbag. 'I've hardly used it.' Verity thought it was big enough for them both to share.

Her eyes were overflowing also and she felt she should leave them alone to talk but she couldn't bear to drag herself away from this spot just yet.

Amelia wiped her eyes. 'Never in my wildest dreams did I ever imagine we'd meet again.'

'You haven't changed a bit, bonny lass.'

'That's not true.' Pause. 'Neither have you.' They both laughed. 'Sit down lass.'

They both sat, Amelia in the middle of the bench with Grandad Ed on her right and Tiny whimpered and jumped up to sit on her other side, his ears cocked, as he stared up at her.

'This is Tiny.'

Amelia stroked Tiny's head and he solemnly offered her a paw. 'Hello Tiny.' She shook it. 'And how are you, Ed?'

'I'm fine. Load of fuss about nowt.'

'That's not what I heard. 'Tell me what happened.'

Verity hovered. 'Would you like a blanket Amelia?' Verity knew how Amelia suffered from the cold, even though she had quite a few layers of clothing on and this was a sheltered spot.

'Here, use this one.' Grandad passed over the red blanket. 'I'm not cold.' Verity felt a pang inside her breastbone as she noticed how his brown corduroy trousers flapped around his legs, he'd lost weight.

'Thank you.' Amelia arranged it over her long legs and looked out to the horizon, breathing deeply of the fresh, cold air. 'I can feel the energy of the sea.'

Verity made to go. 'I'll leave you two to talk.'

'You don't have to go, lass.' Grandad Ed said.

224

'Yes, I do. You've got a lot to catch up on. I'll see if I can fetch some tea and another blanket first though.'

She badly wanted to listen in but knew the right thing to do was leave them in peace.

When she returned with the blanket and a tray laden with vintage teapot and delicate cups, Verity saw that their heads were turned to face each other, Grandad Ed's unlit pipe clamped firmly to the side of his mouth. Amelia seemed to be doing all the talking. They were oblivious to her presence as she approached, then she handed Grandad Ed the blanket and left the tea tray on the ground within reach.

She heard them both speak at the same time. 'Tell me what happened when...'

Then they both laughed. 'You go first, no you go first.'

'I was coming to find you because we'd quarrelled. That day on the parapet of the monument I mean.'

'Do you still remember that day?'

'As clear as the day is long.'

'Me too.'

She watched as Amelia dabbed at her eyes again with Grandad Ed's large hanky and continued talking.

Then she dragged herself away and went to meet Jeremy on the jetty. He was standing looking out to sea, tucking into the remains of golden fish and chips and batter from a paper carton which smelt delicious. He waved the bundle at her excitedly. 'I've just seen a dolphin over there,' he said pointing out to sea.

She followed the direction of his arm and strained to see what he saw.

'How is it going at Sand Steps?' He offered her a chip from the paper.

'Isn't it a bit early for chips?' Verity took one, unable to resist the enticing smell of vinegar. 'They seem to be getting on very well, that is, once they'd stopped crying.'

'I thought so, your mascara is smudged. And it's never too early for fish and chips.'

'Suppose your right.' She reached for another chip and took a few at once. 'Mmm, they're moreish.'

Jeremy licked the salt from his fingers. 'All these heightened emotions may well inspire me to write something.'

225

He scrumpled up the paper and carton and looked around for a bin.

'Shall we walk along the pier? There're a few shops along the marina. We could grab a takeaway coffee.'

'I thought I should give them some space.' Verity turned as they walked along the wooden pier and looked back up to the white building perched on the cliff. 'I'd give anything to know what they're saying right now.'

'It's like being on Long Lost Family.'

'I only hope he doesn't swear too much.'

Jeremy laughed. 'Amelia doesn't strike me as the type to be too bothered about that. They're like chalk and cheese aren't they? What with her cut glass accent and his broad Geordie.'

'Opposites attract. Hard to believe they were born in the same village.' Verity then proceeded to explain how she had asked Grandad Ed to please stop swearing and he had been surprised as he honestly hadn't realised he was doing it.

'Probably done it for years.'

Verity looked down and saw that the sparkle on the golden sands down below was actually patchy white frost. 'I think maybe my work here is done.'

# Chapter 38

Verity gazed up at *The Happy Child* which was now hanging in its rightful place above the fireplace in their living room, resting against a deep pink painted backdrop which matched the child's clothing.

The room was lit by cosy lamplight and flames crackled and flickered in the hearth. Tom was sitting curled up on Amelia's lap, being petted. She loved cats, having admitted she was more of a cat person than a dog lover, and he was certainly drawn to her. Pedro was out for a run with Jeremy, so Verity could spend some time with Amelia.

She had enjoyed showing Amelia around Monument Cottage and they'd finished off the tour in the living room with a glass of wine for Verity and a small sherry for Amelia, with both of them seated on the sofa and gazing up at *The Happy Child*.

Behind them, the curtains were still open at the back window where the side view of the monument could clearly be seen, the pillars outlined in light on its darkened slope. Light from one of the strategically placed side lamps shone directly onto the child's face, illuminating its radiance.

Verity could almost hear the child's laughter, tinkling down through the decades.

'Well, what do you think?'

'Perfect location for it dear. It looks very much at home there.'

'It does, doesn't it?' Verity was very pleased with her purchase.

'I adore what you've done with the backdrop.'

'You don't think it looks too bare without a frame? I got the idea from Monument Manor from the original painting. There was no heavy, gilded picture frame to take the attention away from the magic of the picture, just a plain, red wall hanging. So much more powerful.'

Amelia sipped at her sherry. 'Most agreeable.' Verity wasn't certain she meant the picture or the sherry. Maybe both. 'I'm sure it will bring you much happiness.'

There was silence for a moment. 'Verity I want to say something to you.' Amelia took a final sip and put down her glass on the little side table which Verity had set out for her. 'I just want to thank you with all my heart for all you've done, for me and Ed, for seeking me out and telling me that he was still alive.'

Verity was about to say it was nothing, it was a pleasure, but Amelia was continuing, 'I can't tell you how happy I feel now. It's as if a weight has been lifted from my shoulders. It's the nicest thing anyone has ever done for me.'

She reached over and patted Verity's hand, looking deep into her eyes, her own crystalline blue ones shining bright with unshed tears.

'It was like having a hole in my heart. That's the best way I can explain it. And I never, ever thought it would ever heal.'

Verity felt very warm inside and maybe a little fuzzy around the edges from the wine.

'I'm so glad I was able to help,' she sniffed and squeezed Amelia's hand in return. 'I was worried it would be too much for you.'

'I'm stronger than you think.' Amelia gently reached over Tom on her lap and began rummaging in her roomy handbag which was by her side until she found what looked suspiciously like a freshly washed and ironed version of Grandad Ed's enormous hanky. Had it been laundered by the housekeeper at Monument Manor?

Amelia's tears began to flow more freely now. 'Sorry, dear, it's just that I haven't talked about the past with anyone until recently. So many years of keeping it all to myself.' She blew her nose and wiped her eyes vigorously.

'Oh, please don't be sorry. Would you like another sherry?' Verity asked, rising from the sofa and picking up Amelia's glass. 'Or would you prefer a cup of tea?' Jeremy was driving Amelia back to the Manor House so she didn't have to worry about enjoying a little drink.

'Oh, another sherry would be lovely dear, just a small one,' and she dabbed at her eyes again before refolding the hanky.

Verity took her time in the kitchen refilling both their glasses in order to give Amelia time to compose herself. Glasses replenished and back on the sofa, she was surprised at her friend's next question. Yes, she did think of Amelia as a friend she realised, even though she was so much older.

'Didn't you ever wonder about the child's identity?' Amelia spoke slowly.

Verity stopped mid sip of her wine. 'Oh yes, all the time. Of course, there was no information available so I gave up looking. Everyone said it was meant to be that way, an enigma.'

'That's correct. Jack made me promise to keep it that way. It's the most closely guarded secret in the business. And it added to the allure.'

'Like the Mona Lisa?'

'Yes, maybe. I can tell you one thing.' Amelia leaned forward a little. 'As I've said before, the child in the painting was the happiest and loveliest child that ever did live.'

'I can well believe that.'

There was a loaded stillness in the room, even the crackling of the fire and Tom's purring seemed muted.

'Yes. And that baby girl was mine and Grandad Ed's.'

Verity's jaw must have dropped. When she could catch her breath, she said, 'Really?' She had guessed at this but now it was confirmed.

'Yes. That day up on the parapet, I was going to tell him I was pregnant. That's why I wanted us to run away together before my father tore us apart.'

'What happened to her? She's still alive?'

'Yes, very much so.'

'Oh, that's amazing. I did wonder because your very words were that – *The Happy Child* was surely the happiest and loveliest baby that ever was. *Was* being the operative word. I thought that maybe the worst had happened?'

Amelia shook her head and hesitated before saying, 'No, and the child is a family member.'

'No, surely not,' Verity thought for one heart stopping moment. Please don't tell me. No. Not Violetta. Surely *The Happy Child*, that glorious, delightful baby, couldn't have grown up to become an angry and aggressive white witch? It didn't bear thinking about.

'However, I trust you, my dear. Can you keep a secret?'

'Of course.' Verity held her breath.

Amanda looked around the cosy room and lowered her voice. 'Walls have ears you know.'

Verity raised her eyes ceiling wards where the thump, thump of music filtered down through the thick ceiling and Albie's speakers. 'He certainly can't hear us and Jeremy is out.'

'Then please allow me to tell you.'

'Oh, yes please.' Verity found she was sitting on the edge of the sofa. She breathed again with relief at Amelia's next words and the big reveal.

'*The Happy Child* is Elizabeth Jane Trevalsa. Elizabeth Jane, Eliza for short.'

'Oh,' was all Verity could muster, her heart racing.

'Eliza was my first born. I was fifteen years old when I discovered I was pregnant and gave birth aged sixteen.'

'Thank you for trusting me with such a precious secret. I promise I will never, ever tell anyone.'

'I know that, dear.'

'What happened to you, after that day on the monument?'

'I was banished to the family home in Italy to give birth. Villa Rosa, a beautiful house in Fiesole, not far from Florence.'

'How did you feel about that?'

'I was terrified of my father's wrath. Like a wave, the worry never stopped. I had to learn to live with it.'

'What did he tell you about Grandad Ed?'

Amelia explained that he didn't tell her anything at all and she was too scared to ask. The subject was closed to her and no-one else in Italy knew him or what had happened. Also, the shock of what happened gave her such anxiety and panic attacks that she simply blocked it out for many years, suffering many dark days and nights. She shuddered and there was a long pause.

Verity shook her head a little and patted Amelia's thin white hand. What sort of father would treat his own daughter in that way? She'd thought her own father was bad but one that allowed his own flesh and blood to believe her actions had caused someone to lose their life and to never tell her the truth, to take the knowledge with him to his grave, was far beyond Verity's comprehension. How Amelia must have suffered.

'However, Eliza was a beautiful baby and so easy to love and look after. You see, my mother, who died when I was four, was in a mental

230

institution for most of her married life. I was terrified the same would happen to me and they'd send me away and I'd never see her again.'

'A mental institution? Oh, Amelia, I'm so sorry.' For all her privileged upbringing, Amelia had gone through a lot of heartache.

'Father ruled with a rod of iron. He adored me until I fell pregnant. He was never outwardly violent you understand, in fact he could be very kind. Up until someone dared to oppose him. I knew had to conform to some extent. It was a battle of wills sometimes.' Amelia's voice changed. 'Then I met Jack.'

Amelia went on to clarify that Jack was an artist acquaintance of her father who was thirteen years older. He was Amelia's art tutor and he was kind and generous. They married when she was eighteen and he was thirty-one and didn't have any more children until eight years later.

'I'm pleased you managed to find some happiness.'

'In a sense I wasn't at peace for many years of my married life. Not that I didn't love Jack, I did, we were devoted to each other. But never in the way I loved Ed, you understand. I believe that only happens once within a lifetime, if one is very lucky. And I lived with such guilt. I couldn't tell him, or anyone. Over time, I learnt to live with my secret.'

'What..what did he think about Eliza?'

'He loved her like she was his own. He was a good man. More than I deserved. He didn't ask questions. She was loved by everyone.'

'That's another thing, I always thought *The Happy Child* was a boy.'

Amelia's laughter rang out like the chime of a bell. 'Probably the tufty hair. She did turn out to be a tomboy though.'

'So where is she now?'

'She lives in Italy. She's a retired politician.'

'Never! Really?'

'Yes, she still lives at Villa Rosa with her husband and spends most of her time gardening and writing articles for political journals.'

Verity turned to face Amelia. 'Does Grandad Ed know that he has another child?'

Amelia continued to stroke Tom who purred away in contentment. 'No, I couldn't tell him. I couldn't find the words. He was just so happy to see me and wanted me to know that it wasn't my fault. I

231

didn't want to give him such a shock, with him being in recovery as well.'

Verity nodded. 'It's your decision.'

'I may tell him but not just yet.'

'So, you are going to keep in touch?'

'Oh yes, of course. He's shown me how to work WhatsApp. And I'm going to come and stay at Monument Manor again. It rather felt like coming home.'

'I'm so pleased to hear that.'

'Now, dear.' Amelia put down her glass and sat up very straight. She looked as if she was about to make an announcement. 'Allow me to do something for you.'

'I don't need anything Amelia. Honestly, I'm more than happy with what I've got and the way things have turned out.'

'Oh, but I insist. Wait until you hear what it is, I think you're going to be very happy with what I'm about to say to you…'

# Chapter 39

'Hi Paul, it's Verity here.'

'Hello Verity!' The pleasure in his voice was evident. 'Well, well the day has finally come. I seemed to have waited for ever for you to ring me. I gather this means that you've changed your mind and realised that I am the only one for you?'

'Mmm, sorry, fraid not.'

'Pity. Well, in that case, it must mean that you've got a scoop of a story for me?'

'Not exactly, although I do have a story for you, that's true.'

'Marvellous. I know, let me guess. You are about to reveal to me the identity of *The Happy Child?'*

'Wrong again.'

'Ah, that's a shame. Such news would have catapulted my career into mega stardom. Never mind. Go on then, tell me about this job?'

'I'm getting married.'

'Oh no, my heart is broken. To the Owen Wilson lookalike I presume? Lucky guy.' Verity couldn't help laughing. 'Yes, Jeremy and I are getting married and…'

'Congratulations are in order, I suppose.'

'Thanks very much. I'd like you to run a story for the local paper for the wedding. It's being held at Monument Manor.'

'How did you swing that? I'm impressed. That's a first. You must have made an impression on my uncle.'

'That would be telling. Well, what do you think? Are you up for it?'

'I'd be delighted to cover your wedding for the paper. I'm a professional photographer as well, I'd be pleased to offer my services to take your wedding pics?'

'Of course, that was part of my plan.'

'Ooh, you must have checked me out on the Internet. I'm very flattered.'

'Well, it's 29 January at one pm.'

'Excellent. I promise I won't start singing, 'It should have been me' Verity laughed again.

'See you at the church, as they say, or rather, I should say, see you at the Manor.'

# Chapter 40

They were the only two figures on the stone base of Penshaw Monument and Verity had manoeuvred it so that she and Jeremy were both standing in the very centre, on a round stone which had four diagonal lines leading from it to each far corner of the temple, saying that they would get the best panoramic view for miles around from there. It was freezing.

'If we spin around this way, we'll see the sea and this way, the spire of Durham Cathedral,' she told him, laughing as the wind whipped his golden mane away from his face.

Frost lay in clumps on the grass this clear winter's morning and they could see snow on the Cheviot hills in one direction and a glimpse of the sea, hazy on the horizon in another.

'Ooh, it's chilly up here.' Verity snuggled right into him, hugging him close whilst he put his arms inside her coat so that they were pressed very close together, huddling into the warmth of each other. Jeremy didn't know that in her right hand behind his back, she was holding a small, sealed envelope. She could feel her fingertips pulsing beneath her gloves.

'Well, this is romantic,' he remarked, looking up at the clean, blue winter's sky. 'Did you bring me up here just for a hug this early in the morning? Or to look at the view? Not that I'm complaining.'

'I just wanted us to be alone with the elements for a moment. Listen to that.' The wind was sharp and whistling past the pillars, causing howling draughts to swirl around them.

'Well, we are, apart from Pedro.' He glanced over the edge to where Pedro was happily sniffing around on the grass surrounding the monument, dodging the cow pats. 'But then, we couldn't go for a walk and not bring Pedro along.'

Verity took a deep breath and looked up into his cornflower blue eyes. 'So that's it. I completed my quest. What am I going to do now to fill my time?'

'I think you've been on your own personal journey V. Called Finding Amelia.'

'Oh, by the way, I've got something for you,' and she handed him an envelope.

'What's this?'

'Well, why don't you open it and see?'

'Right, I will.' Jeremy tore open the envelope and drew out the card inside. It was beautifully decorated in white and gold, birds and scrolls, winter berries and leaves and in the centre were the words:

*Jeremy and Verity invite you to celebrate their wedding*

Jeremy's jaw dropped. 'Wow! It's an invite – to my own wedding?'

'Yes!' Verity laughed joyfully. 'Our wedding.'

Jeremy's smile grew. 'You beat me to it. I must confess, I was going to ask you again tonight. Over a special meal.'

'My turn to surprise you.'

'On 29 January! That's only a few weeks away.'

'I know. Why waste any more time?'

'I have no words.'

'What, again? That's so unlike you.'

'No, no, what I want to say is that this makes me happier beyond words. In fact, I'm even happier than *The Happy Child.*' He grabbed her even tighter and spun her round.

'Does that mean you will marry me?' she asked, her hood shaken off and her hair now riffled by the breeze. Not exactly a good look for a proposal, but hey, who cared?

'Will I?' Jeremy scooped her up and swung her round before embracing her thoroughly. 'Of course I will. Just try and stop me.'

'You don't mind the surprise?'

Jeremy beamed. 'Not in the slightest.'

'And what do you think of the venue?'

'I don't know, I didn't look that far down.' Jeremy looked at the card again. 'One pm at Monument Manor. Wow! That's amazing. You've planned all this?'

'Yes, everything's ordered and arranged. I took a bit of a punt, as Greyson would say, and hoped that you didn't want to get married in church again? I know that I don't.'

'You thought right. Not that I care about the venue. Verity, I'd get married anywhere as long as we're together.' Jeremy laughed out loud. 'I'm getting married – at last! Yippee!' and he swung her round and round again to the delight of a couple of giggling kids who had just jumped up onto the platform and were winding their way around every pillar.

'I'm getting married,' Jeremy announced and they laughed.

'Congratulations,' said one.

He reached for Verity again and they embraced.

'I can't believe you've organised all this in no time at all.'

'Well, I do work as an Events Organiser.'

She pulled away to ask, 'Don't you want to know who I've invited? It's just going to be a select few. My dad of course and his lot and Grandad Ed and Amelia are going to come together. Oh, and Sophie and Greyson from work. You can ask who you like as well.' She sighed. 'Unfortunately, my Grandma Anna isn't here to see me get married.'

'I haven't any family left to ask but I'd like Albie to be there.' They kissed again.

'Ugh, I wish you'd just get a room,' a voice behind them said as Albie rocked up. He approached them puffing and panting, dressed totally inappropriately for the weather in trainers, jeans and a thin jacket. He set down carefully the enormous backpack he'd been carrying. 'Have you've proposed yet?' he asked Verity.

'Albie! Guess what, we're getting married.' Jeremy gave him a big hug.

Albie then produced a bottle of champagne and two glasses from his backpack which he handed to them.

'Guess what? I know all about it. Good Luck. You both might need it.'

'Thanks mate. Ah, so you were in on this,' Jeremy qualified. 'Don't normally see you up at this hour.'

Albie flopped down on the stones. 'I wouldn't be normally. Far too early for me. And I don't do exercise – that hill.'

The cork popped and the fizz was poured and Verity forgot about all about the cold as they clinked glasses there in the middle of the base of granite slabs, with the wind howling in and around the pillars.

Albie swung his legs over the edge. 'Thought I might as well pitch in with my news as well.'

'Oh? What news is this?'

237

'I've been offered a job.'

'That's great news mate,' Jeremy hugged him again.

'Well done,' Verity said. 'That's tremendous news. What's the job then and where?'

'It's working as an intern for a film company in Newcastle. And I've got a regular slot on their community radio where I've been volunteering at weekends.'

'That's brilliant Albie,' Verity shook his hand and then thought, oh what the heck and gave him a big hug, thinking how skinny he felt.

'So, you'll be pleased to know I'll be moving out when I get somewhere to live in the city.'

'Oh, that's a shame,' Jeremy said. 'Don't try too hard to find somewhere. You're welcome to stay with us as long as you want.'

'You're invited to the wedding of course,' Verity said. 'Bring your mum if you like.'

'She won't want to come.'

'Rubbish,' Verity said. 'Every woman loves a wedding. Ask her.'

Albie shrugged. 'I might.'

He thrust his gloveless hands deep into his jacket pockets, shivering a little.

'By the way, did you know Pedro has ran off into the woods like a mad thing?'

'It's the cold.' Jeremy whistled and rustled his pocket which meant treats, which Pedro could always manage to hone into from wherever he was, luckily. He came haring back, panting and jumping up at Jeremy for his reward.

'All right if I go back down the hill now?' I'm er…working on a track.'

'Right,' Verity and Jeremy exchanged glances. 'Of course. You go down.'

'I need some scran as well. I'll take Pedro if you like.'

'Sure. We'll follow you down.'

They sat down with their backs against one of the pillars, sheltering from the wind to finish their fizz.

'What was the deciding factor for you V – what made you finally decide you can put up with my surprises and all the daft things I've done?'

238

Verity paused. 'I think it was when you simply dropped everything and came to pick me and Amelia up. No-one else would have done that for me. Amelia was well impressed as well.'

'Can I tell you something?' Jeremy set down his glass. 'I knew when I saw the painting *of The Happy Child* in its place in our fireside that you were ready to marry me.'

'Why?

'I just knew it. Well, let's face it, we're not getting any younger. And if we want to start a family now is maybe the time. And we can create our own *Happy Child* pictures for the wall.'

'My thoughts exactly.'

Verity was almost swept off the edge by Jeremy into a great bear hug of an embrace, which nearly knocked her plastic glass out of her hand. 'At last. We agree on almost everything.'

'And the wedding at Monument Manor is Amelia's gift to us both.' Verity drained her glass.

'How very kind of her.'

'It's the first wedding they've ever held there but they are hoping to go into the wedding market in the future. They've even said we can pick which room we'd like for the reception.'

'I'm so happy that you seem to be excited about marrying me at last.'

'I've always been excited about marrying you.'

'I was beginning to wonder. Especially when that journalist started taking an interest. Definitely a spark there.'

'On his side, never on mine. Oh, by the way, he's doing the review for the paper and the wedding photographs. You don't mind, do you?'

'Not in the slightest. I'm the lucky one. I'm so proud it's me you're marrying not him.'

'And Amelia has arranged for us to stay there overnight for our wedding night as well. In the four poster in the Lavender Room with evening dinner prepared by the housekeeper. Sounds like heaven to me.'

'I can't wait.'

They finished off the wine and put the bottle and glasses back into Albie's backpack which he had left behind for that purpose, as there weren't any bins within sight up here on Penshaw Hill.

239

'I must show you this one thing before we go.' And Verity led the way to the fifth pillar on the south side of the monument, where on the second stone up on the inner side were carved the words - Ed loves Amelia - 1946.

Verity took off her glove and traced the white markings on the blackened stone with her finger, feeling its roughness beneath her skin.

'If I had a pen knife, I'd inscribe our names on there – Jeremy loves Verity - 2015.' Jeremy reached for her hand and covered it with his own. 'As I haven't, I'd just like to say that I love you Verity, with all my heart.'

'And I love you.'

Two lone figures on the monument base, which was an unusual occurrence as there were constant comings and goings up here, they kissed again, secure in their happiness. Another declaration of love for the stones to hold locked tight within, alongside their other many secrets. Silence prevailed for a brief moment until the faint, rhythmical cooing of wood pigeons from the nearby woods filtered through, mingling with the melody of a skylark treading air up above.

Verity looked at the pillar again and imagined the words there, - Jeremy loves Verity – 2015 – directly underneath Ed's etchings. Two totally separate love stories, decades apart. Unfortunately, the proposed declaration of love from Amelia all those years ago didn't happen back then in 1946 and they were separated so cruelly. So much history steeped into these very stones. And so much graffiti depicting many different love trysts. Each inscription would have their own story to tell. She felt lucky she'd been able to discover Ed and Amelia's.

Jeremy reached out his hand to her and as she took it, and he clasped his warm fingers around hers, her heart soared and she felt happier at that moment than she'd ever felt in her life. She was so very lucky that their life together was just beginning and no-one could drive them apart, unlike Amelia and Ed. They had a fabulous wedding day to look forward to and the rest of their lives, if, hopefully, the fates would allow. Verity vowed there and then, never to take her happiness for granted.

As they began to descend the fifty earth steps down the hill towards their home, she looked back and saw the majestic Greek temple atop of a green hill, with hazy blue patches of sky peeping through the gaps in the solid stone pillars. One of those blackened sandstone columns, the one that was second from the right, housed the secret stairway which led up to the parapet. If there had been a roof, there wouldn't have been a parapet atop of the monument at all. How different would Amelia and Ed's story have been if a roof had been built? That was something none of them would ever know.

Yet their story lives on.

## THE END

# Acknowledgements

Thanks first of all, to my wonderful family for their unending patience and support whilst I've been writing this novel. Special thanks go to Luke for all his technical assistance.

Thanks also, to my great friend May for all her ideas, time and reassurance and for helping to make this story as best as it could be.

I would also like to mention my lovely friends at the Romantic Novelists Association (RNA) Northumberland Chapter Writing Group for all their inspirational help and encouragement, especially Caroline Roberts who was part of the reading and critiquing process. Also, thanks to the RNA New Writer's Scheme for the two extremely motivational and developmental critiques I received for this novel.

Thanks to Alexa at the Book Refinery for the cover design.

Last but never least, thanks go to my mother Arlene Smith to whom this novel is dedicated and without whose unconditional love and encouragement, this story would not exist.

Arlene Pearson lives in the North East village of Penshaw and is a writer of blogs, plays and fiction.

Also by Arlene on Amazon

WHERE THE FOUR STREAMS MEET

NORTHBOUND

2.4 TEENAGERS

INSPIRATIONAL PLACES

NORTHBOUND

Printed in Great Britain
by Amazon

20280290R00140